Henrietta Soames was born in 1958 of Hungarian and Czechoslovakian parents. Her stories have been broadcast on Radio 4, appeared in *London Magazine* and been included in anthologies published by William Heinemann and Constable. She lives in London and supports her writing by working as a cleaner, giving lectures and coaching individuals on a wide variety of writing projects.

At the Hall

Henrietta Soames

First published in 1994
by HEADLINE BOOK PUBLISHING

First published in paperback in 1995
by HEADLINE BOOK PUBLISHING

A HEADLINE REVIEW paperback

10 9 8 7 6 5 4 3 2 1

ISBN 0 7472 4615 7

Printed and bound in Great Britain by
Cox & Wyman Ltd, Reading, Berks

HEADLINE BOOK PUBLISHING
A division of Hodder Headline PLC
338 Euston Road
London NW1 3BH

To my sister, Victoria,
who always believes in me

I would like to acknowledge Alan Ross, Heather Godwin and Sheila Fox, who first published and broadcast my stories. Also, Alexandra Pringle for her significant contribution to this book and John Hale for his honesty and clarity of attention. I thank the PCAC for their generous support and my brother, Nicolas Soames, for his unfailing encouragement. I am deeply grateful to Geraldine Cooke for her perseverance and absolute commitment, and to Lesley Levene for her assurance and good humour, and I am indebted to Andrew Hewson for his patience, his confidence and his steadfastness.

I

SHRAPNEL

The rasping of the car over the gravel was like a zip being pulled up, as if the drive knitted together behind, fastening me inside. Relentlessly I was rolled forwards until, acting almost independently of me, the car came to a halt – the handbrake secured, the wheels stilled – and I was here, fixed in front of the house I had avoided for so long.

For a moment I just sat and looked at it: the grey stone walls, the thick ivy – surely that was thicker now, taller? I could hear it tapping against my window in the night, trying to find a way in, and I felt a twist of panic – it's too late to get away now, it's too late. I had a sudden image of turning the car around and cutting my way back through the drive, like a plough forcing a passage out, and then I shook myself. No, I was being silly. This was just going to be a nice, cheap, easy holiday for the twins before they started at their new school next term. It would all be fine.

I heard the twins stirring behind me, waking from the almost supernatural sleep that had overwhelmed them as we came within the environs of the Hall, and I turned around eagerly. 'Are you awake now, children? Did you have a nice – ' But then I caught sight of the great stone wheel leaning against the side of the house, spreading its menace like a dark awning, and I shuddered. Maybe I was wrong. Maybe I shouldn't have agreed to their demands and brought them here. Maybe –

'Mummy, Mummy, are we here now? Are we at Grandma's?'

I grabbed at Christopher's voice as if it was a lifeline. 'Did you have a good sleep, darling?' I reached out to touch his tousled blond hair, my stomach as always turning over at its brilliance.

But he shrugged my hand away. 'Are we here?' he repeated. 'Are we at Grandma's?'

'Now, Christopher,' I began. 'You must remember what I told you. You've got to be good here. You're not at home now and you know your grandmother's very particular about how small children behave.'

But he wasn't taking any notice. He wrestled with his seat belt and pushed roughly at his sister. 'Wake up, Kitty, wake up, slowcoach. We're here – we're at Grandma's.'

'Christopher, don't maul her like that. Let her finish her sleep.'

But he never really listens to me. 'Wake up, wake up, slowcoach,' he said, poking her. 'We're here, we're here.'

'Christopher, don't.' I made my voice stern. 'You must listen to me now. You've *got* to behave here. *No* leaving your toys lying around, *no* slamming of doors, you've got to eat all your food properly and wipe your feet and – listen to me, Christopher, listen to me, or else I'll get – '

But he had turned his attention to the door handle, trying to unlock it now that he'd shed the seat belt. 'Let me out, Mummy. I want to be outside. I want to see Grandma.'

'Christopher, please, don't push me now, I'm warning you.' I could feel panic rising, the house watching me. You can't control them very well, can you, she'd say. Where *are* their manners? 'Christopher, please – '

But his sister was stirring now and her sleepy voice whined. 'I'm not a tortoise, am I, Mummy? I'm not a slowcoach, am I?'

'No, of course not, darling.' I tried to sound reassuring. 'You're a lovely little girl and your brother's just teasing you. Now, please, both of you, I want you to listen to me – '

But Christopher burst in, chanting, 'Kitty is a tortoise, Kitty is a slow, smelly tortoise – '

'Christopher – ' My hand stiffened to punish him.

But even as I lunged awkwardly over the seat it was too late, because he had already flung the door open, and, giggling triumphantly, he leapt out of the car and ran towards the house, the playing cards that had been on his lap fanning out over the gravel.

And it was as if his defiant spring for freedom set in motion the whole wheel of action, because suddenly, as if by clockwork, the heavy studded front door swung open and out stepped Madeleine.

The twins were a good cover. They dragged fearlessly on their grandmother's arms, demanding that she show them her house, her garden she'd told them so much about, so that we had time only for a brief exchange of glances before she was whisked away, the twins chattering furiously beside her.

That's good, that's good, I told myself as I opened the boot and hauled out the cases. They're all getting on well together. It's a very good start.

But I could feel the gravel nipping my feet through the thin soles of my shoes and I walked very uncertainly on my high heels, which weren't giving me the confidence I had thought they would. I could almost hear the gravel laughing – we've got you now, we've got you now – as my ankle skewed suddenly and little sharp splinters jumped into my shoe. We've got you, you're back now . . . Not since my wedding, almost ten years ago, had I heard the cackling of the gravel and then I had ground it down underfoot triumphantly as I walked off on Dan's arm, my knight, my protector, the prince who had rescued the princess and carried her away.

Now, like the mermaid walking on glass, I was actually hobbling forwards. I don't want to be here, I don't want to be here – the cry unfurled before I could stop it, beating like a sail loose in the wind. Why did I agree to this? Didn't I remember?

The dampness of the porch drew me into itself, dousing the hot sun that had beaten on my shoulders, so that now I felt clammy and chilled. I don't want to be here, I don't want – And then I pulled myself together sharply. That's enough, Lydia, I told myself. It's all different now. You're a woman, an adult, a mother. The Hall will have changed too.

Everything will be quite different now.

I stood straight-backed in front of the door and, taking a deep breath, stepped inside. The house welcomed me with cold fingers and musty breath, just as it always had done.

The day before he came we cleaned the house from top to bottom. I didn't know why, of course, and I didn't ask Mother. 'A lady never asks questions,' she always says. 'And you're going to be a lady, a proper lady, Lydia.' She was in an odd, hurrying sort of mood that day and I didn't try to get her to explain things to me. We didn't have any lessons because she said that there were too many other things to do and I was not to get in her way and not to disobey her.

Actually, I don't mind cleaning the house. I never do. Because it means I can go into the parlour and take out all the little things in the corner cabinet – the wooden one with the glass front that has flowers and leaves carved into the glass, so that it's like looking through a forest or a garden. There are silver things – a tiny vase, hardly big enough for a proper flower; some statues, small like dolls, one of a mother holding a baby; and a set of rosy pink and blue cups and saucers that Mother says are very valuable because they're made of mother-of-pearl and which I like because they seem to change colour in the light magically. I always want to play with them as if they were a real tea-set, but I'm not allowed to. I am allowed to clean the things in the cabinet, though – Mother says my hands are small and I can do it better than she can, but she always watches me in case I break something and that takes a lot of the fun away. I wish I could do it on my own.

But that day, the day before he came, she was in a real temper. 'Don't waste time on the cabinet, Lydia,' she said. 'You're to help me turn out this room properly.' I wanted to say that we'd only just done the room a few days ago – it was part of our rota for cleaning the whole house. But I didn't say anything, because

6

she would have been very angry if I'd 'spoken back'. A lady never answers back.

She gave me a soft cloth and a tin of polish and told me to get on and clean all the chair and table legs. Some of them are quite difficult to dust, because their feet are carved into strange shapes like claws and hoofs, and it's a bit scary too, because sometimes I think that they really *are* animal's feet that have been made into tables but might come back to life under my hands while I'm touching them.

Mother was moving the heavy furniture all on her own – she's very strong – and taking the thick creamy-white rug with the pretty blue and green flowers on it out through the garden doors to beat. She has a piece of washing-line strung out on the terrace which she keeps clear of weeds and she slung the carpet over it like a saddle and I saw her beating and beating, as if she was very angry.

'Is this all right now?' I asked her when we'd put the room back to normal and even the drops of the chandelier glistened like snowflakes over our heads.

The room looked so beautiful. Mother had left the garden doors open – 'to air, because it's summer,' she said, but then she went on about the garden under her breath. I didn't listen – Mother's always going on about the state of the garden. I just looked around the room and thought how much I loved it and how beautiful it was and how, when it's just been cleaned like this, I get a funny feeling in my chest, a tingling feeling, which makes me happy.

We never really go into the parlour except on cleaning days, though secretly I do go in there on my own sometimes, just to stand and look, but it's difficult because Mother's always watching me to make sure I'm behaving myself like a lady and I know a lady wouldn't tiptoe into a room when no one was looking. But I loved that room so much. It was different from the rest of the Hall, as if it came from another house altogether – a magic house. None of the other rooms is as lovely. I don't know if it's because of the pretty furniture or the thick carpet –

all deep and soft like warm snow – or the light coming in through the glass doors, but I always felt it was special, and it made me happy and proud to live in a house with that room in it.

'Now we'll do the study,' Mother said, gathering up the dusters and polish and the rags for the floor. 'Come on, child, come on. Don't dawdle. He'll be sure to want to sit in there. He'll be sure to want to see it all, to make sure that it's all here, just as he left it – the Master.' She said that with a funny snorting noise like a horse. 'I'll show him a thing or two. I'm no common peasant girl, he'll see.' She went on like this for a while, but I began to feel excited, because it was the first time she'd mentioned that someone was coming to visit. We don't really see many people. There are the tradesmen who come with the milk and the meat, but Mother says I'm not to mix with them and she likes me to be out of the way when they come. She says they're 'beneath me'. I don't altogether understand what she means. I watch from my bedroom window upstairs when the baker comes and he always waves at me from his van; sometimes he has a young boy with him who's got red hair and freckles just like himself and they both look quite normal to me.

I don't go to the village school – Mother says they're all peasants there. I do my lessons with her. She's very strict. I've learned to write very quickly because she says she's got no patience with children who can't read and write properly. I learned to read quickly too. I sat on a stool at her feet with a book in my lap and every time I got a word wrong she cuffed me over the head. She said it was for my own good and she must have been right, because I can read almost anything now. I like books with pictures best but there aren't a lot of those and Mother says we haven't the money to buy new. In the parlour there are pictures on the walls and when Mother's out beating the carpet I stop cleaning the furniture and look at them. There are garden pictures and horses and deer, and one big scene of a castle with a moat and flags flying. I make up stories about them as if they were in a proper book and I pretend I'm writing the words to go with them.

At the Hall

We live in the kitchen and the scullery mainly, and I do my lessons at the kitchen table now, ever since I spilt a bottle of ink upstairs in my bedroom. So we never really go into the study, not to use it. I suppose it's like the parlour in that way, but we clean the parlour more often. I go into the study sometimes to take a book and Mother doesn't say anything. It's not forbidden, like the parlour.

'Dear God,' Mother said when we stood in the doorway. She wiped her hands down the front of her skirt, not seeming to notice the dust trails she left. I was wearing my pinafore, because she gets angry when my clothes are dirty, but I didn't say anything about her skirt, even though it was one of her good ones.

'We'll have to do all of the books – all of them. Oh, God.' She closed her eyes and for a moment I thought she might cry, which would have been very peculiar, because Mother never cries and she gets angry if I cry, because she says it's babyish and not ladylike and that you must control your feelings. She clenched her fists into hard little balls and banged them against her sides. 'Why did he have to come back?' she cried out. 'Why? Why? Why couldn't he have just left us alone together in peace?'

I couldn't say anything and I didn't dare move. I stood very still beside her, because it frightened me seeing her face all frowning and dark-looking, with her eyes tight shut as if she was turning into a monster. It was the sort of face that she wore when I spilt the ink in my room, and though I didn't think I'd done anything bad this time, I can never be quite sure, so I just stood very still and didn't say anything.

Actually, the study could be a friendly room, I think. Quite different from the parlour and not nearly so pretty, but it has a comfortable feeling about it. There are two chairs in front of the fireplace. One is high-backed, like a throne with big arms and shiny gold-looking studs holding the green leather. The other is an old armchair covered in dark-blue velvety material, all worn and shiny; it looks like a good chair to curl up in with a book. The whole room has shelves of big brown leather books which go from the floor right up to the ceiling. Of course I can't see most of them and I usually take out the ones on the bottom two shelves which have blue and red cardboard covers. Some of them are covered in brown paper and once I found a schoolbook with a lot of very strange names in it, sounding like a sort of pussycat's language – 'iss, uss, iccit . . .' – and inside the cover was written, 'William's First Latin Primer, aged 9¼. The Hall'. That made me terribly excited, as it meant William was only a year older than I was. I was so pleased that somehow there was another child at the Hall – maybe he'd come back here in the holidays or when he was older – that I ran with the book all the way to Mother. 'Look,' I said, 'look what I found. It's from a boy who lives here called William.' She snatched the book out of my hand so suddenly that she let the cooking spoon she was holding over the soup fall on to the floor. 'Where did you get this from?' she asked, glaring at me. I told her. 'Who's William, Mother?' I asked. 'Is he coming to stay here?' But she put the book in her apron pocket – I could see the outline of it against her legs. 'Never you mind, Lydia. Don't ask questions – a lady never asks questions.' Her mouth was all thin, not quite like it is when she's angry but looking as if she might be. 'You're to forget about this boy, Lydia, understand?' She looked at me very hard. 'Put him right out of your head, see?'

But I couldn't forget him, not really. Every time I went into the study to fetch a book, I hoped I might find another message or a book from William. I thought maybe William had been all alone in this house like me and maybe he had wanted friends too. I kept hoping and hoping, but I never found anything else.

In the end we didn't clean all the books, not one by one anyway. Mother said it was just too much trouble and we only cleaned the ones in the first five shelves. I did the ones on the bottom and she did the ones on the top. It took a bit of time, taking them all out and dusting each one and putting it back, and Mother kept stopping to look through the pages. 'Is that a good story?' I asked her when she had one open which had gold on the cover and very thin shivery sort of paper inside.

But she pushed me away and said that I wasn't to breathe on it and spoil it and that they were worth a pretty penny and shouldn't be left idle. 'They ought to be valued,' she said. 'He ought to get them properly valued and insured.'

But I wasn't listening really; she often says things I don't understand and I've learned not to ask her what she means. I was getting hungry. It had been a long time since breakfast. I didn't do the last row of books all that well. I just wiped the tops and the sides and a bit behind, pushed them into a line and left it at that. Mother didn't seem to notice. She was still doing the higher shelves and when she saw I'd finished she told me to dust the desk and the little table and to polish up the big brass ashtray which had dragons running around it and the brass reading lamp. Then I had to get kindling and coal for the fire, which she laid ready after she'd finished her shelves, and we left the room like that.

The hall is very big. It's rather gloomy and I don't like it, even though I have to cross it lots of times a day. The floor is made of pieces of wood like arrows all pointing to the door. Mother keeps the floor very clean – she says it's the most important thing in the house. She gets very angry if I walk over it when the polish is wet, and I can't even tiptoe across, because the polish catches the marks from my feet almost on purpose. I don't like cleaning the hall and I was cross after lunch when I saw her getting the special polish out. She tied two dusters over my feet and I had to shine and shine until the floor looked like a lake.

The only nice thing in the hall which I like cleaning is the grandfather clock by the front door. It's so big I can get inside it and hide, though of course Mother would kill me if she found out. But I like knowing I've got such a good hiding-place if I ever need to use it. The clock bit doesn't actually work. Mother says the pendulum is broken. I wish it would work. When I clean it I always open it up and try to make the pendulum swing like the clock on the mantelpiece in the parlour, but it will only do a few ticks and then it stops again.

There isn't any other furniture in the hall. There are swords and shields on the walls and a big flag hanging down, all of which belonged to my ancestors and Mother says I'm to be proud of. It all looks rather old and dusty to me and I don't like it when she goes on about my ancestors. It's like when she decides we've got to eat properly in the dining-room. That's a horrible room with red walls and huge pictures of people in funny clothes on the walls – all gentlemen, no ladies. Mother's place is at the top of the table and I have to sit beside her and look at the pictures. 'These are your ancestors, Lydia. You're descended from all these important people. They're your heritage and don't you forget it.' They glower and glare at me while I eat my dinner, which is cold by the time it reaches that room, and somehow the vegetable is always cauliflower, which makes me feel sick. Mother doesn't know this but under my place at the table I've made marks with my nails like a ladder. The wood is soft and easy to mark and I do it while we eat to make me feel better. She'd be furious if she ever found out.

It was a long day doing all the cleaning. We don't usually do it all in one go like that. And even when it came to my shining the stained glass on the landing I didn't enjoy it as much as usual, because I was so tired. I hardly bothered to look out through the pretty colours into the garden. It was getting dark but Mother was still busy. Her hair had fallen out of her bun several times and she had pinned it back up again quickly in the way she does, with bits of hair all higgledy-piggledy and pins all sticking out. She had dirt on her face and her skirt, which had been pale blue that morning, was now quite grey-looking. 'You look funny,' I said when I sat drinking my night-time milk in the kitchen. 'You've got smudges all over your nose.' But she wasn't really listening, just nodding at me and looking out of the window at the darkening sky while she muttered to herself,' . . . and maybe we should have done those books all to the top and I'll have to iron all Lydia's dresses and find some flowers to put in the rooms and get extra coal in . . .'

I can bath myself now so I did that, though Mother came up

to wash my hair, which she rubbed so hard my head felt sore. 'You go to sleep now,' she said when I got into bed. She was standing by the door. 'We'll be up early in the morning, because I don't know what time to expect him. He hasn't had the goodness to let me know!'

Although I was feeling sleepy, I looked up and started to ask about what she was saying. 'Who's coming, Mother? Who's "he"?'

And then she came away from the door and actually up to the bed, and I was really afraid for a moment that she was very angry with me, because she never comes to my bed. But she just sat down on the side and I could feel her weight next to my legs, all firm and solid and there. 'You've got to be very good now, Lydia, do you understand?' she said, and she was looking at me in a funny sort of way as if she was asking me a favour. 'You're not to ask any questions and you're to do everything I tell you.' I was nodding, but she was looking away though she was still talking. 'With any luck he won't stay long. There's nothing for him here, he'll see that soon enough. He can go back to his fancy City rooms and leave us alone, but in case he does stay – ' She turned back to me and now she was looking very hard, not angry but sort of forced. 'In case he does stay for more than a day or two,' she said again, 'I want you to be on your absolute, absolute best behaviour. You're to be what I've brought you up to be, Lydia – a lady. He'll be expecting to find a peasant brat and I want him to find that you're a lady. Understand? Understand?' I just nodded again. I didn't dare say anything, didn't dare ask anything, but it must have been all right, because suddenly she put out her hand and stroked my face. 'You're just a child, Lydia,' she said. 'I forget – you're only a child.' I hardly dared breathe under her hand and in a way it was a relief when she got up and went over to the door, though it was a shame too, because it was so nice to have her touch me and look at me like that, as though I was good and all right after all and she did love me.

Before she closed the door she said, 'Remember, Lydia, I'm

doing it all for you. I want you to remember that.'

Then she shut the door and I was alone in the dark. But I couldn't get to sleep, even though I was tired. After a long time I heard her footsteps going all the way down the passage to her own room at the end, where she can't hear me. And I listened to the wind whistling through the little hole in my windowpane. And I wondered about what she'd said and who was the person coming and why it was all so strange. And I couldn't help hoping that maybe, if I showed her I could be very good with this other person, she would stroke my hair and sit on my bed again and look at me in that special way, and maybe I would make her feel proud of me and we would be happy.

'So, this is the child?' He stood in the middle of the parlour, looking down at me. He was tall with white hair and his face was old. Although he didn't have a beard, somehow he made me think of Father Christmas.

Mother pushed me forwards. I could feel her fingers digging in through my dress – the best dark-blue one with the white sash. Mother was wearing her best navy-blue skirt and a white blouse; she'd done her hair up in a different bun from usual and she'd put some lipstick on which made her mouth look all pink and strange. I could feel her hands were wet, as if she'd been doing the washing-up – which was odd, because I knew she hadn't.

'Well, come here, child.' As I went towards him, he looked over at Mother. 'Lydia – her name?'

'That's my name, Mr –' But I didn't know what to call him or what his name was, because Mother hadn't told me, and though I tried to glance back at her to give me some help, she was looking at him and didn't say anything.

'You're very small,' he said, bending down to me, and close up I could see his face was covered in lots of lines like railway tracks and there were deep dents on either side of his mouth. It made me feel sorry for him, because he looked sad somehow.

'Mother says I'm growing,' I told him. 'She says I'll be getting too big for my clothes soon and that I mustn't grow so fast, so I try not to.' I heard a noise from Mother behind me, but he had put his hand on my shoulder and I couldn't turn round.

Then, as he looked at me, I saw that his eyes were getting bigger, bluer, as if they were under water, and I realized that he was going to cry. And I was afraid, because I thought that I must have said something terrible to upset him and Mother had said that if I upset him then he'd do something really bad which would affect us both and it would all be my fault.

I could feel that I was almost going to cry myself, which I knew would be even worse, but suddenly his eyes got still bigger and he said, 'Do you know who I am?' I couldn't say anything, I was feeling so afraid. I just shook my head, even though I know that's not polite.

Behind me Mother said very sharply, 'I haven't told her anything, sir. I thought you'd prefer that.'

But he didn't look at her, he kept looking at me, and suddenly he smiled – not a big smile, but a little one that seemed to be just for me – and I saw he wasn't going to cry and I felt better. 'I'm your grandfather,' he said in a very careful sort of voice, as if he was teaching me something. 'Your grandfather. Do you understand what that means, Lydia? I'm your grandfather and I've come back here to live in my house.'

'But I thought – ' I stopped quickly, because I heard a noise from Mother behind me.

'Go on,' he said. 'You thought – ' But he wasn't looking at me now, he was looking over my shoulder at Mother, and I had a feeling, like balancing on a wall, that I had to be careful.

'I didn't know you lived here too,' I said, looking up at him. 'I always thought this was our house – Mother's and mine. But it'll be nice to have someone else here with us. You're very welcome.' I stopped quickly, because I could see his eyes beetling together and his mouth tightening up and looking grim.

Suddenly he laughed. 'Well, Lydia,' he said, straightening up, 'I'll say this for you. For all your common name, you've a touch of your father in you after all, and he was a bold rascal too in his way.'

My father? How did he know my father? Mother had never talked about him; she said he was dead long before I was born, which seemed to mean that I didn't really have a father, even though in all the stories I read there was always a mother and a father. But you can't have a father who's dead before you, can you?

I wanted to say something like this to the old gentleman – my grandfather – but suddenly he pushed me back towards Mother. 'Run along now, Lydia,' he said. 'I have to talk to your mother.'

Mother had made me practise curtsying and I thought this might be a good time to do one, so before I went out of the room I turned around, looked at him and made the best curtsy I've ever done, then I went out.

His suitcase was still in the middle of the hall. Mother had walked me past it very quickly before, but now I could stop to look at it. It was big, almost as big as me, and made of thick dark-brown leather. There were lots of labels stuck on the sides with pictures of ships and words like 'Ocean' and 'Liner', which sounded marvellous and very mysterious. The shiny brass locks were like knuckles and there was a wide leather strap tight all around it. I thought my grandfather must be very strong to have carried it all the way to our house.

They hadn't shut the door behind me and while I was looking at the suitcase – very careful not to actually touch it – I could hear them talking. Mother was standing just inside the doorway – I could see her through the crack – but my grandfather had sat down. I was very sure of that, because the sofa makes a special squeaking noise when someone sits on it. They were talking a lot. I didn't listen to what they were saying, but I could hear their voices going up and down – his voice mainly, it was deep. I wondered about it all, whether he really would stay in the house with us, which sounded rather nice, even though I was certain Mother wasn't happy about it. And I wondered about how he was my grandfather. Of course, I know that a grandfather is the father of your own mother or father, but Mother had always said that her father had died when I was a baby and she'd never said anything about any other sort of grandfather. Was this old gentleman my father's father, then? And would he tell me about my father? I hoped so, especially as he'd said I was like him.

But when Mother came out of the parlour, shutting the door very firmly behind her, she was angry to see me still in the hall. 'Into the kitchen with you,' she hissed, shooing me ahead of her. When we got into the kitchen, she lifted me, sat me down hard on the table and stared at me. 'How many times do I have to tell you not to listen at doors, Lydia?' she said. 'How many times? Common brats listen at doors. You don't want to be a common brat, do you?' But she didn't stop for me to say anything; she just kept on talking, her words all in a stream: '. . . and making me stand like a common servant girl and not addressing me by my name – not addressing me by any name. I won't have it, I won't have it, I won't – ' And then she turned back to me. 'It's all because of you, Lydia. I'm doing this all for you. If it wasn't for you, I'd never have to put up with this – this – ' But she stopped again. I didn't dare say anything. Her hair was beginning to slide out of its bun and her breath was hot on my face, inches away. 'You listen to me, my girl, and you listen good. You'd better behave with your grandfather, because otherwise he'll have us out of this house quicker than we can say boo. Understand? You're to call him Grandfather – not Grandpa or Grandad or anything common – but Grandfather. Understand?' She gave my shoulders a shake. 'What are you to call him?'

'Grandfather.'

'And what are you to do?'

'I've got to be very good and do everything he says and everything you say, or – or – '

'Or else we'll be out of here lock, stock and barrel and it'll all be your fault.' She lifted me down from the table. 'With any luck he'll only stay for a few days anyhow,' she muttered to herself. 'Now take the best china through to the dining-room, we're having lunch in there, and you mind your manners, girl. I'll be watching you.'

He didn't say much at lunch, none of us said much. I kept my elbows in all the time, like Mother had taught me to with pennies under them, and ate my vegetables – peas, which wasn't as bad as cauliflower. Mother didn't sit at the top of the table, Grandfather did, and Mother sat next to me. I stared at the pictures to see if he looked like the people in them, but he didn't – he wasn't nearly so frightening, even though he was a good deal older.

After lunch he went into the study, where he said he wanted the fire kept up because he was old and felt the cold more. But he said the study should be called the library and that 'study' was a wrong word for it.

Mother said I was to stay out of his way as much as possible and, when I did see him, I was to be on my best behaviour, because otherwise – 'you know what will happen'. She said I was to stay with her and that for the time being we weren't going to do any lessons, though I was to have my books ready in case he wanted to examine them. That worried me. I'm still not that good at sums and, though my writing is getting better, I'm still not very neat with the joining up and sometimes I make blots with the ink, which is very bad and you can't really cover up an ink blot.

Actually, for the first few days I hardly saw him at all. Even so, I still had to keep wearing my best dresses – the blue one and the green one with the flowers, though the blue one is too small really and the material of the green one is so scratchy. And I wasn't allowed to go out in the garden to play, because she didn't want me to make any noise and disturb him.

He kept himself pretty much to himself, though we met for meals, which we ate in the dining-room, where we'd use the best red and gold china with the birds and flowers pattern. Sometimes he smiled at me while we were eating and I think he noticed when I ate all my green beans, because he stopped Mother making me have a second helping by saying he thought I was full. She always served him first and then me and then herself, and she never said anything to him or he to her when we ate.

It was strange having someone else in the house, even though I didn't really see much of him. It made me feel excited to think that I might run into him in the hall or in the parlour, though he never seemed to go into the parlour again after that first day. He slept in the room next to mine, the one Mother never lets me into. She says it's precious, a very special room, and I've only ever looked in through the door. It's a conker-brown room, the walls and the floor wooden like a nut, and there's a very big bed and a cupboard with mirrors in the doors and shelves inside. At night, while I laid awake, I could hear him walking round and putting things away in the cupboard. After a time I'd hear the bed give a big creak and, if I stayed awake long enough, I could hear him breathing slowly and heavily as he slept. It made me feel happy to have someone so close. I even stopped having any of my old nightmares about running through the woods with things chasing after me.

After a few days, perhaps a week, when it all seemed to have settled down, we were in the kitchen and Mother was talking to me about my getting back to wearing normal clothes with a pinafore, and I was thinking that maybe that would mean I'd be able to go out into the garden again, when suddenly we heard a bell ring. It wasn't the front door and it couldn't be the back door, because we were sitting just beside it, but it rang over our heads, and then I noticed something joggling in the box over the kitchen door which has little flags and writing in it. 'Look, Mother.' I pointed. 'It's there.' She looked up and her face was suddenly like thunder, and I was sure she was going to hit me because I'd done something wrong. But she just ran out of the kitchen, leaving me with the big pile of peas to shell and the water boiling for them on the range, even though I was on my own.

When she came back she was very angry. 'If he thinks I'm a servant to be summoned by a bell,' she said, throwing the peas in the water. 'If he just thinks – ' She was slamming the plates and pots from the dresser on to the table so hard I thought they might break. 'If he just thinks – ' She slapped a jug of milk down from the cooler so it all slopped over the side and I quickly got a cloth to mop it up. 'Next time that bell goes *you* can see what he wants,' she said, catching my arm as I went past to wring out the cloth. 'See how he likes summoning his own grandchild with a servant's bell.'

We had our tea in the kitchen and he ate alone in the dining-room. I was afraid he might be lonely in there, but I didn't dare mention it to Mother as she was still in a black mood. But it was nicer eating in the kitchen really – it was friendlier and I could eat more, which I don't feel able to do in the dining-room with all those faces staring down at me.

But just as we'd finished we heard the bell again. I looked at Mother. 'Well, go on,' she said, jerking with her head. 'See what he wants, the lord and master.' She got up from the table and, before I could move even, pulled me out of my chair so that I was standing in front of her. Then she wiped my face with the corner of an old tea-towel and pushed my hair back behind my ears and pulled it hard into a ponytail which she tied with a rubber band from her pocket. 'So stringy,' she complained, as she always does about my hair, even though I have to brush it a hundred times every night. 'God alone knows where you got that from.' Then she gave me a little push. 'Go on, go and see what he wants. He's in the study.'

'But what shall I say?'

She was shaking her head. 'It's all for you,' she said. 'I've done it all for you, Lydia. I won't have you cheated out of what's yours.'

'Mother, what shall I say?' I asked again, but she just pushed me in front of her until I was standing in the hall and she stood in the kitchen-passage doorway, watching me as I crossed over to the library door, like she does when she makes me walk up the stairs with a book balanced on my head to improve my deportment.

I knocked cautiously. My heart was pounding, but I could feel Mother watching me and I knew I couldn't go back to her. After a while I heard him say something, but I couldn't make out what it was, so I just opened the door and went in.

He was standing with his back to me, bending over the fire. It had been a bit cold that day, windy and rainy, all the grass in the garden beaten down.

'Well, don't stand there,' he said. 'Close the door. You know I don't like a draught. Come and help me with this fire. I don't know what sort of coal you're getting in, but it's not drawing the way it should.'

Then he turned and saw me and he looked very surprised. 'Oh, it's you,' he said, but he didn't sound nearly so unfriendly. 'What did your mother send you for?'

'She said I was to come – Mother said,' I corrected myself quickly. 'Mother said I was to see what you wanted.'

He stood there for a bit just looking at me, not unkindly but curiously, reminding me of the coalman's dog, which came out once and found me in the garden and just sort of sniffed and stared all around me without barking or jumping up or making any noise.

Then he sat down in the big leather chair. 'Come here,' he said. 'Let me have a good look at you.'

The study isn't very large, what with all the books and the chairs in there and the desk with the funny rolling-down top. He'd put the little table beside his chair and there was a newspaper on it and a magnifying glass, and when I got closer I saw that the brass ashtray had lots of fat brown stubs that looked like slugs lying inside.

'What are they?' I asked, pointing, though immediately I was worried, because I know that it's very rude to point.

But he didn't seem to mind. 'Don't tell me you've never seen a cigar, child?' He laughed. Then he opened a wooden box that was also on the table under the newspaper and took something out. 'Here.' He smiled. 'Take a whiff of that – the finest leaf.' He held it out for me to look at. 'It's what we won the war for, good cigars like these.'

I didn't dare touch it but went up close and looked, and I thought it was like a long brown sausage. It had a dark-brown smell too, not at all like the cigarettes the butcher's man smokes and has tucked behind his ear when he delivers the meat.

'What are you going to do with it?' I asked.

'Watch.' And he took out a small pair of gold scissors from his pocket and quickly chopped off the end. I was surprised. It seemed a funny thing to do, to have one of these things and then cut it up.

But he still had a lot left of the sausage-cigar. He dangled it out of his mouth and then took a gold box from his other pocket and fiddled with it until, suddenly, it flamed. I jumped back – Mother says I'm never to play with matches and that fire is very dangerous. But he laughed and put the flame to the cigar and, as I watched, he made the flame jump up and down, at the same time blowing lots of smoke out of his mouth.

'It's like a dragon,' I said, very excited.

He smiled and took the cigar out of his mouth and, putting the gold box – he said it was a called a lighter – back into his pocket, said the cigar was lit now and that this was his favourite moment of the day.

'Can you smell the smoke?' he asked. 'Do you like it?'

And I could then. It's funny, I'd actually been smelling it since he came but hadn't really thought about it. It was a lovely, spicy, smoky smell and there were big fat cushions of it all coming out of his mouth as he puffed.

'I saw the butcher's man do smoke rings once,' I said. 'Can you do them?'

'Indeed, I can,' he said. 'Watch.' And he leaned his head back and made a funny sort of gulping noise in his throat and suddenly three perfect rings came out, spinning and spiralling up towards the ceiling.

'Oh – Oh –' Every time he made another one I just said 'Oh'.

At the Hall

It was so wonderful. I thought maybe the whole room would fill up with these lovely rings, they would dance and twist all around us, like in a fairy-story. But suddenly he coughed and there was a big stream of smoke, and he put his cigar down and coughed and coughed into a big checked handkerchief until I could see tears in his eyes. I was worried, so I quickly poured him a glass of something brown out of a bottle that was on the little table, and he took a big gulp of it, but then he spluttered and started laughing until he was coughing and spluttering and laughing all at once, and I didn't know whether to be worried or whether it was all right.

'Oh,' he said, when he'd got his breath back, 'you're just like your father, aren't you? He was just the same. My heaven, I haven't blown so many smoke rings in years.'

He settled down a bit in his chair and pulled me so that I stood just by his knee, and then he reached out and touched my hair that was starting to straggle out of the ponytail. I thought he was going to complain about it like Mother, but he just said in a funny, croaky sort of voice, 'And you're pale and fair too, just like him.'

'Like who?'

'Like your father, child.'

'I think my father's dead,' I said. 'I think so because Mother doesn't like to talk about him. But maybe he's just gone away for a little while and he'll come back soon.'

But he was shaking his head and suddenly, I don't know why, I began to feel very sad and I looked down on the floor at the rug with the swirly red and green patterns that are like dragons and I tried to think hard about them and not cry. But then I felt him put his arms round my shoulders and he stroked me very gently.

'Don't be upset, little one,' he said, his voice all deep and smooth like chocolate. 'Don't be upset. You've got your grandfather here.'

And then he lifted me up so that I was sitting on his knee and, though he had put the cigar into the ashtray, I could smell the warm smoke all over his clothes, and he was rocking me and speaking, though I wasn't really listening but just hearing his words and how they rumbled in his chest and feeling how nice and safe and close it all was.

Suddenly there was a noise at the door and Grandfather stiffened and his lulling voice stopped dead.

'So, there she is.' Mother's voice was loud and harsh. 'I was wondering. Come along, Lydia, you should know better than to go bothering your grandfather. You know he likes to be left in peace. Come along, girl.'

I was already on my feet and standing beside her.

'Was there anything else you wanted, sir?' she asked.

'No, nothing.' But his voice was hard, like hers, and I almost couldn't recognize it.'

'Very good, sir.'

'No, wait,' he called suddenly, when we were already half out of the door. 'You may send the child when I ring the bell in future. I don't want to disturb you from your work.'

'As long as she's not getting in your way, sir.'

'That will be all.'

'Yes, sir.'

When we got back to the kitchen Mother was very quiet. I didn't want to say anything in case I stirred her up, but I did want to ask about why she and Grandfather talked to each other the way they did. It seemed strange to me that they weren't being friendly when he'd been perfectly friendly to me.

'He's quite nice really, isn't he, Mother?' I said when she came into my room that night to check I'd brushed my hair properly before I got into bed. 'He's quite friendly.'

'He's a – ' But she stopped suddenly and then turned a look at me. 'You just do what he says, Lydia,' she said sternly. 'All right? Whatever he wants you to fetch or carry or find or make – anything, understand? Because if you don't, then we'll be thrown out of here with nothing – nothing. Understand?'

But he never asked me to do anything. Whenever the bell rang, I'd go into the library to see him. Mostly he rang because he wanted company and he liked that mainly in the evening, when he was sitting on his own there while Mother and I sat in the kitchen after tea.

'Why don't you sit in the parlour?' I asked him one day.

'A parlour's a woman's room,' he said in his gruff voice, which didn't scare me at all now. 'Too full of fancy knick-knackery – never liked a parlour.'

'Oh, but our parlour is beautiful, Grandfather,' I said. 'I know you'd like it better if you were there and saw it properly.'

He laughed and stood up suddenly, holding out his hand. 'Come on, then, princess,' he said. 'Let's go in there together for a change and we can be lords and ladies.'

It was a lovely evening, the late sun streaming in through the garden doors. He held my hand and I felt very important, because it was the first time I'd ever really been in the parlour without being afraid of Mother. The room looked lovely. Mother and I had done our cleaning a day or two before, so all the furniture was bright and shiny and the room smelt of polish and fresh air.

'You sit on the sofa,' I said, and tried to arrange him so that he didn't look too big and clumsy against the fine carved arms. 'And I'll sit over here.' I went to one of the spindly chairs opposite him and sat well back, though I wished my legs didn't stick out but went down to the floor properly like a grown-up. 'Now we have to have polite conversation,' I said in my best grown-up voice. He smiled. 'Isn't the garden lovely?' I went on, trying to sound like Mother. We both looked out through the doors.

'It's a little overgrown,' he said, a bit sadly, I thought.

'Oh, but I like it like that,' I said quickly. 'I've got hideouts – secret hideouts – I can show you some time, if you want.' I tried to sound as if it didn't really matter.

'That would be very fine,' he said firmly, as if he meant it.

'Oh – good.'

I could see he was looking uncomfortable, so I pointed to the cabinet behind him. 'Look, Grandfather. There in the corner.

Have you seen those things?' I was hoping that maybe he'd say I could get them out – maybe he'd want to look at them properly, maybe he'd see that I really wanted to play with them. 'They're so beautiful,' I said, 'All those little things. Do you want me to show them to you?'

But he just shook his head and stood up and came over to me. 'You really love this place, don't you, princess?' he said, stroking the top of my head gently.

I looked up at him. 'It's my home – our home,' I said. 'Yours and mine and Mother's. We'll all of us always live here, won't we? For ever and ever?'

'Come on, princess.' He held out his hand and I couldn't see his face, because it was turned away, but I could hear from his voice that he wasn't happy and I was afraid I'd said something wrong.

'Don't you really like the parlour?' I got out of the chair.

'There's a lot of memories in this room, princess,' he said. 'When you're older – when you're grown up – then you'll understand.'

'I'm sorry. I didn't mean to – '

But he cut in suddenly. 'Come on, princess, we'll go and make a big smoke in the library.'

'Like Red Indians?'

He laughed.

But Mother saw us coming out of the parlour and said sharply, 'Bed now, Lydia. Leave your grandfather in peace.' I felt his hand tighten on mine for a moment before he let it go. 'And I think it's about time you took out your lesson-books again in the morning,' she went on. 'We can't have you looking like a dunce in front of all the other children when you go to school, can we?'

School? Mother had never said anything about school before. She must be making it up, I thought, to sound good in front of Grandfather. She was always wanting to make things sound good in front of him.

And in fact she didn't mention it again, so I must have been right about her saying it to show off to him. But the books did come out and I had lessons with Mother in the morning until lunch-time, and after lunch I'd be sent off to answer Grandfather's bell. Luckily he always seemed to need me just when I'd finished eating.

On rainy days we sat in the library and he smoked cigars and told me stories about being a sailor. He loved the sea and he said he'd wanted to spend his whole life sailing on it, but then a war came and his father told him he had to fight like a man in the Army. I don't think he liked the Army very much. When he talked about it he'd get a funny look in his eyes and one time he sat without saying anything for so long that the cigar went out between his fingers.

On other days he told me stories about a special underwater kingdom where, he said, I was a princess. I had a huge palace made of coral and there were laughing fish called dolphins to carry me around and do whatever I said. And I'd find treasure and ride on the waves and meet mermaids and have lots of adventures.

He called me 'Lily' instead of my real name, but when I asked him why, he muttered something about 'Lydia' being a tawdry name for his granddaughter. I didn't really understand what he meant, but then he smiled again and said that I was his little flower. 'And you're bright and clever, just like your father, too,' he said.

'Tell me about my father?' I asked. 'Please.' I so much wanted to know.

But he just shook his head as usual. 'Not now, Lily, not now,' he said. 'When you're older – I promise.' And he looked so sad that I knew I couldn't ask any more and that I'd just have to be patient.

On sunny days we'd go outside and I showed him all my hideouts in the garden: the one in the apple tree, high up in the branches, and the little place I'd made in the old greenhouse on the terrace where I kept my treasures – the little glass marbles with the snakes inside and the lovely old pieces of patterned china. He showed me how to get the blackberries off the brambles without getting pricked and we ate them and ate them until we were almost sick and our fingers and tongues were bright blue. Once we shared a bunch of grapes we found hanging from the roof of the greenhouse. They were a bit sour but we ate them all the same. Sometimes as we swished through the long grass he'd say that really the garden ought to be tidied up, but then he'd smile at me and I knew he didn't really mean it. We both liked it the way it was, full of surprises – hidden bushes and flowers and secret places to disappear into.

In the evening, after I'd had my supper, I'd go into the library, where he'd be waiting for me. 'Hallo, Lily,' he'd say, putting down his little gold-rimmed coffee cup. 'Have you come to read the newspaper for me?' Then he'd lift me on to his knee, take the paper from the arm of his chair and put the magnifying glass back on the table, saying, 'There, I don't need that now I've got my Lily here. Your grandfather's getting too old to read on his own without his Lily to help him.'

'You'll never be old, Grandfather,' I told him. 'Never, never.'

And as I read the words out, he smoked his cigar and the room fogged up so that it was like a secret club for just the two of us. And when I went up to bed my night-dress was all spicy and sweet and smelling of him, so that it was as if he was with me all night.

It was getting colder, autumn was coming, and one day when I was sitting on the little footstool at his feet, listening to him telling me a story, he suddenly stopped right in the middle. I looked up and saw his face was all twisted, as if he was going to cry, and his hands were sort of clenched like bird's claws on the arms of the chair.

'What is it, Grandfather?' I cried. 'What is it? Is something wrong? Are you all right?' But he didn't say anything and I was so frightened I just ran out of the room, calling for Mother.

But by the time we got back to him he seemed to be fine again – a bit pale-looking, but he was sipping some of the golden brandy cordial that he liked and reaching out for a cigar.

'I'm perfectly all right,' he said in that funny voice he used to Mother, when she asked what was wrong. 'Thank you.'

'It's the damp, princess,' he said to me when she'd gone. 'It's just the damp. Soon I'll be fit as a fiddle as usual.'

But he looked very peculiar and not at all well, though he tried not to show it, and over the next few days I watched him carefully to make sure he didn't do anything to make his damp worse.

Mother was starting to grumble about making up two fires for the library and the parlour. She said we needed to air the parlour and it was a waste to have a good fire going in there and not being used. So Grandfather and I sat in there together in the evenings, though it wasn't the same as being in our library, even though the parlour was still beautiful, especially with a big fire burning in the marble fireplace. He looked smaller now than when he first came and I noticed that his tummy didn't reach out to his trousers like it used to, but he started wearing a pair of jolly red braces and we made a joke of it when I pulled the elastic so that it twanged on his shirt.

It was nicer when Mother didn't sit in there with us. Somehow it was always rather uncomfortable when she was in the room too. They didn't talk to each other. Mother would sit doing some mending and Grandfather would sit reading his paper with his glass – not asking me to help or anything. And though I was allowed to play with the little things from the corner cabinet, somehow, even though I'd get all the little tiny cups and saucers arranged and the little statues and the heart-shaped pincushion with the pretty coloured pins in a nice pattern, it just wasn't the same with them both being there, watching me.

We were sitting in the parlour one evening. It was already dark, though not yet bed-time, and Mother had gone out to the kitchen to get something for my supper. He beckoned me over to him. There wasn't enough room for me to climb on his knee on the spindly chair, so I went over and leaned against him and he put his arm all round, holding me tightly.

'I want you to know, Lily,' he said in a different, hard voice –

not cross but firm, 'that I'm going to look after you when I'm gone. I'm going to make sure you'll be all right.'

'But you're not going anywhere, Grandfather,' I cried. 'Please, please, you're not going away anywhere. Don't go away.'

Then his eyes got big as plates, like they had that first time, and I was afraid that maybe I'd upset him, though I knew he wouldn't be angry at me, but I didn't want to make him cry. 'Oh, don't go Grandfather.' I put my arms around him and hugged him as tightly as I could. 'Don't go, please.' I could feel his bones all hard and sharp on his chest. He'd got so thin since the summer, he didn't even fill the chair up like he used to, and I felt terribly afraid that somehow he would sort of melt away, and that was what he meant by going. 'We'll make you special things to eat,' I blurted. 'Good things – nice things, to make you big and strong again, and then you won't want to go anywhere else. You won't want to leave me. Oh, I'll be very good, Grandfather, I promise – '

'Lily, Lily, my princess.' He stroked my hair. 'I don't want to leave you – '

'Then you won't. You promise – promise, Grandfather?'

He took a breath and stood up suddenly. 'Come here,' he said, crossing over to the cabinet. He opened the door and reached into the back. 'I want to show you something.' He took out the long, narrow, ivory tube case that has pretty carving round the side and always rattles when I dust it, as if there's something inside, though I've never dared try to open it. He twisted it between his hands and it came apart. 'Oh,' I said, because I was afraid it might be broken, but he just put the two halves back in the cabinet and turned again to me.

'This is for you, Lily,' he said, and he was holding out a key. It was a medium-sized key and had an old worn label hanging from it with some writing on. 'This is the original key to the Hall,' he said. 'Look.' He bent over, pointing, and I saw that the writing was in very old-fashioned letters, but I could still read it: 'The Hall'. 'Of course, it's not the same lock now. This is many years old. My father gave it to me when he – when I – '

He broke off, stammering a bit. 'When I was the right age,' he said. 'And now I want you to have it. It's symbolic, Lily. You understand?' I nodded hard, though I didn't understand really, but he was looking at me so strangely, so meaningfully, I didn't want to let him down. 'When you're older, then you'll understand,' he said. 'Then it'll all be clear to you. But for the time being, this is just so that you know I'll look after you. For ever and ever, I'll look after you.'

'And you won't go away?'

He put the key into my hand and shook his head. 'No, princess, I won't go away.'

'Promise?'

'Now you look after that, my Lily,' he said all in a hurry, and I thought he must have been afraid that Mother might be coming back soon. 'Keep it somewhere safe – somewhere only you know about – and remember what I said, all right?'

'I'll do whatever you want, Grandfather,' I said, slipping the key into my skirt pocket. I would find a special hiding-place for it tomorrow, not in my room, because Mother might find it there, but in the greenhouse – yes, that was a good idea, and I smiled. 'I'll put it in a really special place, Grandfather – somewhere nobody can ever find it.'

And he looked happier now, smiled and patted my head. 'You do that, princess.'

'I won't tell anyone. It'll be our secret, won't it?'

'That's right, Lily, it'll be our secret.' And he held out his hand for me to take and I felt his fingers all big and strong and firm, holding my hand and making me safe for ever.

It got cold. I had to wear woolly tights and jumpers and even Grandfather wore a cardigan over his shirt. Mother kept me at my lessons sometimes till almost tea-time. She had a big book with special tests in it that she said I had to get right and learn if I was to be ready for next term.

Sometimes his bell would ring and ring and it was ages before Mother would let me answer it. Grandfather never got cross with me but I heard him talking to Mother once when the library

31

door was open, saying things about his bell not being answered and his dinner not being so good and who did she think she was to give him such cheek. But I ran away before I heard any more, because his voice was loud and hard and it frightened me.

He still sat in the library during the day and one day – it was a Saturday and there were no lessons – Mother went out with her shopping-basket to go down to the village to get extra vegetables, because she said there hadn't been enough in the delivery van that week. She left me work to do – I was to clean the banisters all the way up the stairs, and dust and polish them thoroughly. Although Grandfather hadn't rung his bell, I knocked on the door and went into the library just to see if he was all right.

'Hallo, Lily,' he said, smiling like he always did when he saw me. 'Have you come to sit with me?'

I explained about Mother being out and my having to clean the banisters and said I was sorry to disappoint him, but all of a sudden he got out of his chair – he had to push on the arms now to stand up – and said in a jolly voice, 'Well, my dear, then I'll keep you company.'

I was very surprised and even more so when he asked for a cloth too and he said we'd race each other up to the landing, where the stained-glass window is. It was a lot of fun and we made a game of jumping over the stair-rods, so that when we arrived at the landing we were both out of breath.

I always stop at the landing when I'm dusting the banisters. I like looking at the colours and shapes in the glass: they make a lovely pattern on the floor and when the sun shines through in the afternoon the light is all green and blue and floating.

'It's like being in the sea, isn't it, Grandfather?' I said, as we stood there looking at it. But he laughed and said it was much nicer than being in the sea, much prettier and not nearly so cold.

'Do you see that coat of arms?' he said, pointing to the picture in the glass at the top of the window. 'That's our family coat of arms – yours too, princess. It's the same that's on the flag in the hall, do you see?'

I hadn't noticed this before, even though I must have seen the picture every day, and I felt a bit silly and stupid for being so blind. But when I admitted this he just smiled and said, 'Now, now, princess, no need to take on like that. All soldiers make mistakes, you know.'

'But *I'm* not a soldier, Grandfather,' I said. 'Not a proper soldier like you were.'

'You've a soldier's blood in your veins, my Lily,' he said. 'And you can be proud of that – though you'll never have to go to any war, thank God.' His voice was shaking a bit, like it always did when he talked about war. 'You'll never have to fight in those damned trenches,' he said. 'I'll make sure you never have to fight at all.' Then in a twinkling his voice changed and he said, 'Do you know what glass is made of, Lily?'

'No.'

'It's made of sand.'

'Sand, Grandfather? Really?'

'That's right, princess. Not a very promising material, I grant you, but look what you can make of it. It was your father who taught me that, princess – he was keen on science and making things. He'd have made a fine engineer, maybe even an inventor, if he'd – ' But he stopped suddenly and, though I was hoping like mad that he'd say more, I knew better than to ask him. Instead, I thought to myself, I'm a soldier, I'm Grandfather's soldier, and I imagined myself riding on a big white horse with the flag of our coat of arms – my coat of arms – fluttering in the wind behind me. When he asked me why I was so quiet and what I was thinking about, I told him and he looked very pleased and proud of me. 'Ah, Lily, Lily,' he said, 'you're worth more than all of us put together.' Then, because we'd finished the polishing, we went into the library and I read the paper to him till Mother came home.

But one morning when I was getting up I suddenly heard terrible noises coming from his room. It sounded like the noise a rabbit makes when it's caught in a trap – I saw one once when I was playing in the woods at the bottom of the garden – squealing and sort of thin screams and whining. Something was very wrong and, even though it was forbidden, I ran out of my room and straight into his to see what the matter was.

He was lying in the big bed looking small and all twisted up and his hands were crumpled into fists, beating on the covers.

'Grandfather, what is it? What is it, Grandfather?' But he didn't answer me, he didn't even seem to know I was there, and I ran down the stairs and fetched Mother.

By the time she came up he'd gone quiet again, but his face looked very white and I could see blood on his lips, as if he'd bitten them.

'I'll call the doctor,' she said, standing at the door and looking down at him. But he shook his head and said he'd be all right, though his voice didn't sound all right at all – weak and wavering.

'Come out of here, Lydia.' Mother took my arm and pulled me out with her. 'Leave him alone.'

'But, Mother – '

'Do as I say, child. Don't answer me back.'

But he looked so forlorn lying there and I couldn't concentrate at all on the lessons, because I kept thinking about him. We usually stop for my milk half-way through and Mother has a cup of tea. I watched her pour it out, all strong and brown how she likes it, and after a moment I asked her if I could take a cup up for him.

She shook her head. 'Your Grandfather doesn't want to be disturbed, Lydia. Leave him alone. Now, we're going to do history next. Have you got your book with you?'

I lied then and said it was up in my room, though in fact it was in the library – I'd been looking at it with Grandfather the day before. I was terrified she'd know that I was lying, but she just clicked her tongue and told me to go and fetch it.

I went straight up the stairs to his room, knocked very softly on the door and went in.

He was sitting on the side of the bed in his dressing-gown, feeling with his feet for his slippers. 'Hallo, Lily,' he said, his voice trying to sound cheerful. 'Did you want me?'

'Are you all right, Grandfather?' I ran towards him. 'Are you all right? Shall we fetch the doctor?'

'Doctors – quacks, the lot of them,' he said. 'I don't need any doctor. I just had a bit of a turn, that's all. Gave you a fright, did it, princess? No, there's nothing to worry about.'

All the time his feet were sort of swimming around, looking for their slippers, and I knelt down to help him. They were very cold, his feet, and sort of bigger than they had been and a funny blue colour. It was actually quite hard to push the red-leather slippers on and in the end I could only get them half-way, so his feet stuck out over the back.

But he didn't seem to mind. 'That's lovely, princess, that's lovely. Now you run along and get on with your lessons and leave your old Grandfather to get dressed.'

Still, I didn't like leaving him and I lingered by the door. 'Are you sure you're all right?' But then I heard Mother calling for me from downstairs and I had to go anyway.

For some days after that he didn't get up till nearly lunchtime. He was walking differently now and when I tried to take him out for some fresh air in the garden, he leaned on my arm and we had to stop every few steps for him to get his breath. In the evening we sat in the parlour and, though I brought in the little footstool from the library and he told me stories, somehow it wasn't the same as when we were just us together.

'You let him talk to you, Lydia,' Mother said. 'He's an old soldier and old soldiers like to talk about their wars.' But he never talked about any war, just about the underwater kingdom and my cave there, with all the treasure in it and my garden full of wild seaweed floating over my head.

In the mornings I'd hear him whimpering like the rabbit, but I learned not to call out for Mother, because he told me not to and said I had to be brave like a soldier and that I wasn't to cry. I went in to help him with his slippers and sometimes Mother would let me take him up a cup of tea, though she grumbled about him making us fetch and carry extra things, though I didn't mind. And sometimes it was very hard not to cry when I saw him lying there with his face all thin and bony and creased up; sometimes I had to dig my nails hard into my palms or really bite my lips almost till they bled to keep the tears down.

Then one day he didn't get up at all. Mother went in to him in the afternoon, but she shut the door and I couldn't hear what they said. She was inside for a very long time and when she came out her mouth was all tight and I knew better than to ask her what was happening. Then she put on her best coat, the one with the fur collar, and put on her best gloves with the buttons and said she was going to fetch the doctor and I was to sit with Grandfather till she came back.

That was the first time he explained to me about the Ship Room. I was sitting on his bed beside him and he told me how really this room, his room, was the inside of a ship. 'The clouds outside through the windows are the sails and this big bed is the master cabin and we're floating off to sea, princess, with the wind in our face and our flags flying high . . .'

After that we always played the Ship Room game when I was in with him. The doctor left a lot of medicines and Mother said I was to help do my share and that she had enough on her plate without looking after a sick old man as well, so she showed me how to measure the medicines and I would give them to him every morning when I went in. He made a funny face but he always took them and said they made him feel better, and it made me feel very grown up to be in charge of them.

Mother didn't seem to mind so much about the house now and it started to get very dusty. When I sort of hinted that we hadn't cleaned the parlour for a long time, she just said it didn't matter any more because there was no one to see it. 'It can all go hang,' she said, 'all of it. I wasn't born to be a housemaid.'

It was going to be Christmas soon. All along I'd decided that he'd be well by Christmas, because it was impossible that anyone could be ill at Christmas. Every day when I got up and dressed and went into his room and found him still lying there, looking all pale and thin, I thought, but it will be all right soon, because it'll be Christmas soon and on Christmas morning I'll go in and find him up and dressed and smiling at me. 'Good morning, Lily,' he'll say. 'I told you I'd get well again.' But sometimes, when he was looking very ill and didn't even answer me and barely opened his mouth for the medicines, it seemed as if that lovely Christmas day would never come.

My heart was really beating when I got up on Christmas morning. I dressed quickly and then, holding my breath, I knocked on his door and went in. But it was just as I'd imagined. He was up and dressed and sitting on the edge of his bed, smiling and smiling at me, and I ran into his arms and we didn't say anything much, just sat there together feeling very, very happy. It was the best Christmas present I could ever have had.

I helped him downstairs – he still had to lean on my arm a bit, even though he said the medicines really had cured him – and we went into the dining-room to have lunch properly. It was almost like the first time when he had just come, except now he smiled at me and I wasn't frightened of him at all, and when he sent Mother out to fetch something from the kitchen he took all the horrid Brussels sprouts off my plate and put them on his, even though he didn't eat them.

After lunch we went to sit in the parlour while Mother did the washing-up. I'd made him a picture of a ship sailing on the sea with our magic kingdom all drawn in underneath and he said it was very good and the nicest present he'd ever had. There was a big fire blazing in the hearth and I'd specially cleaned the room when Mother wasn't noticing the day before, so now it looked all gleaming and lovely. I sat at his feet on my footstool, both of us close to the fire, and I thought I'd never ever been so happy, because it was all right now.

Then he said, 'And I've got a present for you too, princess. Do you want to see what it is?' And he put his hand in his pocket and pulled out a big, round, smooth sort of ball of glass. 'Careful,' he said when I went to take it, 'it's heavy.'

I held it in both hands very carefully and it sort of nested there. There was a kind of picture in the middle, like a flower, made of white glass with a little yellow centre.

'It's lovely.' I hardly dared speak. 'Oh, it's beautiful, Grandfather.'

'It belonged to my mother,' he said. 'She used it to hold her papers down when she was writing her letters out in the garden – she liked sitting out there writing. I remember seeing her use it when I was a little boy the same age as you, princess.'

'Were you a good little boy, Grandfather?'

He laughed. 'Once my father had beaten some sense into me,' he said. 'I was always trying to run away to sea.' His voice went quiet and he sighed. 'I'd never have left my mother, though,' he said. 'If she hadn't died so young – I would never have – it would have all been different.' He was staring over my head as if he wasn't seeing me at all. 'You don't realize,' he said suddenly, 'how the things that happen to you when you're a child affect the whole course of your life. You don't see that at the time.' He sounded very sad and I sat very still, holding my lovely present, not wanting to disturb him. But all of a sudden he seemed to remember me. 'And do you see that flower in the middle?' he said, pointing to it with his quavery finger. 'Do you know what it is? It's a lily – like my Lily.'

'Oh, it's the most wonderful present I've ever had, Grandfather. Thank you, thank you.' And I jumped up from my stool and hugged him and hugged him until he laughed and said I was squeezing the very breath out of his body. Then he told me to fetch him a cigar from his box in the library and, though he cut it and lit it, he didn't seem to puff on it as much as before and a lot of it just lay in the ashtray, but he said that obviously it would be a while before he got his palate back again and that he would have to work up to it gradually.

After Christmas it was very cold – no snow, but the windows were covered in ice and there was frost all over the garden. It was windy too and every night the ivy batted on my window, like someone trying to get in.

At the Hall

Mother called me into her room one day. I never usually go into her room – she says it's her private place and anyway I don't like it in there. It's very dark and there are big cupboards and it's all neat and very tidy because, she says, 'A lady is never untidy, her things are always in good order.'

She was sitting at the dressing-table and watching me in the mirror. 'Don't slouch, Lydia,' she said. 'Hold your head up. God knows, you'll never get anywhere in life looking like that. I don't know where you get those looks from. Head *up*, Lydia.'

It's a very big room.

At last, when I was next to her, she turned away from the mirror and said, 'Well, I've got a nice surprise for you, Lydia.' She was smiling and using her pleased voice, and I thought that maybe it was something to do with my birthday, which is soon after Christmas, and maybe she'd got me a new dress, because I'd grown out of a lot of my old ones and I didn't like to tell her that even my shoes were getting a bit tight. I smiled back as much as I could and hoped and hoped that it would be a blue dress or a green one, because they are my favourite colours.

'I've arranged for you to go to school,' she said, still smiling. 'It's a boarding-school and you'll start next week. I've already got your uniform sent and you can try it on if you want.' She pointed with her head.

The uniform was lying on the bed. I hadn't noticed it when I came in. It was red, blood red. It looked like meat from the butcher.

'Well, what do you say, Lydia? Well?' Her voice was getting cross now, but still I didn't know what to say. Boarding-school? Going away? But what about Grandfather? How would he – 'Well, don't stand there gawping, child,' she said, angry now. 'Not catching flies, are you? What do you have to say?'

'I – I – '

I could see her eyes all drawing up close together and beetling at me. 'You understand what I'm telling you, don't you?'

'Oh – yes, Mother.'

She smiled suddenly. 'You know, they were very impressed with your schoolwork. They think I've done a really good job with you.'

I just nodded, but it seemed to make her cross again. 'Really, Lydia,' she said. 'I did expect rather more from you than this – a little gratitude would be in order, you know. It hasn't been so easy getting the money out of your – ' But she broke off. 'And you'll be mixing with some very high-up people,' she started again. 'People from your real station in life – ladies' daughters, like I've brought you up to be. So what do you say, Lydia?'

'Oh – I – '

'Where are your manners, girl?'

'I – I mean – thank you, Mother,' I managed to stutter out, and she finally nodded and looked satisfied. But all the time I was thinking, What about Grandfather? How would he manage? Who would make sure he took his medicines? Who would take up the paraffin for his little heater to keep him warm? Who would he talk to? How would be ever get properly better if I wasn't there to look after him?

He was staying in bed all the time now. He said it was just a little 'lapse', but he was getting even thinner and hardly eating anything. His nails had grown very long – 'Long as a Chinese conjuror,' he'd say with a funny smile, holding them up to look at them. 'I'll get them cut soon.' When I sat on the bed holding his hand, they would dig right into my palm when his pain came. But I didn't cry – he didn't like me to cry – and I didn't call out for Mother – he didn't like me to do that either, and I never showed him I was frightened.

But I couldn't help crying when I told him about the school. 'I don't want to go, Grandfather,' I said, sitting beside him on the bed. 'I don't want to go.'

'There now, Lily, there now.' He didn't seem to mind that I was crying and just patted my hand, his nails lightly scratching my fingers. 'It's all right,' he said. 'Going to school is a good thing. You're going to learn a lot of new tricks to teach your old grandfather, aren't you?'

'But I don't want to go. I don't want to leave you – '

'Remember, Lily,' he said. 'You're a soldier – a brave little soldier – and a soldier always obeys orders, even when they don't like them.'

'But what about you, Grandfather?' I was crying even more. 'How – how will you – '

'Do you know what I'll be doing, princess?' he interrupted me. 'I'll be sitting up here in bed, or downstairs in the library, and I'll be looking out through the window down the drive and watching for my Lily to come home again. Now, don't cry, princess. Remember – step by step, step by step, the army marches on to victory . . .'

But the night before I was to leave I couldn't sleep at all. I kept turning over and over in bed and every time I opened my eyes I could see the uniform lying on the chair opposite, like a wolf waiting to eat me. And then, even though I knew it was forbidden, even though I knew Mother would kill me if she saw me, I got out of my bed and, opening my door very, very quietly, slipped into the passage and went next door to see him.

There was a night-light burning in a little saucer by his bed and he was mumbling – he couldn't sleep either, he was saying, the pain keeping him awake, all those old wounds trying to heal but too late though, too late, he was too old for his body to knit together again . . . I stood in the doorway, shivering in my thin night-dress and listening to him rambling and moaning, and suddenly then I saw his pale stubbled face and his hollow cheeks and his eyes sinking back in his head, his lips sort of grabbing at breath, all blue and wet with spit dribbling over them, and then I knew, I just knew, that something was going to happen – something terrible, something that would make it never the same again.

I pulled back the covers and very gently climbed into bed with him. 'Ah, Lily,' he said, as he put his arms around me.

'My little Lily.' His fingers were soft as a bird's wing on my head.

I stayed there all night. My head rested on his chest and I felt his breath become deep and even, rocking me to sleep. When I woke in the morning I felt very happy. I cuddled up to him. Everything was all right.

And then I remembered.

There were ten beds in the dormitory, five on each side. Mine was half-way down the middle. The other girls looked at me without really smiling and asked a lot of questions: 'Who are you? Why have you come in the middle of the year? Where do you live? What does your father do?' Like a flock of birds circling and swooping and pecking around me.

Every morning when I woke up I'd think, This is one morning less. And every lesson when it was over, This is one lesson less. And when it was very bad and the others were teasing and laughing at me because I didn't know how to play their games, I'd hear Grandfather telling me to be brave: 'You're a soldier, Lily, a brave little soldier.' And I'd imagine a helmet like a mask to cover my face so that no one should see that I was upset.

I think it was on my birthday that the teacher took us to the History fair, or it was some time just after – I'm never too sure of the exact day when my birthday is and anyway I didn't say anything about it. But she took us to a special museum and we listened to a talk with pictures up on a screen and then we were all allowed to run around outside. There were some tables set up with things for sale and on one of them I saw the book. It was a special-looking book – not very big, but the covers were made of wood instead of leather. The man behind the table told me that the book was the story of a shipwreck and that the covers had been made from the very wood of the ship itself. I'd brought my purse with the taxi money in it that Mother had given me to get back home from the station at the end of term and, without even once thinking of what she'd say, I just handed over all the money and bought the book, even though it would mean a long walk for me.

When we got back to school I practised my italics until they were perfect and then I wrote 'To Grandfather, from his Lily' inside the cover. It looked beautiful and the rest of the term seemed to go much quicker, because whenever I was upset I'd look at the book, at the pictures of the ships and the old spidery writing on the thin paper, and I'd think of how pleased Grandfather would be when I gave it to him.

And then at last it really was over. I was on the train and then I was at the station, leaving my case, and then with just the book in my hand I was running, running, all the way down the road until I was at the gates with the trees arching over my head and I could see the Hall there at the end. And then I was running down the drive and into the house and straight up the stairs and I only stopped for a moment to get my breath back and straighten my skirt, because a soldier is never dishevelled. And then finally I was pushing the door open and running inside. 'Grandfather, Grandfather, I'm home – I'm – '

But there was something wrong, or my brain was thick, slow like mud somehow, because I couldn't quite recognize the room. The bed was made up and the medicines were cleared away; the cupboard doors were open and all the shelves empty. There was no dressing-gown on the bed or leather slippers on the floor, and even the ship in a bottle, his pride and joy that he'd made himself, wasn't on the little folding bookcase where he could see it first thing in the morning.

Maybe he's in another room, I thought slowly. Yes, of course, I realized, how silly of me, he must be better now and he's downstairs, waiting for me in the library. And I was just about to run downstairs again when I heard a shout from the window.

'Lydia? Lydia, is that you? I didn't hear the taxi. Come down at once, please, I want to talk to you.'

I went over to the window, but the sight of Mother was even more confusing. She was wearing muddy boots – oh, and *trousers*. What would he say? He'd be so angry. 'Women should look like women, act like women . . .'

I opened the window and leaned out. 'What are you doing up there?' she shouted. 'Come down this instant.'

'But, Mother – '

'Don't argue. Oh, and Lydia – ' And I thought, Yes, now she'll explain it all, now she'll tell me where he is. 'Lydia, bring me the change from the taxi, will you? I gave you more than enough, you know. There must be some change.'

I didn't say anything. I closed the window and walked away from it. I put the book down on the bare table by the empty bed. And all the time I was thinking, it has happened, it has happened. I walked very slowly down the stairs. He's not here, I told myself, he's not here and it's happened. As I walked I could feel my face tightening up again with the helmet all frozen on, like at school. I went outside to where Mother was standing, waiting for me in her dirty workman's clothes.

She took me round the side to the garden and at first I just stood there, gawping. It looked completely different. The long grass had been cut so it was flat all the way down to the woods. At first I thought that somehow I was in the wrong place, but then I looked again and I saw the apple tree, except that it was lying on its side and there were big holes all over the ground where the flowery bushes had been.

'Mother, what will – ' I started to say, but as I turned to look at her I suddenly stopped.

The greenhouse. It wasn't there. It wasn't there. The greenhouse wasn't there. Where it had been was a big, clear, dry piece of earth.

'Mother – ' I cried, running towards it. 'Mother, where – what have you – where – ' I was gibbering, stuttering, and I knew she'd be angry, but I couldn't think about that. My greenhouse, my special place – gone. And suddenly I remembered my key, Grandfather's key. It was in there. I'd left it in a little pot under one of the old workbenches in a place nobody would ever find. I was on my knees now, scrabbling in the dry, dusty earth, but there was nothing, nothing, not a shred of wood, not a sliver of glass, nothing. 'Oh, Mother, Mother,' I wailed, not caring any more how angry she'd be. 'Mother, what's happened? Where has it gone?'

'That's enough, Lydia.' She stood over me. 'Stop blubbering like a baby. Really, I don't know what you're making such a fuss about. An old greenhouse – It was high time it came down. It was an eyesore quite apart from the danger – '

'But – but I had a – I had – things in there, special things, things that were mine.'

'There was nothing in there,' she said. 'I checked it myself before the workmen came. Nothing but a load of old rubbish – pots and so on – nothing worth keeping. Now, Lydia – ' She looked at me hard. 'There's going to be a few changes here now. Lydia, Lydia, are you listening to me?'

But it was so hard to listen. I had to keep swallowing to try to stop crying, and I kept thinking, My key, my key, I've lost Grandfather's key.

'Pay attention, Lydia. I want you to listen to me now. Things are going to be very different from now on – '

'But what about Grandfather?' I couldn't keep it in. It just burst out of me. 'What's he going to say?'

But she just smiled, as if she wasn't frightened at all. I didn't like the way she looked all pleased with herself. I didn't want to see it. 'That's just what I'm saying, Lydia,' she went on. 'We don't have to worry about your grandfather any more, that's the joy of it. You see, we're quite safe now. We're quite, quite safe.' She looked very happy.

'But, Mother – '

'And you don't have to call me by that name any more, Lydia,' she interrupted. 'I've never liked it – it's sentimental and quite unnecessary. You're old enough now to call me by my proper name. Now – ' She was smiling her decided smile and I just looked up at her numbly. I didn't want to hear any more, I didn't want to know any more, I didn't want any of this to be happening. 'There's a lot to do to get this garden into shape,' she was saying, 'and that's what we're going to do. Starting right now. So run into the house and get some old clothes on and you can start to help me lay out the markers for where the flowerbeds will be, all right?' She looked at me and smiled suddenly. 'And I tell you what, Lydia,' she said. 'As a special treat I'll allow you to keep the change from the taxi money all for yourself. How about that?'

We worked in the garden every day. We laid out lines of string marking the ground and Mother said those were the places we had to dig over. She did the digging and I carried away the weeds. She told me to put them all in a heap where the greenhouse had been, and every time I went there I kicked around the earth a bit, hoping that maybe, just maybe, I might find the key, but of course I didn't. Some men came and they sawed the apple tree into logs and Mother said we could burn it over the winter and it would smell nice on the fire. I didn't want to think about that.

She wore trousers all the time now and didn't seem to care about the house and how it looked. The floor in the hall got very dirty and covered in bits of mud from where she walked about with her big boots on. When I tried to say something, she just laughed and said it didn't matter any more and that she was liberated from house-cleaning. But I took the polish and the dusters and went into the parlour on my own – she didn't seem to mind that any more – and while she was busy outside I took all the things from the corner cabinet, cleaned them and put them back, and I dusted the chairs and polished the tables. Then I sat on my little stool and closed my eyes and tried to imagine Grandfather was there with me. But it was very quiet. And suddenly I realized that the clock wasn't ticking on the mantelpiece. Grandfather always wound it up in the evening, just when I was on my way up to bed. Always, when I came out of the kitchen after I'd drunk my milk, he'd come out of the library at exactly that same moment and we'd go into the parlour together and he'd take out a big key from somewhere inside the clock and wind it up. 'There,' he'd say, 'all ready for a new day.' But when he'd been ill, he hadn't been able to do it and the clock must have stopped ages ago, but it was only now I noticed and I didn't know how to wind it myself. The chandelier was tinkling over my head though the little pieces of crystal were dull and not sparkling any more and I just covered my face with my hands and cried.

I was ill in school that summer and they had to send me home in the middle of term. They said my temperature was too high and I should be at home resting. They sent Mother a telegram and she had to come and collect me. She was angry about that and when we were alone she said I was just putting it on, but I didn't care any more about her being angry. I felt very tired all the time, tired and hot. I didn't want to eat anything, I just wanted to sleep. I fell asleep in the train and when I woke up I was in my room and my case was on the chest at the bottom of the bed. I don't really remember it very clearly but I think I stayed in bed a long time and Mother – Madeleine – came in and out a lot. I just wanted to sleep and sleep and sleep for ever.

When I began to feel better, Madeleine said I should come downstairs, because she didn't want to keep fetching the trays from upstairs. It was sunny and she said I could sit in the garden, but I didn't want to sit out there. It looked so strange now. There were lots of places where the earth was bare and ugly, with no plants or grass covering it up. Madeleine was very brown from spending so much time outside and I don't think she'd have minded even if I'd got brown, though before I'd always had to wear a hat.

But I didn't want to think about how things had changed – it hurt my head to think – so I just spent the days sitting quietly on my own with a book in the parlour, not really reading but looking at all the nice things and feeling safe and peaceful with them around me.

One day when I came down with my book I heard voices from inside the parlour. For a moment, just a moment, I thought, it's him, he's back, he's back, and I ran in without stopping.

Madeleine was sitting on the sofa. I noticed immediately that she was wearing one of her skirts. Opposite her, in the other chair, resting his feet on my little stool, was a man – a strange man I'd never seen before. He had a cigarette between his fingers and the smoke was coiling up and spreading out through the room.

'Say hallo to Mr Stein, Lydia,' Madeleine said, as I stood there. 'Heavens, child, where are your manners?'

I must have said something, because all of a sudden he was standing up and looking down at me. He wasn't very tall, but he sort of felt tall. He was wearing a smart blue suit and had a tie like a bow at his throat. 'Hallo, Miss – ' But Madeleine stopped him. 'Just call her, Lydia,' she said, 'that's quite enough for a little girl.' He turned back to me. 'Hallo, Miss Lydia,' he said, and his strange voice seemed to laugh at me as he spoke. 'What a beautiful girl you are.' 'I'll make the best I can of her,' Madeleine said. He laughed. '*Ach* children,' he said, 'only problems, my friends tell me.' Then they both laughed and looked at me.

I didn't like him. He had thick black hair that was streaked with white, like a badger, and a funny accent that sounded like the rooks in the woods. Though he smiled at me a lot and tried to make me shake his hand, I didn't want to. There was something about him that made me think of the wolves in fairy-stories that gobble you up. Maybe it was his smile. He smiled a lot and Madeleine smiled a lot with him. I didn't want him in my parlour.

After a while Madeleine told me to leave them, because they had things to discuss. But I didn't close the door completely and I stood beside it and listened to her telling him about how I'd been ill and it had been even more of an expense and so she hoped they'd be able to do business.

Then, as I watched through the crack of the door, I saw him suddenly pick up one of the spindly chairs and turn it over, almost as if he were going to clean it. 'Very nice,' he said. 'Very nice, very good quality.' Then he went round the whole room, touching all the things in it and speaking to Madeleine and writing things down in a little book. I couldn't really understand it at first, but then it came to me that maybe he was from a special place that cleaned things properly. And because we hadn't done the cleaning for so long, maybe he was going to do it for us. And maybe he might even repair the wonky leg that had broken on one of the tables and stitch up the material on the sofa where it had come away on the back. I felt much better once I'd realized this and I was sorry I'd been so unfriendly to Mr Stein. And when I saw him standing in the middle of the room, looking up at the chandelier, then I was absolutely certain, because the chandelier was really very dirty now, far dirtier than I'd ever seen it before, though it still tinkled beautifully in the draughts. It'll all be lovely again, I told myself as I ran upstairs to watch him leaving, it'll all be just as it was.

I watched from my window as he shook hands with Madeleine in the porch and when he went to his car that really decided me. It was a big shiny silver car without a single spot of dirt. Nobody but a proper cleaning person can have a car like that, I thought, and I smiled and waved from my window, even though he didn't see me as, with a flash of his gleaming black shoes, he got into the car and drove away.

I was feeling much stronger now and started to go back out in the garden. It was sunny and warm and I wanted to play down in the woods, but Madeleine said I wasn't to play there any more. 'Don't you know?' she said, looking at me very hard. 'There's pilots down there left over from the war. You don't want them getting their hands on you, do you?' 'Not real ones?' I said. 'Real enough, my girl. Now don't go down there any more, you hear me? You can stay up here where I can see you.' She went on and on about it and in the end I gave up. I didn't want to argue with her and I was scared of what she was saying, scared of the woods and what might be in them, though I'd never been scared of them before. But now everything was different.

The van didn't come until a few weeks later. I'd quite forgotten about Mr Stein. Madeleine and I were busy planting the ugly, stumpy bushes she'd bought, setting them out in straight lines in the new beds. I thought they looked horrible with their spikes and their rusty-coloured leaves, but Madeleine was very happy. 'Your father would be proud of me,' she said. 'He'd be proud of what I'm doing.' Usually she hardly ever mentioned my father but this time, instead of being pleased at hearing about him, I just thought how Grandfather would have hated all this change, like I did.

We had nearly all the bushes planted when we heard wheels crunching the gravel and suddenly an enormous elephant-like van came up through the trees and stopped outside the house. I wanted to laugh, but Madeleine dropped the fork out of her hands, pushed the hair back from her face and said she was going to be busy now and I was to stay right there in the garden and not move.

I waited until she'd got to the van and then I took some small steps forward. There was writing on the side of the van and I wanted to read what it said, but I couldn't get close enough. Then, as I stood watching, about five or six men got out of the back, all wearing long brown overalls – they fluttered around Madeleine like a group of moths. Then another car came up the drive and stopped beside the van. I recognized it at once, of course – it was so bright and shiny – and when Mr Stein got out and shook hands with Madeleine I felt quite excited, because at last now the parlour would be properly cleaned. They all followed Madeleine into the house.

It's very difficult to look in through the parlour doors from the garden without being seen. I decided that if I lay down very flat and wriggled my way close to the doors, they might, if I was very lucky, just be too busy with the cleaning to see me. And I wanted to watch to see how they did it. Maybe I could learn something for later, because surely they weren't going to come every time. I did wonder a bit about the big van, but then I realized that there must obviously be a special machine in there to do all the cleaning, so I crawled up as close to the doors as I dared and waited.

At first they all stood around in a clump talking. Then the moth-men nodded to something Mr Stein said and started picking up the chairs and carrying them to the door. I couldn't understand that at all. Surely they were going to bring the cleaning machine in from the van, weren't they? And it wasn't till two of them had got either end of the sofa and were carrying it out that I finally understood – they were taking the furniture *to* the machine. Of course. How could I have imagined that they would bring a big machine in through the doors? They would take the furniture to the machine and it would clean everything and then they'd bring it all back.

The room seemed to be getting very empty and, though I understood what was happening, it made me feel strange to see it looking so bare. Everything got taken out – the pictures, the little tables, everything. Then finally there was just the corner cabinet left and I thought, no, they can't need to take that. Because I had only just cleaned the little things inside it the day before and they weren't at all dusty. Mr Stein opened the door and I saw him put his hand inside and one by one take all the things out, wrap them in cloths and put them in a case at his feet. Then the moth-men came back in and lifted up the cabinet and took that away too. They all went out. The room was empty and suddenly I was very, very worried. It wasn't right, it couldn't be right. And I was just about to run inside when the men came back with Mr Stein. He pointed to the floor and up at the chandelier and they nodded, and he went out again and they did something on the floor and two of them walked out with the carpet like a giant sausage under their arms. The other two were putting up a little ladder and I could see them fiddling around with the chandelier.

No, this wasn't right. I ran round to the side of the house to see what was happening. There is a big stone wheel there that I am forbidden to go close to. Madeleine says it is very precariously balanced and that it will crush me if I go anywhere near it. I've always been afraid of that wheel, ever since she told me about the children it did crush, and I've never so much as touched it. But this time, because it was important, because I was desperate, I went right up next to the wheel and hid beside it, where I knew no one could see me. It was very cold crouching there and I could almost feel the ghosts of those dead children trying to catch me, but it was the only place to hide and I had to watch, had to see what they were doing to Grandfather's things.

Madeleine was smiling and shaking hands with Mr Stein. 'I just can't tell you how grateful we are,' she said, as he handed her a small piece of paper. 'I simply don't know how we would have managed without you.' 'The pleasure is all mine,' he said. 'I hope you won't miss these treasures.' He waved his hand to where all the furniture was looking very strange, standing out on the drive. Miss them? What did he mean? He wasn't going to take them away, surely? 'There are more important things in life than old pieces of furniture,' Madeleine replied. 'You're a wise woman,' he said, smiling his wolf smile. 'And you would still be interested in some of the other pieces?' Madeleine asked. He nodded. 'Of course, of course. At any time when you wish to contact me I will do my best to be of service to you.'

The moth-men were putting the furniture in the van now. I saw it all go – the tables and chairs, even the carpet, all rolled up. I closed my eyes when they lifted in the corner cabinet. When I opened them again, the furniture was all packed away and two of the moth-men were carrying a large bundle wrapped in sacking. It fell open when they lifted it into the van and I saw the chandelier. It was all going, all of it. The men got into the van. I saw Mr Stein and Madeleine shaking hands, then he picked up the case from by his feet – the case that had all the little things in it – and he got into his car and drove away.

I didn't wait any more. I was running, running, not to the house, not even to Madeleine, because it was too late for that, too late for it all. I was running down the garden, through the soft beds, kicking the bundles of new plants, never minding that my legs were getting scratched and bleeding. I wanted to run away, away – I wanted to run away and never come back. Let the pilots get me, I thought, running to the woods. I don't care any more. Everything's gone and I don't care.

She caught up with me just before I reached the woods. She grabbed hold of my shoulder and swung me round. She was panting and her face was all smeared and dirty, her eyes round and hard, and her hair straggling over her shoulders. 'How dare you disobey me?' she shouted. 'How dare you?'

But I didn't care any more. I didn't care even if she hit me. There was nothing to care for any more, nothing, it was all gone, all taken away. 'I hate you,' I screamed. 'I hate you. I don't want to be here with you. I want to run away. I want – I want – ' But I was crying now. I'd never shouted at her before and I was afraid and angry and upset all at once. 'I want my Grandfather,' I sobbed. 'I want him – I want him back. Where have you put him? Why have you taken away all his things? They're his things. Put them back. Tell that Mr Stein to put them back.'

'Don't be such a fool.' She was shaking me. 'Don't you understand? We're free – free. Your grandfather's dead. We don't ever have to live with that miserable old bastard again. We're free, you and I, free.' And then she suddenly sat plonk down on the ground, still holding on to me, but with her other hand grabbing handfuls of earth and running it through her fingers. 'We got what we wanted,' she said, 'and now we're free – free to do what we like. Who cares about that old furniture? I'm not a housemaid and neither are you. I'm not going to waste my life cleaning all day. There's the garden to do – the garden is what's important now. We'll buy some nice comfortable furniture we don't have to clean and don't have to tiptoe around.' She had let go of me now and was burying both her hands deep in the soil, like a dog digging for a bone. 'We've won, Lydia, don't you understand?' She was laughing. 'We've won. I played the game for both of us and we've won. I've won for you. Because don't you ever forget this, Lydia – ' She suddenly turned to me. 'I did it all for you – *all* of it. And it was worth it. God, in the end it was worth it.'

But I didn't say anything. What was there to say? And I didn't even try to run away. What for? There was nowhere for me to go. I just looked at her sitting there, scrabbling in the dirt like an animal, and I thought, I hate you. I hate you and I'll hate you for as long as I live. I'll never stop hating you and one day, one day, I'll get my own back, just you wait and see.

I stood in the pool of the hall, the suitcases like rocks around me. I was aware that soon those rocks would dissolve, forced open by the pressure of these insistent waters, and all the contents – clothes, shoes, books, toys – would soon become part of the landscape of the house from which I would no longer be able to distinguish myself.

But I just stood there, open-mouthed, marooned in the cold heart of the house, that no man's land I used to cross holding my breath. It looked so cluttered, so dirty. The floor was scuffed, unpolished; I could feel the rough, untreated wood scratching the soft leather of my suitcases with hard, spiteful nails. If I looked hard enough I could still see the faint outline where the flag had hung, the hooks where the swords and shields had been displayed, though the walls themselves were grimy, the paint cracked and peeling. Oh, God, I should never have come back . . .

'Ah, Lydia, there you are.'

I jumped. 'Madeleine – yes. I – I was just taking the cases up.'

'No need for that,' she said crisply. 'Later.' She stood sturdy and imperious, her iron-grey hair twisted into a tight knot at her neck. Although I am taller than my mother, I always feel she is looking down on me. But then I noticed she was wearing the new skirt Dan and I had given her for Christmas, in an attempt to wean her away from her shabby gardening clothes, and so I told myself sternly, She's making an effort, you can too.

I tried to smile.

'We'll have tea now,' she went on. 'It's all prepared on the terrace. Come along.' And she was so certain of being obeyed that already she was turning away and I, like a sleepwalker, was taking a step to follow her before I pulled myself back.

'No – ' I tried to cover the cry quickly. 'I mean, not just yet – in a moment – ' She turned round to give me a hard stare. Oh, God, the fish look, stern and unblinking . . . 'I just want to unpack some of our things,' I rushed on. 'You know how creased everything gets in a suitcase.' There, surely she'd approve of that?

But she just looked at me for a long moment, then sighed heavily – like bellows, I remembered suddenly, the childhood image horribly vivid, bellows puffing out the smoke of her anger. 'Well,' she said slowly, the annoyance clearly marked in her voice. 'Tea *is* ready, you know. I don't want to let it get cold.'

'I'll only be a minute.' I grabbed my chance as an artiste grabs her trapeze. A minute would be all I needed to recover my bearings and settle myself, settle the past that was being kicked up all around me like a drift of leaves. I must see myself here as an adult, independent, and I must remember Madeleine as that dislocated old woman on her annual Christmas visit to us in town, standing awkwardly by the tree as she received her presents. 'I'll only be a moment,' I said again as I snatched at the cases. 'I promise.'

But she stepped forwards. 'We'll do it together, Lydia,' she said smiling. 'It won't take so long then. Here – ' She reached out a strong, sunburnt hand. 'Let me take one. You can't walk up the stairs in those shoes anyway, you'll break your neck.'

'No – ' My cry was desperate now, with not a shred of gauze to cover it. No, not together, not Madeleine's hands unpacking the clothes and stitching them into the fabric of the house. I lunged at the cases and began half carrying, half dragging them up the stairs. 'No – you have your tea and stay with the children. I really won't be long.'

But it was as if her eyes drained the strength from my arms. The cases dragged on my shoulders and each step closer to the stained-glass window on the landing was a step snatched from defeat. I'll be all right at the window, I told myself, if I get to the window it'll all be all right. Because I had always rested at the window. On the way up to my room at the end of term, it had always been the first mark of reprieve from the cold clutches of the hall, something familiar, something permanent, something Madeleine could never get rid of or change.

I put the cases down at last and looked out through the lozenges of glass. They were very dirty, cobwebs in the corner which automatically I wiped off with my hand. I must show this to the twins, I thought, Kitty especially will love this. But where were the twins? I tried to peer through the glass. I must keep them in sight. They can't be allowed to run riot, not here. Where were they?

'A moment, Lydia.'

I started, turned round quickly. What was she still doing here, watching me? 'Yes.' I answered, a little irritably, a little defiantly.

'I don't think,' she began slowly, 'I don't think – I've explained about the rooms.'

The rooms? I looked at her. There was a familiar smile on her lips which made me uneasy. 'What about the rooms?' I said. 'I'd thought Kitty would go in my – in the Rosebud Room and Christopher would go in the spare room and – and – ' But she was smiling that smile, the surprise smile that always danced out of my reach like a fisherman's fly on the water – I've got a surprise for you, Lydia, you're starting school next week . . . I've got a surprise for you, Lydia, I've had our bedrooms done. There, doesn't yours look pretty with all the little rosebuds?

'No, it won't be like that, Lydia.' She was shaking her head. 'You see, they're *both* going to sleep in your old room. I've set up the camp bed in there.'

'Both?' I was taken aback. Was it so long since she'd seen the twins that she'd forgotten how naughty they could be about going to sleep? 'But Madeleine, there's no need. You know they're much better about sleeping in their own rooms now. Of course, it's very thoughtful of you.' I managed to smile gratefully. 'But I'm sure they won't be a bit frightened being here, and anyway – ' I tried to laugh it off – 'you know what it'll be like if they're in together, they'll be up half the night fooling around and – '

'Not in this house they won't.'

'But why can't one of them sleep in the spare room?'

'Because I'm sleeping in the spare room.'

'But – but what about your room?' I was confused now, the rooms spinning over my head like a merry-go-round.

'You're sleeping in there.'

'Me?' I was shocked. Sleeping in her room – Madeleine's room, with those twisted briars creeping up the walls and the garish fat blooms spying on me? No. No. Never.

'I thought you'd appreciate the extra space.' She was really smiling now, as if she enjoyed my confusion.

'But what about the Ship Room?' I cried out before I could stop myself. 'Why can't I sleep in there?' Because in the end it had really only been the promise of the Ship Room that had persuaded me to come down.

Madeleine's laugh was serrated: 'The "Ship Room"?' she questioned. 'Oh, you mean the Brown Room. No, I'm afraid you can't sleep there, Lydia.' She paused, and there in the deep I saw a glint of movement.

'Why not?'

'I've, well – ' She broke off and took a step forward, idly stroking the newel post at the foot of the stairs with her thick garden-stained fingers. 'Didn't I mention it to you?' she said. 'No, come to think of it I don't think I did.' She paused again, and there it was just beneath the surface, finally swum up from the deep, the fat fish of her surprise.

I stood very still. 'What didn't you mention?'

'I've invited a guest down for a few days while you're here.' She sounded casual, but I could hear glee in her voice. 'Should I have told you earlier? I don't think so. It really wouldn't have made any difference, would it?'

'A guest? Who?'

She hesitated again, seemed about to speak, but then suddenly she changed her mind. 'We don't have time to go into it all now, Lydia, we'll talk about it later. You just go upstairs and sort out your things.'

'But, Madeleine – '

'I think that'll be all for now, Lydia,' she said briskly, turning away. 'I'll be out on the terrace with the twins. We'll wait tea for you. Don't be long, please.'

And she swept out of the hall, leaving me standing up there by the window like a child in a game of king-of-the-castle when all the other children had gone. The field was mine, but the suitcases leaned against me heavy as corpses.

I thought I had prepared myself for the Rosebud Room. When Dan had told me that he'd be on tour with the orchestra all summer and we wouldn't be able to have a proper family holiday before the twins started at their new school, and when I'd succumbed, finally, to the twins' pleading and agreed as a special treat to bring them down to visit the Hall, I'd gone over and over the place in my mind, disinfecting it of all the unpleasant memories, scouring it clean so that my return would find it sterile and fresh and undisturbing.

But now, as I entered the room – my old room – the tight little yellow buds with the rough-haired stems clawing up the walls made me shudder with a familiar nausea. Even though the paper was faded now and the buds I'd picked away with my child's fingernails were flat and empty and not the new growth I used to fear, still the densely packed, prim flowers made me feel trapped, as if in the palm of a tightly-clenched fist.

It won't matter to the twins, I told myself as I heaved their suitcase on to the bed. They won't notice anything, they won't care. But even though I unpacked carefully, methodically, still the tendrils of the room reached out to catch me – the ink stain on the floor, the tiny hole in the windowpane through which the wind whistled in the night while the ivy creaked and strained, trying to reach me . . .

No.

At the Hall

I stood back from the empty suitcase and tried to look round the room calmly. It doesn't look nearly so gaunt now, I told myself, with the twins' things softening it. Their toys and books look very good on that chest of drawers, even if it is shabby. No, it's all fine, it's all going to be fine. I tucked Kitty's owl into her bed and Christopher's teddy into his and tried to push out of my mind the thought of them lying pale in that frozen spring bower.

But as I came out of the room, I realized with a slump of despair that I wouldn't be able to hear them if they called me in the night. My suitcase was waiting outside Madeleine's door at the far end of the corridor, from where nothing could be heard. I hesitated. No, I'd unpack my own things later, when it was dark and I couldn't see the roses.

And I meant to go straight down the stairs for tea on the terrace. I was even bracing myself for the next encounter. But it was as if my body had moved forward of its own accord. Two steps and I was outside the door – his door. Like a child again, I looked furtively over my shoulder, then gripped the handle and slipped inside.

The Ship Room – our ship, princess, all shipshape and watertight, eh? But it's the Brown Room now, I reminded myself, pushing aside the memories that tangled over my head like strands of seaweed. I'll have to remember that. Certainly it looked impersonal enough. A meagre bed in the corner, with a drab brown cover thrown over it. A table, a chair, a washstand.

But standing there in the heart of that nut-brown room, couldn't I catch a faint whiff of his cigars? Maybe trapped in the curtains? Or in the walls themselves, seeped in over time, as the heavy scent of tobacco had seeped into his clothes, his hair, his skin? Surely there was something – some little trace?

Then I noticed the bowl of roses on the windowsill and I remembered Madeleine's mystery visitor. Who was it? I was too old, surely, for her to play these guessing-games. But whoever it was – and certainly Madeleine knew few people, not liking to 'mix' with the neighbourhood – I resented them coming down and stealing this room from me, this one little oasis of peace that would have kept me watered and refreshed for the whole difficult holiday.

Maybe they won't stay long, I thought, as I went back to the door. Maybe when they leave I'll be able to sleep in here after all. The thought gladdened me and I shut the door gently, carefully, unable to break the habit of years ago.

'Your tea is cold now,' Madeleine said acidly as I stepped out on to the terrace. 'We didn't wait. Christopher and Catherine were a little - impatient.'

'Oh, I'm sorry.' I pulled the wrought-iron chair out so that it screeched on the flagstones. 'Sorry,' I mumbled again.

'I'll have to make some fresh.' Madeleine reached for the teapot.

'No, no. You don't have to,' I said quickly. 'I can drink it cold – I prefer it cold, actually.' And before she could stop me, I'd grabbed hold of the pot – God, how that fat brown belly used to leer at me over my vegetables – and poured the thick, dark liquid into my cup. 'Lovely,' I said, taking a great gulp of the bitter brew. 'Just what I wanted.'

'If you say so.' Her voice was stiff with disbelief.

We lapsed into silence.

Oh, God, I thought, why is this so difficult? Surreptitiously, trying to avoid looking directly at the garden, I glanced round for the twins. Where were they, my anchors, my buoys, who would keep me from floating adrift in this cold sea? Would they suddenly pop up there amongst the avenues of bird-leg roses I was trying so hard not to see? Or were they in –

'I sent them off to play,' Madeleine intercepted me. 'They're in the woods. I hope that's all right?' she added with a show of deference.

In the woods? You're not to go playing down there, Lydia, the pilots will get you . . . I was so surprised that I missed the rest of her sentence. 'What?' I said stupidly, when she looked at me for a response.

'Not "what", Lydia, please.'

'Sorry.' I pulled myself to sit straight, concentrate, but the little metal points of the chair were cutting into my back. 'I, I didn't catch – What did you say?'

'I merely said – ' But she was sighing irritably now at having to repeat herself and I winced. Oh, God, she's going to be angry, please don't let her be angry. And then I was so appalled at hearing that child's prayer leap so readily into my mind that I almost missed what she was saying again. ' . . . and rather overexcited, the journey, I imagine. They just need to run off a little of their high spirits.' She looked at me, waiting.

'Yes – yes, of course,' I agreed quickly. I took another sip from my cup, but even as I drank the sour, cold tea I could feel Madeleine's will reinforcing my movements like a steel corset. Hold the saucer *with* the cup, Lydia, properly, girl . . . I felt hot and dirty, the sweat of apprehension pricking under my arms. I'd like a bath, I thought. A long, hot bath. But there would only be the old stained tub that took ages to fill – just two inches, mind, Lydia; there's not enough hot for you to waste . . .

'Actually,' Madeleine said suddenly, leaning forward, 'now we've got a moment, I wanted to talk to you about the twins. This new school you're thinking of sending them to . . .'

'It's all decided,' I said quickly. 'They'll start there in the autumn.'

'Do you really think that's wise?' She was crumbling a piece of bread as she spoke, rubbing it between her thick fingers till the table was covered in little pellets. And don't play with your food, Lydia. I've told you before, if you waste it you'll go hungry . . . 'You know, they're very young, don't you think?'

I looked at her astonished. Since when had that made any difference to you? I thought. Since when did you care about a child's age?

'What do they think themselves – the twins, I mean?' she went on. 'I haven't had a chance to ask them myself yet, but – '

'And I would prefer it if you didn't,' I cut in. 'The twins are absolutely fine about it. Dan and I have explained it all to them, they've been down to the school, they understand they'll be boarding there and they're both perfectly happy about it. In fact, they're quite excited,' I added. 'Though you know what children are like – they try not to show it, of course.'

'Of course,' she echoed drily. 'But – they are very young,' she said again. No more than I was, I thought, eyeing her coldly. 'Are you sure they understand just what – '

'Madeleine, I really do think that I – that Dan and I know what's best for our children,' I said firmly. 'It's a lovely school, huge grounds for them to run about in, and they're going to get a much, much better education than we'd be able to give them in town, all right?'

'But what about the money?' She was gripping on to the subject like a bulldog. 'Surely it's all going to be far more expensive than that small, progressive day school they've been going to?'

'Actually,' I said, barely managing to hold on to my temper, 'it's not all that expensive really. And Dan's got a regular income from the orchestra now which he will probably be able to supplement with some extra teaching – he's been invited to give some master classes while he's on tour,' I added, hoping to distract her. 'And – well,' I went on, trying to sound casual, 'I'm going to be free too without the twins around, aren't I? So, I've been thinking that I might be able to find myself a job – start a career, even.' There, it was out, the secret wish that I'd nurtured without telling anyone – a life of my own at last, some freedom, some independence. I love my children. God knows I'd give up my life for them if I had to, but in a way that was what I had done and it was hard bringing them up with Dan away so much of the time, hard to have a family so unexpectedly, so unplanned and not just one child but two. I'd sacrificed myself for them without any complaint, any compromise, for eight years and now it was time I had a little freedom, a little of my own youth back before it completely melted away.

I tried to look at her straight, unafraid, while I waited for her response. I told myself that whatever she said, it didn't matter, my mind was made up, the decision taken.

But she looked away from me, looked down the garden so I couldn't see her face, and her voice when she spoke was subdued. 'Well, Lydia,' she said. 'I'm not one for interfering, as you know. I just thought you might – might reconsider – for the children.'

'I'll bear your opinion in mind,' I said coldly, aware only of a dull disappointment that she should appear so indifferent to my own fledgeling plans.

'Still,' she said, turning back to me, 'at least they can have a good holiday here before they start.'

'They've been looking forward to it.'

'Well, as you know, Lydia, you could have brought them down to the Hall at any time. It's not for the lack of invitations.'

We were treading on very thin ice and, though I tried to meet her gaze levelly, my eyes kept sliding off.

'Anyone would think,' she continued, 'that you had some sort of bee in your bonnet about coming here.' She paused and then added heavily, 'The Hall is your home, Lydia, after all.'

Our eyes met.

But at that moment there was a loud shrieking as the twins swooped round the side of the house towards us.

'We've been playing lions and tigers,' Christopher shouted, and I was so relieved to see him, my darling golden boy, that I didn't even think to reprove him for his loud voice. 'Look, Mummy, I'm a lion and Kitty's a tiger. Look – look – ' And roaring wildly he crouched on all fours and sprang down the terrace steps.

Kitty was sidling up to me, soft, pliant, her skin smooth under my fingers. I wanted to lift her on to my lap, to feel her warming me. 'I'm not a tiger,' she said. 'I don't want to be a tiger.' She was twisting her plaits round and round her fingers and the ribbons had come undone. 'I don't want to be a tiger,' she said again.

'Stand still, darling,' I said as I turned her around and pulled off the ribbons. 'Let me do your hair.' The strands were silky. If

I bent over close enough I could even smell the baby-powder smell that permeated her skin. And I had a sudden rush of love for her and her brother, these mysterious separate beings who had grown in my belly and for whose sake I tried to do everything.

'But I don't want to be a tiger,' she said, wriggling.

'Stand still, darling.'

'I don't.'

Christopher bounded back up the terrace steps. 'Kitty is a tortoise,' he chanted irritatingly. 'Kitty is a – '

'Christopher,' I warned. 'Don't.' I tied the final bow in Kitty's hair and pushed her away. 'Now, remember what I told both of you about behaving?' I eyed them. 'Remember?'

'But I'm not a tortoise.' Kitty's lip was trembling, her face creasing. If she starts to cry now, I thought, there'll be no end of a scene. It's the end of a day, she's tired, overexcited –

'Of course you're not a tortoise, darling,' I said, my hand reaching for the sugar bowl. 'Here, have a – '

'But he says – '

'Christopher, for heaven's sake tell her you're sorry.'

'But I'm not. I think she *is* a tortoise.' He glared obstinately.

'Christopher, please.' I could feel Madeleine's cool gaze on my back. Why did the children have to show me up like this? 'Here, darling – ' I made one last attempt with the sugar lump. 'Kitty, you have this and – '

'But I don't want to be a tortoise,' she shouted, ignoring my outstretched hand. 'I want to be – I want to be – '

'You can be an eagle.' Madeleine's voice broke in, firm and strong, and Kitty looked over to her immediately. 'You can be an eagle,' she went on, smiling encouragingly. 'And an eagle can see very far, can't it?'

Kitty jumped up and down, suddenly excited. 'I'm an eagle – an eagle,' she cried, and danced around the terrace, her arms out wide. 'I'm an eagle and eagles can do much cleverer things than boring old lions.' She was taking little hops and skips into the air.

'Lions can kill more things,' Christopher put in.

'But eagles can fly, can't they, Grandma?' Kitty ran up and, flinging her arms around her grandmother, gave her a warm kiss.

'I think it's time for bed,' I said. 'Time for your baths anyway.'

But they both ignored me. 'I'm an eagle – an eagle,' Kitty was shouting persistently. 'And you're just a boring, smelly old lion who can't do anything.'

'I can tear you into little pieces,' Christopher shouted back.

'You'll have to catch me first.'

'Children,' I warned. 'Remember what I told you.'

But the squall flared up suddenly. She pushed him, he pulled her plaits and before I knew what was happening they were locked together, rolling over the terrace, tearing and punching each other viciously.

'That's enough,' I shouted, very angry now, as I leapt out of my chair. 'Christopher, Kitty, stop it. Stop it – *now*.' I grabbed hold of their shoulders and pulled them up. 'Stop it this instant.' I was livid. 'Don't you remember what I told you? What do you think your grandmother's going to say?' I could feel her eyes taking it all in. 'She certainly isn't going to want to have you in her house again if you behave like this.' They were hanging their heads now, panting, dirty. 'I'm ashamed of you both.' I thundered. 'And I want you both to – '

'I think that's enough, Lydia.' Madeleine's voice broke in. 'They're only children.'

'Oh – ' I dropped my hands as a sudden bolt of tears choked my throat. But I was a child and you . . .

'Come along, Christopher, Catherine.' Madeleine's voice, though stern, was not censorious. 'You can both help me to clear the table. We'll take this all inside, if you please.'

The children gave me a very wide berth as they went to their grandmother and silently took the crockery she held out to them.

'We'll let your mother rest for a while,' Madeleine said to them. 'I think she needs a little peace and quiet after her long drive. Come along.'

They made a little procession – Christopher with the milk jug and Kitty with the sugar bowl, both carefully avoiding my eyes as they followed their grandmother inside.

It doesn't matter, I told myself as I sat back in my chair, it really doesn't mean anything. I kicked off my ridiculous shoes, finally tipping out the shards of gravel. They're only children, I reassured myself. But their little defection sliced small and deep like a paper-cut.

I lay awake in the bed – Madeleine's bed – shuffling through the day as if it were a pack of cards I was trying to sort into suits. But it would not be ordered so easily. As if some mischievous joker ran about the piles, flicking them out of their places, so the day fragmented into a series of disparate incidents.

The twins had not wanted me to read them a bed-time story. They had allowed me to undress them, wash them, put them into their pyjamas. They had even seemed to accept my apology for shouting at them and had let me kiss them and stroke their soft hair as I brushed it, before dancing lithe and joyous again down the long corridor. But when they had clambered into their beds, looking, I thought, so small, so vulnerable in that spartan room, their faces jaundiced by the mustard rosebuds, they had pushed away the book I'd picked up.

'Grandma's *telling* us a story,' Christopher said. 'A real one – not one from a book.'

And like a babushka from a fairy-tale, Madeleine's head suddenly appeared round the door. 'Oh, you've got your mother here with you,' she said, starting to withdraw. 'Then you don't need me.'

But the twins immediately howled in protest. 'Grandma, you promised,' Christopher cried, rearing up out of the bed.

'You promised,' Kitty echoed. 'A story, you said, a story.'

So Madeleine came stiffly into the room. 'Well,' she said, not without a note of gratification in her voice, I thought, 'if you're really both so keen . . .'

She looked at me expectantly, the twins looked at me

expectantly and suddenly I could feel them all pushing me out. But I didn't want to leave, not yet, not like that. I felt so terribly ashamed of my anger that afternoon. Maybe they haven't realized how sorry I am, I thought as I bent over them. Maybe they don't see how much I really do love them.

'Good-night, Mummy.' Christopher kissed me briskly as I stroked his buttery curls, lying on the pillow like flakes of croissant. God, to think that I had almost – But no, my heart still turned over when I remembered that secret visit to the clinic – only a quick operation, they'd said, very straightforward. It made me feel sick just to recall it. No matter how desperate I'd been at finding myself pregnant, I could never now forgive myself for even considering . . .

'Can we have the story now, Grandma?' Christopher broke in. 'I'm really looking forward to it.'

And I had to go.

Lingering outside in the corridor, I heard Madeleine's voice begin. 'Once upon a time there was an old woman, and when she brushed her hair night flew out . . .' And I felt rising again that bolt of tears – but you never told *me* stories . . . And, too, I could feel myself pricked by little thorns of bitterness that the twins – my twins – should be so prodigal with their affection.

Then, finding myself outside the door of her room – my room – I was unable to delay any longer and went inside. Banks of roses in full-breasted splendour burst out at me from the walls – pink, purple, crimson, orange. The garish colours were an assault. Great waves of pot-pourri, nauseatingly sweet, overwhelmed me. I held my breath and ran to open the windows, but they were all jammed or locked or sealed up with old paint. 'Oh, God.' I let go of my breath and just slumped down on the hard chair beside the ugly dressing-table. God, I hated this room.

I made myself get up and fetch my suitcase from outside the door, but as I swung it on to the bed I noticed the embroidered pillowcases. There, you remember you're not just a nobody with old flannel sheets. You're a lady, from the Hall and don't you forget it . . . The rough knots would worry at my skin all night.

I forced my attention back to my case, but hesitated to open it and put my things away. In a night, a day, my clothes would become stained with the heavy scent of rose and lavender. In the same way, though my face and hands were sticky with sweat, I didn't want to wash them, because the perfumed-soap would seep into my skin to make my own body betray me. In the end I just sank down on the soft bed, indecisive, uncertain, feeling defeated as I tried not to breathe in the horrible cloying sweetness of the room.

After a while there was a discreet knock on the door. 'Dinner is ready. You can join me now, please,' Madeleine's voice announced. I went downstairs.

My place was set, as always, opposite the portraits. As I took my seat I felt automatically under the table for the little marks I had made with my childish fingernails. Yes, it was still there, that impotent ladder of defiance.

It was a quiet meal. Chastened by my outburst with the twins, I felt guarded and defensive. I ate carefully – Elbows *in*, Lydia, you're not learning to fly, are you? I wanted to get this stilted intimacy over with as quickly as possible. But Madeleine had opened a bottle of wine and after two glasses her face became flushed and her eyes darted up and down from mine like minnows. It took me a little while to realize she was excited about something – the surprise guest, maybe? She kept starting conversations and then cutting them off abruptly when, not responding, I allowed them to peter out.

'Coffee in the Garden Room,' she said, when at last we stood up. 'No, don't come with me. Just go in. I'll bring it when it's ready.'

You must make an effort, I told myself sternly as I crossed the hall. She's making an effort, you've got to make an effort too. Pull yourself together. So it was without really preparing myself that I just opened the door and stepped inside.

The Garden Room.

At the Hall

The Garden Room that had been my parlour but which now had evolved into an extension of the garden like a shed.

Two great chintz-covered sofas sat opposite each other on either side of the fireplace, sagging under the weight of books and catalogues. In places the flowered material had worn through completely and stuffing and springs burst out like strange plants eager to reach the light.

The floor was now covered in coarse rush-matting, frayed and crumbling, which split into little puffs of dust under my shoes. Around the edges, where the matting stopped, the floor was stained with soil and dark splashes of fertilizer. There were rings from where buckets had been left to stand. A rusty watering-can stood brashly in front of the fireplace.

Even the mantelpiece was a mess of seed packets and small hand-tools obscuring the swags of marble fruits and flowers. At each end was a tawdry vase containing a great bunch of roses, but the blooms were drooping, the water in the dirty glass green and brackish and wrinkled petals had fallen on to the hearth, where ash from an old fire was covered in dust and studded with knots of crumpled paper.

I stood frozen, horrified, but when I saw his chair standing over by the garden doors I had to bite my lip hard to keep myself from crying out. The green leather was torn, stuffing spilling out from the seat and arms. The decorative wooden baubles had broken off so that the back looked lopsided and the delicately carved spindles between the legs were crudely held in place by ugly strips of masking-tape. All around the chair straggled plants that stood on the chipped remains of the gold china dinner-service, the floor beneath them gritty from where they had been clumsily watered.

'Well, sit down, sit down.' Madeleine bustled in with a tray before I could collect myself. 'No need to stand there gawping, is there?' She put the tray down on a rough wooden table piled high with gardening books and took her place in the chair.

'But it's – it's – ' I stammered weakly, gesturing to the room. 'It really doesn't look very – '

'It's the height of the growing season,' she interrupted roughly. 'I've better things to do with my time than shilly-shally indoors.'

She poured the coffee and handed me a cup. Though it was chipped and the handle had been broken and glued on carelessly, I could still recognize the fine gold tracery inside the rim. 'I really don't think it's right – ' I made one more attempt as I cleared a space for myself amongst the catalogues on the sofa. 'I mean, the value of the house will – '

'The value,' she snorted contemptuously. 'The value indeed, Lydia. It's really none of your business how this room looks. I like it like this and this is how it will stay – it's homely. Value indeed.'

I let the subject drop. She was sitting there on her throne, strong, confident, as I crouched on the sofa beneath her gaze. Who was I to challenge her?

As I watched, she took a sip from her cup and then put it down on a pile of magazines at her feet. And there it will remain, I thought suddenly, remembering another hallmark of apparent sophistication – the cup never completely drained, the plate never scraped clean. I used to trace her passage through the house by the half-filled cups left on tables and mantelpieces. And yet I had seen her in the kitchen drinking glass after glass of water, pouring it down her throat. I had even seen her drinking from the tap in the garden, scooping up the water in her muddy hands as it ran down her chin and over her shirt, like a navvy on a hot day.

'I've got something I want to show you.' She broke the silence suddenly, getting up and poking amongst the clutter on the mantelpiece. 'It's an idea I've had.' She turned back to me with an envelope in her hand. Her eyes were glittering. 'Go on, take it. Have a look. Tell me what you think. I'll explain it all in a minute.'

She stood over me as I opened the envelope. There were some slides inside. 'Go on, look at them,' she said impatiently when I hesitated. 'You have to hold them up to the light.'

I picked one out at random – they were in no particular order as far as I could tell – and, holding it up to the naked bulb that dangled from the ceiling, made out a drawing of a tree in a courtyard with a group of people sitting beneath. The drawing was very detailed; even on the slide I could make out the features of the faces. It looked very well done.

'Go on, go on,' Madeleine urged, when I put the slide down. 'Look at the next one. Look at them all.'

I went through them one after another. They were quite faultless, but there was something strangely cold about them. As if the artist – whoever it was – had bleached the scenes and the people in them of all feeling. It made me feel uncomfortable. There was something too revealing, too naked about these pictures. They were pitiless, unforgiving.

'That's a self-portrait,' Madeleine said, as I held the last slide up to the light. 'Sophie Dario her name is – foreign, I think. She looks quite young, doesn't she?'

The face on the slide was staring at me so hard that I flinched. There was no actual expression, but in the tight-set mouth and fixed gaze there were determination and a purpose that almost mowed you down to look at.

'She's pretty, don't you think?' Madeleine said, when I put the slide down.

I shrugged noncommittally. Pretty was the last word I'd have thought of. Cold, yes, uncaring even – she had a look like a nun, not saintly, far from it, but as if she was dedicated to something she would let absolutely nothing stand in her way of achieving. I thought her almost frightening.

'You see – ' Madeleine took back the slides, bundling them into the envelope. 'You see, Lydia, it's like this.' She paused, turning the envelope over and over in her hands. 'I've been thinking for some time that I want to do something for the twins. No – ' She held up her hand, halting me. 'Don't interrupt. Let me explain it all properly.' I sat back warily as she took a breath. 'You see,' she began again, 'I've watched them changing so fast, growing up so fast, and I felt I wanted to do something –

to make some sort of record of them, something permanent, something that would last. I really couldn't think what. And then it came to me.' She smiled suddenly, unexpectedly, her face lighting up. 'It was when you were showing me those photographs you'd had taken – remember? Last Christmas. Well, it just came to me then that what I'd *really* like to do would be to have some *proper* pictures made of them both. You know, for posterity, to keep here for them at the Hall with the other family pictures.'

'What other pictures?' I broke in.

'You know, the ones in the dining-room,' she said impatiently.

'The portraits?'

She nodded.

'You mean,' I said slowly, 'you're thinking of getting portraits painted of the twins?'

'Painted – or drawn,' she said quickly. She had put the envelope back on the mantelpiece and was pushing the pins in her hair with nervous little stabbing movements. 'Though I must say, I think to have them drawn would be better, because it would be easier on them. Though,' she rushed on, 'Simon says that Sophie's *such* a good artist she really wouldn't have to do more than have them sit for the odd half-hour or so, reading a book or playing quietly or something. He says a few sessions like that would be quite enough and – '

'No, wait – wait a moment. You're going too fast. Who is this – '

But I couldn't stem the flow. 'And then,' she heltered on. 'When you told me you were all *really* coming down for the summer at last, well, I was even more pleased because it meant that the work could take place here, at the Hall, which would be *so* much more fitting, do you see?' She was looking at me eagerly, as if actually asking for my approval. 'I really do think that it would *mean* something.' Her eyes were almost pleading. 'Don't you agree?'

I had to pick my words carefully. 'I think it's an interesting idea,' I said slowly. 'I don't know what the twins would say about it though?'

'Oh, I'm sure they'd love it,' she said with a laugh. 'You know, all that attention. And it's bound to be very educative for them – I mean, maybe we'll be able to persuade Sophie to give them some lessons. Simon says she's really very good – well, you can see that for yourself, can't you? I do think – '

'Who's Simon?' I interrupted before she could go on. 'Where does he fit in? I thought you said this Sophie person was the artist?'

'That's right.' She nodded. 'And she *is* good, isn't she? You must see that?'

'I don't know,' I answered truthfully. 'She's very accurate, if that's what you mean – it all looks very true to life . . .' But did I really want that chilling gaze turned on my children?

'Simon says she's going to be really – '

'No,' I broke in firmly. 'Let's get this in some sort of order. How did you actually meet this artist and – '

'Oh, I haven't met her yet,' she said, sitting back down again on her chair. 'Simon's done all the – '

'What Simon?' I broke in again. 'You keep mentioning this Simon. Who is he?'

'Oh, you remember Simon,' she said carelessly. 'Surely you can't have forgotten how good he was to us? Simon – you know, Simon Stein, the man who helped us when – '

'Mr Stein?' My voice rose, I could feel the hair on the back of my neck prickling. 'Madeleine, you don't mean – '

'You know, I don't think he's changed at all,' she ran on. 'As soon as I spoke to him I recognized his voice immediately . . . rather older, I suppose – well, he must be in his sixties now – but you remember what a distinctive accent he always had?'

'Madeleine, but – '

She overrode me. 'You see, when I first decided on the idea, I didn't have a clue how to go about it – you know, how to find an artist, would they be any good?' She settled back comfortably into her seat. 'But then I suddenly thought that the one person who might be able to help me was our old friend, Mr Stein – '

'No – but, Madeleine – '

'After all, he did have such good taste, didn't he?' she swept on. 'Always dressed so well, you know, looked so distinguished, remember? So when I was with you at Christmas I looked him up in your telephone directory – after all, Stein is a rather unusual name. And what do you think I found?' She leaned forward. 'Stein's Gallery, that's what I found. Stein's Gallery. Isn't that incredible?'

She paused, but now I was too shocked to say anything. I could only sit there and let it all spill over me.

'I telephoned as soon as I got back here – I didn't want you to know anything about it yet – and of course it *was* him. He owns a gallery now – he was always so enterprising – knows all about artists and was absolutely charming.' She smiled. 'He was so surprised to hear from me. Well, it had been so long. But he remembered you – asked after you. He always had a soft spot for you, Lydia, treated you so respectfully, I always thought.'

Simon Stein, I was thinking. Mr Stein. Why should *he* come back into my life?

'He hasn't married, you know,' Madeleine was rattling on. 'It's such a shame, really. I think he'd have loved a family. All his people were killed in the war, he told me once, just briefly. He'd been in a camp, you know. When they set him free and he came over here, he had absolutely nothing, just the clothes they issued him with. No money, no property – nothing.'

'Made up for it quickly enough,' I muttered before I could stop myself.

She looked at me sharply. 'That's not very charitable, you know, Lydia.'

'I don't feel very charitable about that man,' I said.

She tightened her mouth disapprovingly. 'I don't think there's any need for *that* sort of attitude, Lydia,' she said tartly. 'But then, charity has always been in rather short supply with you, hasn't it?'

There was a pause. I watched the warmth ebbing from her

face, until it became hard and stern as usual. How dare you contact that man? I wanted to say. How dare you resurrect that nightmare? But I said nothing, the words choking inside me.

'Anyway,' she continued, her voice cold now, 'to cut a long story short, Simon told me he'd recently come across a new artist – he specializes in new artists apparently – but this particular one, Sophie Dario, he was very interested in. He sent me those slides – ' She gestured with her head – 'and said he'd try to arrange something. When I found out you were coming down for the summer, he said he was sure it could all be fixed up to tie in with that. I thought it would be a nice surprise for you.' She looked at me resentfully, but before I could respond went on, 'However, it seems there's been some sort of hitch – I don't know what exactly. When he rang the other day, he said he'd explain it all when he got here. He said – '

'He's coming here?' I nearly jumped out of my seat. 'Here? When?'

'He's arriving tomorrow,' she replied coolly. 'That's why I needed the Brown Room free. He's a very busy man, you know. I think he'll only be able to stay for a few days.'

Mr Stein, I was thinking, that man – here? Dear God, could this get any worse?

'You're very quiet, Lydia,' she said, standing up and reaching for my coffee cup. 'Why don't you go to bed now?'

'Madeleine,' I managed to force out. 'Madeleine, I – I really don't want this – '

But she was putting the cups on the tray, her back to me, and didn't seem to hear.

'You know, Lydia,' she said, picking up the tray and turning to face me. 'I'm arranging all this for your benefit – yours and the children's. I hope you can remember that.'

Now, as I lay in the bed – Madeleine's bed, with the cold sheets trussing me like winding-cloths – I felt the blunt edge of my own impotence hacking me. I don't want to be here, I don't want to be here . . . But my childhood chant was empty as an old snail shell and instead I could only feel the grip of Madeleine's will like fine roots planted in all around me.

There was something drilling, something shrill and insistent drilling into my sleep. What was it? Workmen digging up the house – digging up the foundations? I awoke suddenly. The phone was ringing. I grabbed my dressing-gown and ran out of the room. The bright sunlight streaming through the stained-glass window on the landing dazed me, so that I stood confused for a moment. Where was I? Oh, yes – but where was Madeleine? Surely she could hear? And then suddenly it stopped.

Blinking and rubbing my eyes, I went back down the corridor and into the Rosebud Room to check on the twins. The room was empty. Were they up already? Outside? What time was it? God, I'd slept so badly, snatching at moments of sleep as they swept past me – but then I'd never really slept well in this house.

I noticed the tray on the floor outside the door of my room. There was a note propped between the cold teapot and the cup. I opened it and scanned the contents quickly, but before I could react the phone rang again and this time I was quick enough down the stairs to answer it.

'Hallo?'

There was silence at the other end and I was about to put the phone down when a voice spoke uncertainly. 'Madeleine? Is that you?'

'Madeleine's not here at the moment. She's gone out – ' With the children, my children, she's stolen my children. 'This is her daughter speaking.' I crumpled the note in my hand and firmed my voice. 'Was it important? Would you like to leave a message?'

But there was a burst of laughter. 'Lydia? Lydia? Little Miss Lydia, is that really you? Oh, but your voice – you sound so – so – '

No, I leaned against the wall weakly. Oh, no.

'But you know who this is?' he went on, his accent rasping his voice. 'You can guess, yes?'

At the Hall

I gritted my teeth. 'Mr Stein,' I said.

'Simon - please, call me Simon. We are old friends, no? Well, Lydia, my dear, how are you?'

I shuddered. I could just see him sitting at a big empty desk, sleek and complacent in a tailored suit, a cigarette between his clean fingers.

'Your mother tells me you are married now and have two fine children,' he went on, seeming not to notice my silence. 'Has she told you about her little surprise?'

'Yes – yes, she has mentioned something.'

'You will be so happy with the pictures, Lydia. Sophie is such a fine artist.'

But I was gathering myself together now. 'Madeleine mentioned a problem?' I said.

His voice lowered. 'A tragedy, yes. I will explain it all when I see you, but I am still very optimistic for the commission. I am certain I can persuade – '

'Was there any message for Madeleine?' I cut in.

But it was as if he didn't hear, or didn't want to hear my shortness. 'Tell me, Lydia, and how are you? How is life treating you? Are you happy?'

'I'm fine – thank you.' But I was forced to respond. 'And you?'

He sighed. 'Well, life goes on, day to day. My accountants are unhappy because I don't want to show the sausage-makers in my gallery, but they are not artists those people – *ach*, their paintings one after another like sausages, all the same. But my accountants like them because the frankfurter-collectors like them and so they all try to push me, push me, all the time. Do you want a job, Lydia?' he said suddenly.

'A job? I – no – no – ' I stuttered.

'A pity.' He sighed again. 'I could do with a person like you to take over this place for me. I'm getting a little too old now for all these games and I don't need the business – I have enough money. Your mother tells me how capable you are with your children and your husband. Are you sure you wouldn't – '

'Quite sure,' I said firmly. Did he honestly think I didn't remember?

'Well,' he wheedled, 'maybe we can talk about it when I come down to the Hall, what do you say? Maybe part-time, maybe – '

'Was there a message?' I cut in sharply. 'For Madeleine?'

'Ah, yes.' His voice deepened. 'Tell her, if you would be so kind, that I am deeply sorry but I am delayed – ' My heart rose – 'A meeting here today – a collector, you know, one of the better ones, not a frankfurter.' He laughed. 'But it is only for today, tell her. I will let nothing stand in my way tomorrow.'

Twenty-four hours, I thought, at least I have another twenty-four hours. 'I'll tell her,' I said, trying to keep my voice even.

'You will tell her how very sorry I am?'

'I'll – Yes, I'll tell her what you said.'

'Then I look forward to seeing you tomorrow, Lydia.'

'Yes.'

'Goodbye.'

I slammed the phone down. 'You – you – ' But I couldn't pronounce the word: bastard, bastard – those rows of girls jeering at me in the dormitory and I never knew how they found out. A horrible word, a word that smelt foul as excrement on the pavement. But I still couldn't use it, not even for him. And how would it be when I actually saw him – when he was actually here? How would I cope with that?

Sunlight was streaming through the stained-glass window, but the pit of the hall felt very cold. I shivered, feeling suddenly vulnerable standing there in my thin dressing-gown, the hall pressing in, watching me. And it was so quiet. Oh, where were the twins?

The note was still in my hand. I smoothed it out and read it again. Her handwriting was thick, stolid: 'I have taken the twins for a little outing. We will probably be back after lunch. Help yourself to food from the pantry. I'm sure you will appreciate the peace and quiet. M.'

Tearing the note into little pieces I flung them into a corner.

How dare she just take the twins like that, how dare she? And what had she said to make them leave without even coming in to see me? 'Your mother won't like you to wake her, not when she's asleep.' Yes, something sly like that. Maybe she'd even reminded them of the row yesterday? Oh, yes, she'd tell them anything to get them on to her side, wouldn't she?

I closed my eyes. Oh, God, I should never have come back here . . . No. I forced myself upright, forced my eyes open. No, I wouldn't give in. I'd get dressed, go out, take the car – anything, anything. Purposefully I started to cross the hall. But what if something happened to the twins and I wasn't here when they tried to reach me? Of course I couldn't go out. I was stuck here; I couldn't get away.

And then, as I stood uncertainly at the foot of the stairs, I caught sight of the library door. I made no move towards it, but I could see vividly, clearly, as if it was just in front of me, my own small hand reaching out to turn the stiff, shiny brass handle. Hallo, Lily. Come to help me read the newspaper . . .

God, I'd been so young, so young. I could see it all as if through the wrong end of a telescope, my little figure standing there by the arm of his chair, looking up at him so innocent, so ardent.

I was outside the door now, the handle cold under my fingers. I turned it, stepped inside and for a moment, just a second, the room was as it had been – the shelves full of books, the big roll-top desk, the chairs pulled up close to the comfortable warmth of the fire. But then I caught sight of my muddied reflection in the grain-speckled mirror, I smelt the damp and must of mice, saw the little bell-push wrenched furiously from its socket and I was back in the sacked empty room with the dirt and the cold, hard shock of it all.

I should not have come back here, I cried to myself. Oh, God, I should never have come back. But my cry was the cry of one already falling, my head already beneath the waves, and the house simply swallowed up my words indifferently, as it had done with a lifetime of my avowals.

* * *

It would be another hot day. I dressed turning away from the glare of glass on the dressing-table and made up my face from my compact; I couldn't bring myself to look in my mother's mirror – who knew what reflection I'd see?

Again I visited the twins' room, checking the neatly made beds and folded pyjamas for some sign of my children. But there was only Madeleine's hand smoothing the sheets, tucking in the toys and choosing the clothes they would wear as she carried them off like a witch in the night . . .

I went downstairs, made myself coffee and carried it outside. I would sit and read; it would be restful, quiet – I could do with some peace, couldn't I?

But a light breeze kept ruffling the book. Birds chattered noisily over my head, while insects whined past my ears before landing on the pages looking like little points of exclamation. I read the same paragraph four times before I realized that I hadn't got a clue what it was saying and then finally I flung the book down on the table and looked out. The garden . . . It was unavoidable.

There, laid out in front of me, ringing the lawn in a rainbow arc, were the roses. Each one a statue, a spear – straight-backed, clipped, pruned, sprayed into production. Crimson, yellow, orange, pink, they wrapped up the garden like the ribbon on a present, each bush studded with flowers gaudy as bows. The broad sweep of lawn was striped like a deckchair – no daisies, mosses, weeds. The grass was shorn short as the hair on the head of a soldier.

Here it was, Madeleine's garden, the garden that had swallowed up my house. It was formal, exposed, not a secret corner or an unknown nook. Broad and swept and clean, a skeleton masquerading in a velvet cloak, the bare bones of production stripped of the mystery of fecundity. A garden of strictures, rules – Don't you dare go anywhere near those bushes, Lydia . . . Don't walk on that new turf. A summer garden that was as cold as winter. God, how I'd hated those bushes.

At the Hall

How pleased I'd been when frost blackened the premature shoots. And I could still taste the salt blood of revenge watering my mouth when greenfly or mites or birds or moles had wrestled with Madeleine to preserve their kingdom. But she had won in the end. She always won in the end. With traps and poisons, with sprays and washes and bait, she stamped out all the wild uprisings and planted the avenues of roses that now stood obedient as soldiers to her command.

I could hardly remember it as it had been before – the thick clumps of grass, the meandering paths, the apple tree, the greenhouse . . .

No. I stood up sharply. I wasn't going to remember. It was all over, finished, past. I must keep busy, I told myself, I must do something. But what? I looked down the garden and smiled suddenly as the idea stuck me. I know, I'll make up the vases. Won't Madeleine approve?

I found a trug and a pair of secateurs in the scullery. There were some vases in there too – not the lovely old crystal ones but earthenware jugs that would do. I couldn't find any gloves.

Roses are not kind to children. If a ball is lost, it cannot easily be hunted in a thicket of roses. They used to snag my dresses, prick my hands, jealous of any other presence than that of their votary. Look at these blooms, Lydia, look. Can't you see how beautiful they are? But I was too small to see the blossoms, only the thorns that threatened my eyes and rasped in the wind like a knife being sharpened.

But they were tame now. Just large bushes with heavy, overbred flowers stuck crude and garish on fragile stems. They stood docile as a cow, relieved to be milked of their blooms. Some broke into a shower of petals when I touched them; others were sticky with insects, which I squashed and left in a silent tangle of wings and legs.

I carried my basket back to the house conscious of a victory. How easy it had been to raid Madeleine's sanctuary table, raping the bushes of their precious flowers.

I smiled to myself as I stood in the scullery, stripping the leaves and crushing the stalks. And it was a pleasant task, arranging the flowers in the vases. I concealed the bruised stems and displayed only the fat, stupid, heavy-scented blooms.

But the taxi didn't arrive till late in the afternoon. While I waited, anxious, fretting, I roamed without purpose through the dirty, cluttered rooms. I kept finding things – the stool, now three-legged, propped on a pile of gardening magazines, its tapestry cover frayed and moth-eaten; his magnifying glass, astonishingly intact, weighing down a clump of seed packets; the little ivory paperknife he opened his letters with in the morning, stuck roughly into a pot to prop up a wilting plant. And as I wandered I was pursued by memories, voices, scenes I didn't want to recall, each room stained with the grime of the past.

When at last I heard the gurgle of the taxi, I ran to the front door and flung it open. 'Christopher, Kitty – Darlings, where have you been? I've been so worried.'

'Oh, we've been fine,' Christopher answered, grinning up at his grandmother. 'You needn't have worried, Mummy.'

'Come here, darlings.' I knelt down on the gravel, holding out my arms. 'Come here. Let me hold you both.'

Was there a little hesitation? No, maybe not. I could feel Madeleine watching as I clasped the children to me, burying my head in their hair.

'You smell all salty,' I said, kissing Kitty's head. 'You smell of the sea.'

'That's where we've been, Mummy. It was brilliant.' Christopher pulled himself free of my arms. 'Granny took us to – '

Granny? Dear God, Granny? I glanced up at Madeleine, but she was simply smiling – complacently, I thought.

She caught my eye. 'I must apologize for bringing the children back so late,' she said stiffly. 'I take full responsibility of course.'

But before I could reply Christopher tugged my arm. 'And

we saw ships, Mummy, *huge* ships, and Granny said that if we were really good, then we could go in one tomorrow and – '

'And she said we could go swimming too.' Kitty danced up and down, just out of my reach. 'Can we, Mummy? Please – please, can we? Granny says – '

'Darlings.' I tried to laugh. 'Don't call you grandmother – that. You know she doesn't like it. She's "Grandma", remember?'

'But she said we could,' Kitty burst out suddenly, rushing up to her. 'You said, didn't you, Granny? You said – '

'Kitty,' I warned, seeing the beginning of a storm.

But Madeleine cut in smoothly. 'Really, Catherine, you are so excitable, child.' I watched hungrily as she stroked my daughter's head.

'But you said, Granny, you said – '

She smiled down on her fondly. 'That's right, Catherine, I *did* say you could call me "Granny" if you wanted. Grandma is a bit of a mouthful for a small child, isn't it?'

'You see?' Christopher flashed back at me triumphantly. 'I told you, Mummy, I told you – '

'That's enough, Christopher,' I said crisply.

'Well,' Madeleine said after a moment. 'I think it must be time for tea. You two stay out here with your mother and I'll get it ready.'

'We could help you, Granny,' Kitty suggested, 'if you want?'

'I'm sure your grandmother wants a bit of peace and quiet,' I put in quickly. 'After all – ' I laughed – 'she's had you all day. She could probably do with a rest, don't you think?' The gravel was biting into my knees and I felt ridiculous kneeling there. 'Help me up, darlings,' I said, holding out my hands. 'I've got quite stiff down here.'

They didn't say anything, but with their hands safe in mine I felt better. 'Well,' I said brightly, looking down on them. 'I think we've just enough time for a little walk together, what do you say?'

'All right,' Christopher said offhandedly.

'But will we be back in time for tea?' Kitty exchanged a glance with her grandmother. 'And I can have my special cake?' she added shyly.

'Of course you can.' Madeleine smiled back.

'Right then,' I said briskly, 'let's be off.' And I walked swiftly round the side of the house, whisking my children out of sight.

I found myself taking them down through the woods, towards the pilot pit. Obviously Madeleine had seen fit not to scare them with that horrible old legend, so it would be all right.

I held on to their hands tightly. No, I wasn't going to let them go. For the rest of the holiday I'd make sure they stayed with me. She wasn't going to get another chance to steal them away.

It was cooler under the trees and we stopped in a clearing while I pulled my sleeves down. Released from my grasp, the children wandered half-heartedly amongst the fallen branches. Christopher scuffed at the leaf mould with his feet.

'Don't,' I said sharply. He looked at me indignantly. 'I don't want you to ruin your shoes, darling,' I added, softening my voice.

'Granny let us paddle in the sea, didn't she, Kitty?' She nodded. 'I got wet right up to there – ' He drew a line over his chest. 'The waves were so big they nearly went over my – '

'Don't fib, Christopher.'

He looked at me sullenly. 'We *did* go paddling, anyhow.'

I took a deep breath. 'So, you had a lovely time, then, with your grandmother?'

'Oh yes,' they chorused.

'You didn't miss me, then?' I just couldn't keep the question back. They hesitated. 'Never mind,' I said quickly. 'All that matters is that you had a good time.'

'Oh, we did.'

'It was *so* good – '

'Can we go out again with Granny tomorrow, Mummy?' Kitty asked. 'Please?'

'I was hoping – ' I tried to sound casual – 'that we three might go on a nice little outing of our own tomorrow. What do you think?'

There was a pause.

'Can Granny come too?' Kitty asked.

'You'd want her to come, would you? I was thinking it would be just the three of us.'

Christopher picked up a stick and started to peel it. After a moment he said slowly, 'If we all went together, then nobody would feel left out.'

Unlike today, I thought in stubborn silence.

'And if we all went together,' he went on carefully, 'it would be even nicer, wouldn't it?' He nudged his sister.

'Oh – yes, Mummy,' she said. 'We'd like it even better, wouldn't we?'

They were both nodding furiously, their heads bobbing up and down on their slender necks, and I was suddenly, horribly, reminded of the fragile stems of the roses I had crushed so ruthlessly. Oh, God, I realized with a jolt, what was I doing to them? What was Madeleine making me do to my own children?

'Yes, of course,' I stammered. 'If – if that's what you want.'

'Oh, thank you, Mummy.' They both beamed. 'It'll be really good.'

'Really the best.'

'Really, really – '

'Really and really and really – ' They were both giggling.

'All right, that's enough,' I snapped.

Christopher threw his stick down, a pure white strip on the amber wood floor. 'Can we go back now? I'm hungry. I'm sure tea's ready and Granny's got us each a special cake – '

'Mine's got cherries on it – '

'Mine's chocolate.'

And mine?

'Can we go now?' he asked again when I didn't reply.

'What? Oh – ' I looked at them standing there so keen to be gone. 'Give me a kiss first,' I said.

They both obeyed. And then I had to let them go.

I watched through the trees as they ran up the garden, the lawn springing their steps like a trampoline. I had to clench my fists to keep from crying out after them. The leaves shivered over my head.

'What have you been doing to my children?'

'Ah, Lydia, there you are – I was wondering. Help me with the tray, would you? I don't know where the twins have run off to. I saw them a moment ago, but they seem to have disappeared again. Are they with you?'

'What have you been doing to them?' I gripped the edge of the rough kitchen table, still panting from my long run up the lawn. 'I want to know – now.' I slammed my fist down, all the frustrated anger of the last twenty-four hours suddenly erupting.

'Really, Lydia.' Her voice was cool, distasteful. 'I don't have any idea what you're talking about.'

'Oh, yes, you do,' I shouted. 'Those children are *mine*, do you hear? I won't have you taking them away.'

'Lydia, there's no need to – '

'I won't have you telling them lies and getting them on to your side and turning them against me, their own mother.' I was trembling.

'Lydia – ' The complacent smile was gone now and her face looked shocked. 'For heaven's sake, what's come over you? Of course the twins are your – '

'I love my children, Madeleine, which is more than can be said for you. I love them and I won't stand by and watch while you try to take them away from me.'

'For goodness' sake, stop being so utterly ridiculous,' she snapped. 'I took the twins out for the day, that's all. There's absolutely no need for you to work yourself up into a frenzy about it. I'm their grandmother. It's perfectly reasonable that I should – ' She broke off, looking at me angrily. 'You're not a child, Lydia, so I can't demand an apology, but if you honestly think that I'm going to put up with accusations like these being levelled at me in my own house – '

At the Hall

'In *your* house?' I broke in. 'Really?'

'You know what I mean.'

'No, I don't.' I looked at her coldly. 'Since when has this been your house?'

'Lydia, as long as I'm living here – '

'You live here with my permission, Madeleine. Maybe you've forgotten that?'

She looked round uncomfortably. 'I really don't think there's any need to go into all that now.'

'Oh, no? You know, Madeleine,' I said after a moment. 'I could sell the Hall for a very great deal of money if you weren't living in it.'

'No, you couldn't,' she retorted sharply. 'Under the terms of your grandfather's will, the Hall is to be passed on to your – '

'Under the terms of his will, the Hall *and all its contents – all* its contents, remember? – belong to me.' I looked at her. 'But there isn't a lot left of the contents, is there, Madeleine?' I went on. 'Let's face it, you and Mr Stein made a pretty penny out of that lot, didn't you?'

Her face was white. 'That – was a very long time ago, Lydia,' she said uncertainly. 'I - don't think you've tried to understand – to see my point of view. Your grandfather was not such a wealthy man. There were things I had to provide – clothes, books, your school fees – '

'There was enough money for that and you know it,' I hissed.

'But there was nothing for me,' she cried suddenly.

'No.' I paused. 'There wasn't, was there?'

'I had to live on something,' she ventured after a silence. 'Surely I had a right to that, didn't I? To something of my own?'

I just looked at her.

'I did so much for you, Lydia,' she said. 'It was all for you really. Can't you see?'

'Oh, yes?' I laughed. 'The garden was for me too, was it? All those bloody roses,' I went on. 'You don't have to tell me where the money went, Madeleine. We've only got to look outside to see it.'

'But you don't understand, Lydia,' she burst out. 'I wanted something for myself – something of my own.'

'But it wasn't yours to want.'

'Oh – but – '

'It was mine,' I shouted. 'And it still is mine – ' I waved my arm – '*All* of it.'

She was silenced. She stood with her back pressed against the old stone sink, hands plucking her skirt, head bowed, avoiding my fierce gaze. I felt a rush of triumph. A victory, finally I had beaten her. It was a sweet moment.

Then, slowly, she looked up, not directly at me but over my shoulder through the open door to the hall. 'It's like one of those ancient tragedies,' she said, her voice small, distant. 'Where the one thing you take great steps to avoid is exactly the thing that happens to you in the end.' She turned to me. 'With your education, you should know what I mean.' The look on her face was eerie.

'I – I don't know,' I said, discomforted. 'What *do* you mean?'

She sighed. 'I should have guessed it would happen in the end. I suppose you could say I've been a bit of a fool.'

'Madeleine – ' She was frightening me now. 'Madeleine, what are you saying?'

'The thing is,' she continued, her voice menacingly calm, 'I just didn't expect it from you. From your grandfather – yes. Every day that he was alive, even when you were at school, I was afraid that he'd – ' She broke off.

'Honestly, Madeleine.' I tried to laugh. 'I don't know what you're talking about. Now let's just – '

'But I should have guessed really. You *are* his grandchild after all and so very like him, aren't you, Lydia?'

I looked away, began putting the cups and plates on the tray. 'I'd rather not talk about him, if you don't mind,' I said. 'Now, let's just get all this – '

'I could tell you things about him, you know.' Her voice was very steady. I could feel her eyes boring into my back. 'Things that might give you a very different picture of your sainted grandfather.'

'Has the kettle boiled yet?' I fussed with the tray. 'I could really do with a nice cup of – '

'He used to – '

'No – ' I cried. 'Don't – don't, please.' I turned to face her. 'Please, Madeleine, leave him be.'

She held my gaze for a long moment. 'I didn't stand a chance with you, did I?'

I made no reply and we waited in silence for the kettle to boil. I nudged it around the hotplate, watching eagerly for the little tendrils of steam to emerge. If I could just get outside, see the children, put this terrible row behind me . . .

But when it was finally boiling, with the clouds of steam obscuring her face as she poured the water, she said suddenly, 'I'll be out of here by Christmas, Lydia. All right?'

'You'll – what?'

Calmly, she put the kettle back on the side and replaced the lid of the teapot. 'The Hall,' she said. 'It's quite simple. You can have it back. I'll leave.'

'Madeleine, what are you saying?' I couldn't read her face at all, it was blank, a stone wall. 'For heaven's sake,' I spluttered, 'we've just had a few words, that's all. There's no need for you to take it so seriously.'

'Oh, but I do, Lydia.' She turned, looking at me unflinchingly. 'You see, I've lived here once with that fear hanging over me and I'm not going to do so again.'

'But – I didn't mean – '

'I know *just* what you meant,' she cut in. 'As you reminded me, this is your house. I won't forget again. Now – ' She reached out to take the tray – 'shall we have tea?'

'For God's sake, Madeleine – ' I grasped her hand, but she shook me away.

'Don't, Lydia.' Her eyes were very fierce. 'Don't.' She lifted the tray. 'Now, we'll say no more about it. I want the twins to enjoy their holiday.'

'Madeleine, please, listen to me.'

She stopped in the doorway glancing back at me, and suddenly as I looked at her I thought, My God, she's got Kitty's eyes – Kitty looks just like her grandmother . . .

'You know, Lydia – ' She gave a bleak smile – 'it never really was my place here, even after all I did. It was always much more yours – and your grandfather's.'

Then she was walking away.

By the time I had swung my car out on to the motorway all I could feel was an immense relief to be away. I'd been mad to have gone down there, crazy to have thought it could work. The whole thing was like a bad dream from which now, at last, I was just waking. It's a storm in a teacup, I told myself, as I drove very fast down the long, straight road – ridiculous, the whole thing will soon blow over. But it haunted me, Madeleine's figure etched on my driving mirror as she stood in the porch, watching me drive away. She was adamant, she would leave the Hall, and nothing I could say or do would shake that.

I fled.

The twins were silent on the back seat. When I had told them we were leaving they'd laughed as if I was joking. And not until I'd actually started packing their things had they realized I was serious.

'But *why* do we have to go, Mummy?' Kitty pleaded, staring at me with Madeleine's eyes. 'We haven't done anything wrong, have we?'

'Of course you haven't,' I tried to reassure her. 'This is nothing to do with you.'

'Then, why?' Christopher questioned belligerently.

'It's – it's – ' But what could I say when they looked at me, their faces crumpled with confusion? 'It's just best,' I said weakly. 'Now let me get on.'

'But we want to stay here,' he persisted. 'We like it here. We want to stay with Granny.'

'Christopher – '

'I don't want to go – I don't want to go – I don't want to bloody go!' And he hurled himself at the suitcase, throwing the clothes on to the floor.

'Christopher,' I shouted. 'That's enough. Stop it.' I pulled him away. 'You're too young to understand. Now don't argue with me.'

He stood there, trembling, his face a fixed bayonet of accusation. 'I want to stay here with Granny. I don't want to go home with you. I hate you.'

His words had cut through me as a blade through paper. Oh, God, the icy hatred of children – didn't I know just how long it could last?

But now as I peeped at them in the mirror I reassured myself. No, they'd forget – all children forget. It would all smooth over. Even though they sat mute and sullen, staring blankly out of the windows.

All through the journey I made unnecessary stops and, under cover of filling up with petrol, bought sweets and crisps and drinks, tossing them lightly into the back seat. But they brushed them aside disdainfully, my thirty pieces of silver.

'We'll have a lovely time at home,' I said to the silence. 'We'll go to the park – and the zoo – and swimming – '

'We were going to go swimming in the sea with Granny,' Christopher burst out resentfully.

'Well,' I said brightly, relieved that at least I had provoked a response, 'I'm sure we can do that too. And maybe – ' I had a flash of inspiration – 'maybe we can all go to the airport together to welcome Daddy back from his tour. What do you say – an exciting trip to see all the aeroplanes?'

But they didn't say anything.

I was very tired when I finally pulled the car to a stop outside the house: tired of driving, tired of the silence, tired of Madeleine standing there in the porch.

I woke the twins and took them inside. My house – thank God – shuttered and still but clean of memory, unfingered by the past.

But in the end it was not so easy to fall asleep. Madeleine stood there, the twins clinging to her hands. I should have kissed her, I thought, muddled by tiredness. Maybe I did, didn't I?

But we had not embraced. It was a habit we had never got into.

The twins demanded reparation for their holiday and I paid in full. Trips to the zoo, the park, the swimming-baths – but not the sea, none of us mentioned the sea. And slowly, gradually, over pints of milkshake and cola, mountains of chips, pounds of chocolate, they allowed me to come close to them again. Yes, I thought, as I washed their lithe, slippery little bodies, rumpled their hair and read them stories at bed-time, I knew it would all blow over.

Of course, I made the twins write thank-you letters to their grandmother as soon as they came home and I checked them afterwards – ostensibly for spelling – but they received no reply. Well, that was blowing over too, I told myself. And of course, eventually, I'd phone Madeleine, or write. I'd make the peace, there was no need to have a feud. But somehow, as the summer wore on, I never quite got round to it: it was always too late, I was tired, I wasn't in the right mood . . .

And yet it was hard for me to forget. However much I tried to push it away, the visit flickered on the edge of my sight like a flashing light I couldn't ignore – Madeleine standing in the porch like an abdicating queen; the roses braying in the garden; the cracked coffee cups; the dirty, scratched parquet in the hall . . .

In the thick, hot nights of that sultry summer I dreamt – but no, I told myself, I slept soundly, deeply, undisturbed by the firings which peppered my restless nights with ancient shot. But those denied dreams spread a weary film over my days, making me sour and bitter.

I woke one morning at dawn. Suddenly it was all very clear. It was the last summer – the last summer . . . I got out of bed and reached for my clothes. He needs me, Grandfather needs me . . . And then suddenly I was awake, sitting on the edge of my bed, rigid with shock as his touch, his voice, his breath, dragged me with a yearning I had thought never to recall. It was as if my visit had sprung open a locked compartment from which a mess of feelings showered down inescapably, like a blizzard. And all the memories were stirred, rising like shards, hard little relics breaking the surface of my mind. No, no. I tried to push them all away. No, I don't want to remember, I don't want to feel it, I don't want to lose it all over again . . .

But like the fine shoots of a plant squeezing through concrete, so the Hall seeped into my life. Dan sent me roses on our wedding anniversary, the twins gave me scented soap. The cleaner left for her fortnight's holiday and the house clogged up with dust. In the evenings, after traipsing round school-outfitters, I was too tired to do any more than kick off my shoes and slump in a chair. 'We'll go away for a few days before you start school,' I said to the twins. But they just looked at me sceptically with their grandmother's eyes.

Their uniforms were blue and green – good safe colours. They stayed very quiet while we tried them on and seemed to be quite indifferent as we bought kitbags and trunks and tennis racquets, showing not the slightest degree of interest in anything connected with their new school.

Dan had stayed on for the master classes after the rest of the orchestra had returned. Of course I was sorry that he was away, sorry too that the children wouldn't see him before their term started. But it would be easier, I thought, to get them settled into the school without him. He'd never been so certain of the decision as I was, and I was afraid that if he was here he might somehow persuade the twins that they didn't want to go. Of course I missed him, but then I'd got used to missing him, he was away so often. All the more reason, I thought, for me to find a career of my own. And our marriage would survive. A little less love, a little more compromise – we'd rub along. It was a long time since I'd thought he'd be the answer to everything.

'You'll write every week on the cards I've given you?' I pleaded as I stood with the twins in the huge beamed antechamber that smelt so familiarly of polish and vegetables. 'Promise? I'll want to know how you're getting on, if you're happy, if everything is all right. Promise you'll tell me – promise?' They nodded miserably, looking strange and vulnerable in their new uniforms. Christopher's hair had been cut too short and it bristled under my hand. 'You'll keep your cap on, won't you?' My voice wavered. 'I don't want you catching cold.' And for once he didn't even attempt to dodge, just stood there, blinking. 'It's for your own good, remember? You'll both be very happy.' I pulled them towards me, kissing their wet eyelashes, then ran out to the car before my own tears could dissolve my decision.

It was autumn. The mornings were tinged with mist and a hint of winter crisped the air. People wore thick coats with scarves hiding their faces. The shops displayed red and gold and purple – the colours of Christmas.

The twins had settled down and were sending me their postcards. They were blandly informative – their teacher was all right, they were learning a foreign language, on Wednesdays they had sausages for lunch and went swimming.

I had not yet found a job or settled on an appropriate avenue to begin my career. Of course I looked in the papers and sent off for brochures about training courses, but nothing seemed very inspiring. Sometimes the days looked rather long and empty. But I kept myself busy – wrote to Dan, who'd be back at Christmas, and cleared out several cupboards so that the house was nice and tidy. I was considering replacing the beige of the drawing-room with a pale blue, but I didn't like the thought of all the upheaval.

As Christmas approached I made my preparations and did my shopping, joining the crowds that sprawled in an untidy sea over the pavements. The twins were demanding expensive presents and I knew that in the end I would buy them all, just to stave off the splinters of guilt that still ached in me whenever I saw my own carefully stamped and addressed postcards waiting on the hall floor.

I sank down in a chair one evening exhausted. Around me, scattered all over the drawing-room carpet, were the boxes and bags and packages of presents for the twins. The department store had been a nightmare, the air hot and thick, people clustered around the stands like bees on a honeycomb. The weary assistants had been surly and short-tempered, the powder worn through on their faces so that the creases showed hard and obvious in the glaring lights. When I'd finally reached the mecca of the revolving doors, I'd been too drained to do any more than fall into a taxi and come home.

But now I looked at the presents with satisfaction. I'd be able to get them all wrapped up and hidden away without any danger of the twins finding them. Yes, I thought, relaxing at last, it had been a good day. It was nice to have the shopping done early and not in a rush at the last minute. And I'd noticed a course for a career in advertising that sounded very interesting.

I started in surprise when the doorbell rang. I wasn't expecting anyone. I opened it cautiously. An old man was standing on the step, half turned away – I could see the white hair lapping over his neck. He was carrying a large black portfolio.

'Yes?'

He turned around.

'Oh,' I gasped, my hand to my mouth. 'Oh, Mr Stein. What – what are you – '

He didn't hold out his hand but inclined his head. His hair was white all over now, but he had the same deep-set dark eyes, though his face was heavily lined, folded with age.

'I – I was just passing. I – I was hoping for a few words with you, Lydia. If it is not so very inconvenient?'

Inconvenient? There is nothing I need to hear from you, I wanted to shout. But years of training to be polite pulled me back from the door and I simply allowed him to enter.

'I – I will not take up very much of your time,' he said, following me into the drawing-room.

I didn't offer to take his coat but indicated a chair and took a seat opposite.

'This is – very unexpected,' I said, when the silence became intolerable.

'Yes – yes, it is.'

He undid the buttons of his coat but didn't take it off. I noticed that beneath it his suit was crumpled; there were little burnholes on his shirt and he wasn't wearing a tie. Not quite the dapper Mr Stein.

'This is really a – how do you say? – impulse, yes. Just an impulse, Lydia. You understand?' He paused, smoothed the thick hair back over his head.

I waited.

'I – I think I can understand that you are not – pleased to see me.' He glanced at me expectantly, but I wasn't going to give him any help.

He took a breath and, touching the portfolio by his legs as if for confidence, began again. 'I – I want you to know, Lydia, that I – I – ' But then he broke off again, smoothing his hair back, a nervous gesture.

For a moment I was almost tempted to offer him a drink, but I remained in my chair.

'I – I have an apology to make to you, Lydia,' he said abruptly. 'You see – you see – ' He began to hesitate, but with an effort he forced himself onwards. 'You see, I did not know when I bought the – the antiques from your house that they were your possessions – your personal possessions – your inheritance.' He glanced at me, but I remained icily impassive. 'I did not know,' he went on, 'that the Hall was *your* house – that it belonged – that it all belonged – to you. I – I did not know.' He was turning a little ring round and round on his finger. 'It was only today – your mother explained it all to me, Lydia. This afternoon before I left she finally explained – '

'You've been to see Madeleine today?' I broke in, surprised.

'No, I left there today. We've been there for some weeks – '

'We?'

'Myself and Sophie Dario. But you already know about the commission?'

'I know Madeleine had a commission in mind,' I said. 'But I had assumed that without the twins the whole thing would be cancelled?'

He smiled. 'Your mother is very generous.' I winced. 'Very kindly she decided to honour the agreement with Sophie. I think your mother saw how important this commission was for her. And I suppose your mother wanted some – memento for herself now that she is leaving.'

'Leaving?' I looked at him incredulously. 'Madeleine is no more leaving the Hall than – than flying to the moon.'

He shook his head. 'No, I'm sorry, Lydia, but your mother has quite made up her mind. Of course I have tried to persuade her not – '

'Oh, that's ridiculous.' I laughed. 'She's just making a big fuss over nothing. We had a – a little disagreement, that's all.'

'Yes, I know,' he said. 'Your mother has explained it to me – today she has explained everything – and even though I do not agree with her decision to leave, I can understand – '

'She's not leaving. She'll never leave, not in a million years,' I scoffed. 'The only way she'll ever leave that place is feet first – understand?'

But his face was solemn. 'You see,' he went on in the same calm, even tone, 'she is going abroad – '

'Abroad? Madeleine? Don't make me laugh.'

He bowed his head. 'Naturally,' he said slowly, 'you would have some – difficulty trusting my word.'

There was a pause.

'So – you came to see me – to apologize?' I said coldly.

He said nothing, inclined his head.

'For – for taking my things – my inheritance?'

His eyes pleaded.

I looked at him sitting there so small and humble in my fine drawing-room, his legs neatly pulled away from the sprawl of parcels on the floor.

'I don't think I can forgive you,' I said.

He made no reply, just closed his eyes for a moment, then, tightening his fingers on the portfolio, made as if to get up. 'Of course – ' His voice was shaky, his accent suddenly more pronounced, clipping his words so that they hopped and stumbled like a maimed bird. 'I – I – it is very understood – understandable. Please – you must excuse me for being – for taking up your time.'

'No, wait.' I held up my hand and he looked at me hopefully. 'Before you go – ' I tried to keep my voice firm, to stamp out the pity – 'Tell me what's been happening – at the Hall. You say you've been there for some *weeks*?'

He nodded. 'I have even ignored my gallery. *Ach* – ' He waved a hand – 'that joke I will give up now, anyway.'

'But why – I mean, what have you been to the Hall *for*?'

He tapped the portfolio. 'To help with the drawings, to give advice, to – '

'But what drawings?' I frowned. 'Drawings of what?'

'They are the drawings that – ' He broke off and looked at me with a sudden eagerness. 'Maybe it is – maybe you would like to see them?'

'I don't know – '

'I have them here.' He stood up, looked over his shoulder to the dining-table at the far end and headed towards it. 'I have brought them ready for framing.'

'Well, I'm not sure I – '

But already he had laid the case on the table and was unzipping it, his movements quick, excited. 'Come,' he said, 'let me show you.'

With some reluctance I went over to him. The drawings were in a pile, face-down on the table. They were very large. He turned the first one over.

I didn't recognize the place at first; I was lost in a sort of grudging admiration – how very clever she was to get all that depth of room on to the flat sheet of paper. But then he turned over the next and I gasped. 'No, it can't be – it can't – '

Because there in front of me was the parlour. The parlour as it was, as it had been. Light streaming through the open terrace doors on to the thick carpet, glinting the chandelier so that I could almost hear its fine music tinkling over my head . . .

'No, no – it can't – '

But there were the fine-legged tables, the embroidered cushions on the spindly chairs – even the cabinet in the corner, the etching sharp and crisp on the glass . . .

'What have you done? What have you – '

I pushed his hands away and turned the drawings over one after another. God, it was all there, all of it – some rooms drawn twice from different angles. The library, its shelves full of books, the roll-top desk, the fat decanters and even a newspaper folded over the arm of his chair. The hall with the flag and the swords and shields ranged up the walls, the grandfather clock in the corner . . .

'What is this? What – is this?'

Tears blurred my eyes. God, I didn't want to see this, I didn't want to remember. But it was like a drug; I had to look, had to turn the sheets over. The Ship Room with the great bed and his sea-chest at the foot of it; a view of the stained-glass window with the coat of arms bright and clear; that lovely sweep of staircase where he would stand at the bottom wishing me good-night and following me with warm, loving eyes as I went up to bed . . . Oh, but it hurt, hurt to see it again as it had been, hurt to remember coming back from school to find another set of objects missing whilst in their place, like dragon's teeth, the garden sported a double row of roses . . .

No, no – I didn't want to remember.

I tried to gather the drawings into a pile but my hands were shaking so much they wouldn't stay in order and then suddenly an odd, small drawing fell out.

It was Madeleine. But she was gaunt. Deep lines on her face, and the flesh that had been so staunch and robust was now limp, crumpled. Her mouth hung loose, her eyes stared vacantly out of the picture. Even her hair that had been so tightly coiled into the spring of her bun now straggled listlessly over her shoulders. The drawing looked like a death-mask.

I was so shocked that for a moment I couldn't speak, just stared at the hideous portrait. 'But, but – this is appalling,' I whispered. 'Is it some sort of joke?'

'This is no joke,' he said gently, taking the picture out of my hands. 'Sophie is a good artist.'

'But, but this isn't true?' My voice rose sharply. Had I the drawing in my hand at that moment, I would have torn it from top to bottom. 'Madeleine isn't like – that.'

'She is very changed.' His voice was sad.

'But why?' I had pulled out one of the chairs and now I sat down, my legs weak. 'Why? Is she ill? Is there – '

'She is leaving, Lydia,' he said firmly. 'I – I think this upsets her so deeply.'

'But she isn't leaving. You keep saying that she's leaving, but – '

I saw pity in his eyes as he looked down at me. Pity, as if for a fool, a child. Had I been such a fool? But what had I done? I'd done nothing.

'Go down and see her, Lydia, before it is too late. She is your mother, after all.'

'But I can't – I can't.' I was sobbing now, my face in my hands, tears crushed between my fingers.

'Ah, Lydia.' His hand brushed the top of my head, light as a moth. 'The past makes us all prisoners.'

What time was it? I was still sitting on the hard dining-chair. Had he gone? I looked up. Yes, yes, he'd gone.

Stiffly, I got up, poured myself a drink. I took it over to the armchair feeling dazed, tired, my mind wandering. What was it Grandfather had always said?

'I don't like to drink on my own, princess. Here, you have a little drop with me.' And he'd pour a trickle into one of the thimble sherry glasses and I'd clink it against his tumbler and coax him to talk.

'Tell me about your battles, Grandfather. Were you very brave?'

'Brave? No. I stopped a few pieces of shrapnel, if that's what you mean?'

'What's shrapnel?'

'It's – well, princess, it's a sort of medal soldiers win in wars – a special medal that you wear inside your body.'

'Is it real?'

'Oh, yes, it's real.'

'Can you see it?'

'Not always – but you can feel it, though.'

'But what does it do? Does it stay there for ever?'

'Well, princess, this is a special medal. You see, one day – maybe years and years later – the shrapnel will decide it's time to come out – you've had the medal long enough now, you don't need it any more. And though you may have got used to it – got attached to it, so to speak – you just have to let it go. Do you see, princess? The war is over and those old medals must be taken away and forgotten. Ah, but you're too young to understand. Later, when you're older, my little Lily . . .'

No. No.

But it was too late, I couldn't fight, couldn't push it back. The drawings forked like lightning behind my eyes and slivers of memory pinned me to the chair.

In the morning I went down to the Hall.

II

INTERNAL
LANDSCAPES

Madeleine

August
They've put me in this big back room and I don't like it. It's dark and gloomy and smells of mould. Ma would have a fit if she saw it; she wouldn't let a room get all musty like this. I hate it. I hate it here. I hate the way they look at me – that stuck-up Lisa, who thinks she owns this horrible house, her going on about her 'Master', and what he'd say if he saw just 'what I was'. Like I'm some sort of insect, the way she looks at me. I won't be looked at like that.

'*Miss*' Madeleine, she calls me, and sniffs at the 'Miss' to make sure I get her point. No one's thought of being nice to me or asking me what I want. No, they just bundle me up here like I'm some disease they're afraid of catching. Well, it isn't my fault, none of it's my fault. And I didn't have anywhere else I could go. If Da finds out where I am, he'll kill me for sure.

August
It's so dark in this house that even when it's sunny and hot outside, like it is now, it doesn't warm the place. In here, I'm cold all the time, and if I go out for some air or to feel the sun on me, that Lisa shoos me back inside like she's ashamed of people seeing me.

I've got absolutely nothing. The clothes I stand up in and this diary book that Ma gave me last Christmas to do my exercises in. She was keen on my schoolwork. She wanted me to do well. 'You do your homework, Maddy,' she'd say. 'I'll do the milking and no one will be any the wiser.' Miss Sykes said I was good, that if I worked hard and did all my lessons, I could go places, that's what she said. 'We can make something fine of you, Madeleine.' Ha, if she saw me now, she wouldn't be so proud of her star pupil.

'Everyone should keep a diary,' she used to say to the class. 'It's excellent practice for the mind and sharpens the faculties of observation.' Of course everyone else just laughed at her, like they did at her accent and the queer clothes she wore and the way her hairpins were always falling out of her bun. But I liked her. I thought I'd be a schoolteacher, someone important, like her. Fat chance now. Fat chance then, really. Though I did work. Even when Ma couldn't stop Da from hauling me out of lessons to help with the potatoes or the hoeing or the lambing, I'd work at night when he was asleep so as I shouldn't slip behind in the class.

God alone knows where Miss Sykes is now. Up North with her own people, helping with the war like everyone else. She should have stayed here. If she had, it wouldn't have turned out like this. She could have spoken to Da maybe, done something . . .

Don't know why I'm thinking of her. And it's stupid to be writing all this down. But I've nothing else to do and no one will see this anyway, no one will check it for spelling or grammar. It's ages since I've even looked at a book. Long before William, it was, when Da took me out of the school. 'You're finished with all that now, girl. You're a tenant-farmer's daughter and don't you forget it. All that book-reading's no good for the likes of you. Won't tell you when to get in the harvest, will it? It's thanks to workers like us that them teachers can fill their bloody bellies . . .' On and on and on. If he could only have heard himself. But I suppose, thinking of it, that if it hadn't been for him – I mean, if I'd have gone to that college place Miss Sykes talked about, I'd never have met William. I wouldn't have been in the dairy that day. So it's because of Da, really. Ha, I'd like to see his face if I told him that.

I can hear the planes overhead. Horrible noise. Lisa will be in soon with the tray. She'll slam it down and look at me like I'm dirt on her shoe, something smelly the cat brought in.

At the Hall

But I'm glad I'm not on the farm. I'm glad I'm away from Da and him going on and on, and his belt, and that look in his eyes on a Friday night. But I hope the enemy does invade and he gets killed in that stupid Home Guard regiment of his. Because it's his fault Ma died. It's his fault I'm here in this place with no money and nothing of my own and a stuck-up servant hating me.

August

One day just runs into another. I don't remember what day of the week it is. I only know when it's Sunday, because Lisa goes to church then. I can just picture her sitting in the pew, looking all prim and pious so that no one can see what a cow she is. Ugly bitch.

Of course I don't go to church. In my state. I wouldn't dare. They'd stone me, those gossiping good-for-nothings. Anyway, who wants to sit in a gloomy cold place that's full of lies. Da goes, and look what good it does him. Ma? Yes, Ma would be sad that I wasn't with the Lord. But what help did that Lord ever give her? Never stopped Da on a Saturday night. Never stopped that drinking and swearing and breaking of the best china, did He?

So, I know it's Sunday because Lisa goes away, stays the night with her Ma in the village and leaves me alone. Of course I'm meant to stay up here in this big dark room – food on the tray – but no stopping me. Last Sunday I had a good look round. I wanted to find a picture of William. I went into his room. That nice brown room we stayed in together. I like that room. All small and cosy. It's warmer than the rest of this graveyard. The walls are all wood-panelled, lovely old wood, smooth, the grain all shining. And that big bed where he lay with me, his skin all white next to mine so brown. A lady and a blackamoor, I joked to him; he was the pretty lady with his fair skin and his white-blond hair and I was the swarthy man. Yes, *I* said that, me, Maddy. Only he didn't call me Maddy, like everyone else did, the kids teasing me at school – 'Who's mad then, Maddy . . .'

No, right from the start, when he stood in the dairy with the bandage slipping off his head and the flower in his uniform tunic, right from then, he called me 'Rose'.

August

I went into the garden today while Lisa was out the front – not that I think she cares so much really. Nothing shows yet. But the garden . . . Well, I wouldn't call it a garden. A bloody wilderness more like. I don't know why it's been so let go of. You can see there used to be plants all neat in the borders, dull plants to be sure – lavender, rosemary, nothing bright – but good enough and all just left to grow wild with the weeds over everything. A couple of fruit trees that could do with a good pruning too. Waste. And when I think of the whole country turning over their little handkerchieves of lawn to grow carrots and potatoes for the bloody war effort, it makes me sick, the waste of this place. When I think of how Da made us dig up all Ma's flower garden, the spring bulbs, the roses, the lilies, everything, just to put in another corner of turnips, and Ma not even complaining as she pulled out the plants, though it broke her heart. And here's all this land going to waste – I get so angry I could shout. So, this is how the gentry live, Da, doesn't matter to them, does it?

So, I thought I'd just clear a little patch to let those flowers breathe at least. If they were going to be there at all, it wasn't nice to see them all choked up with the weeds like that. And the touch of the earth was good. Nice, rich soil, though I could feel with my fingers it could do with some muck come autumn. And I was enjoying myself, the sun on my face, fresh wind – I've been so shut up in that ugly old house.

But then Lisa came out, shaking her fist and shouting at me. 'Don't you dare touch the Master's garden. You leave it alone.' And I didn't answer her back, though now I wished I had. I just let her go on ranting at me, though she didn't try to hit out at me this time – she's learned that I can give as good as I get; I haven't lived with Da without learning a few things. But I sat back on my heels and just thought how like a chicken she looked, clucking and squawking, her hair all white and brown, speckled like an egg. And I thought, no man's ever looked at you, you stupid chicken, and that's why you're on your knees to your bloody Master. Don't do that, she says, fifty times a day, the Master won't like it. Don't move the ornaments. Don't go into the Master's study. Don't touch the Master's war mementoes. Like living in a museum. But I looked at her shaking her fist at me and I suddenly thought, if it hadn't been for William, I could have ended up like that, all thin and scrawny, with no one but a master. But I've had a man of my own and in the end I'm worth more than her and she knows it. I've had my William.

August
I do miss him. I think maybe if I write him down then it'll be like it was when we came into this house – but it was a different house then, not gloomy like now, but dark and full of secrets. The furniture all wrapped up and a stale smell like the inside of a suitcase all shut up. But we loved it. It was our secret place, our house. And we joked about in the rooms and played with the old weapons in the hall and laughed. Yes, I made him laugh, me, his Maddy, his Rose. And the little red wound on his head was all smoothed out, because he was happy, and he looked well and rosy, not the pale ghost of a man who'd stopped to ask for some milk at the dairy because he was too tired to go on walking. And by the time he left with his brass belt gleaming and his uniform nicely pressed, his wound was healed and clean, all new skin grown over. And ready to get smashed and burned and –

No. I won't think about that. I see the planes overhead flying every day. There's big air fights going on. Sometimes I see one falling, but I don't shout, not like Lisa and the others in the village. There's a man in that plane and I don't care if he is the enemy. William was in one of them and I know what he didn't tell anyone, what he didn't even put into words to me. I know that he hated it. For all he was good, for all he was brave, for all he'd got some medal, he hated it, feared it, wanted it all to stop. He was probably relieved when they shot him down and it was finally over.

But the real joke is this. He only went in to the Air because he was afraid of the sea. Afraid of the sea and he was drowned in it, the water rising up around him and him trapped in that little cockpit like a rabbit in a snare. Bloody joke. He never dared tell his Da, but I'd like to. I'd like to tell the Master just what I think of him and his lot, moving people like William around as if they're just pieces of feed to be thrown into a trough. Much they care, sitting in their snug offices. And William not wanting to go to war and ending up dead anyway. Defying his Da and going into the Air and not the Navy like the Master wanted. Well, I hope the Master has it on his conscience. I hope it haunts him till the end of his days.

Bloody war. Doesn't solve anything. Our men, the enemy men, they're all the same stripped down. All of them dolled up like Da in his Home Guard uniform, marching round like he's some sort of general while Ma cooked and cleaned and did the cows and hoed and planted and her never thanked, never noticed. Except when the shirt wasn't ironed right for the parade – oh, then he noticed all right. And she'd be down on the floor with the hot iron burning her arm where he'd thrown it. Bloody coward. If he saw a real enemy he'd run a mile. He could only ever fight people like Ma and me who don't fight back. But now I'm gone and Ma's dead and he can't ever touch either of us again.

September
It's hot. I don't like it. It never bothered me before, but maybe now with all this extra weight and everything . . . And I feel so tired. Couldn't help with the harvest now. God, when I think of the hay I used to make, how easy it was lifting it on to the trailer. The one thing Da liked me for – 'She's a good worker, our Maddy.' But with the strap hanging from the wall, who wouldn't be?

My legs are all swollen up. I don't like it. And my belly is starting to stick out. It's so hot. Even the weeds in this wild garden are wilting. William said they never came down here much any more, that's why the place was left. Even before the war it was shut up. Only opened in the summer, when he'd come back from his training or on holiday from his fancy school and university. Properly educated, my William was. But he still loved the place. 'It's home, Rose,' he said, as we looked out through the window of his little brown room. 'I never forget the Hall.'

Two weeks. That's all we had. Two weeks. And even then we didn't know each other for the first three days of his leave, not till he came into the dairy on Easter Monday with that flower in his buttonhole and his face white as the milk he wanted. He sat on a churn and took the flower out of his smart blue-grey tunic and gave it to me – in exchange for the milk, he said, as I wouldn't take any money. And he laughed and said I was pretty. Me. Me. He said *I* was pretty.

I know I'm not pretty. I used to look and look in the mirror in Ma's bedroom but my face never changed. When Da was out, we'd put milk on my freckles and buttercream on my hands to make them soft. And Ma'd put by cream from the dairy and extra bread from the baking to make me fat, but it never made any difference. I was thin and tall, like a beanpole, Da used to say – 'Nothing on you to get hold of, Maddy.' Not that it stopped him trying on a Friday night, when his fat belly was full of beer.

I'm letting my hair grow now. I don't need to keep it so short. I only wish William could see me now that I'm a bit plumper and my hands softer and my hair longer. Because I was ashamed of how I looked, the roughness of my hands and my hard bones that jutted into his stomach. And my front that was as flat as a boy. And the ugly, coarse, dark hair between my legs. But he didn't seem to mind. 'You're my beautiful Rose,' he said. And when I pretended to scold him and said it was a sin to tell lies, he pushed me back against the bed with his white hand on my

111

brown skin like a stamp on a slab of butter – 'You're my beautiful Rose,' he said again, and kissed me and kissed me until I all but believed it.

No one would understand. They'd say I was a tease, that I was after his money – or worse, that I'm a – But I didn't know nothing about William and he knew I was a tenant-farmer's girl right from the start, but he didn't care. And it was him I wanted. Not his money or his medal or even his house. I didn't know about those things and I didn't care. It was William I wanted. William I got.

September

Lisa's been even more sour than usual. When I tipped my tea into my saucer to drink it, she snatched it away and said if I was to stay here I would have to learn to behave properly – 'Like a lady,' she said. 'You're not on the farm now, *Miss* Madeleine. You're at the Hall and it's time you started to learn some decent manners.' Stupid stuck-up cow. As if she's such a bloody lady. But I didn't say anything. She writes to the Master every week and I don't want him getting an even worse picture of me than he probably has already. So, I'm to eat my food more slowly and take little sips of tea from the cup, never mind that it's scalding hot – and likely as not learn to prink my bloody finger out as well.

September

I'm sitting up here in a strange little room I've found. It's very small and looks down the drive, so I can see all the trees turning yellow, the leaves curling up at the edges like tiny hands.

I like this room. There's a funny old table that's all leaning over with just one big leg in the middle and a comfortable chair I'm sitting in. I'm going to stay in here in the day. It's out of the way and Lisa can't say anything. And it feels so cosy and nice after those horrible big dark rooms that feel like people have died in them.

I'm looking out of the window and thinking of William, how

he lay propped up on his elbow, smoking one of his cigarettes – 'You mustn't let them beat you, Rose. Never let them beat you.' He looked fierce; even his skin was darker with all the sun from his leave. And I thought he was so handsome lying in my arms, mine, ugly Maddy who'd never had a boy even look at her before. 'Why did you choose me?' I said. 'There's plenty of prettier girls.' 'You're beautiful, Rose,' he said. And he bent over me again and we did it again, only this time he was rougher and pushed my legs apart and I had to bite my lip not to cry out. Not like the first time, when he was gentle and stroking me over and over till I was live and sharp everywhere like an early strawberry. 'I want to forget,' he said, panting in my neck so that I could feel his tears on my shoulder. 'You make me forget.' He was going back the day after.

Two weeks. And the days clicking past like the hands on a clock. He was lucky to get the leave at all, he said – 'Just in time to meet you, Rose.' Lucky? To be wounded as he crashed his plane. Lucky? And they only gave him two weeks before parcelling him back up into the seat to fly over the sea, chasing the enemy, the enemy, always the enemy. Bastards.

But I didn't say anything to him. I kissed his eyes and his hair that was shining as a buttercup, and nibbled his lips when I dared. Because he was mine. Mine. And I loved him. And he was my man.

September

Yes, autumn's coming now. The trees look tired and dusty with all this summer; they want their winter, they want their rest.

Today, sitting up in this porch room, I looked down the drive and it seemed almost like the trees were trying to wave me out; they kept pointing up the drive to the gate. But I can't go. I've nowhere else I can go. Da'll kill me if I show up there. And anyway, I'm thinking I have a right to be here, as much as if I was properly William's wife. He would have wanted me to stay here, I know. Except that last night I dreamt I saw William and he was telling me I should go, that I shouldn't stay here, that it would be bad luck for me. But it was only a dream.

I wish I had a picture of him. There's nothing here. Not even a scrap of paper with his handwriting on it. I wish I could stay in his little room. I wish he was here. I wish I wasn't so alone. I wish –

October
Lisa brought out a package today. 'From the Master,' she said, opening it. It was full of new clothes, warm clothes, and a new ration book in my name. And a ring. I was pleased with the clothes, I've been getting worried, because these old ones are getting so tight. But I laughed at the ring – 'A bit late, isn't it?' I said. Lisa scowled, her face all red and folded like the comb of a cockerel. 'You're to wear it,' she said. 'For seeing the doctor and such.' 'But we weren't married,' I said. 'Shut up, girl.' She grabbed my hand and forced the ring on. 'You're married now,' she said. 'Master says so.'

It's tight on my hand because my fingers have swollen with the water. And it looks wrong. My hand's too red and the nails are all bitten and my fingers are stubby. It rubs. But I don't dare take it off. It'll be winter soon and cold and the war and the bombs and there's nowhere else . . .

And now I'm thinking of Ma's ring, all thin and worn on her hand when I sponged it and laid it out, with the powder covering the bruises and her hair spread over her shoulders so that none of the marks should show. She looked absent. Oh, I know they say the dead look peaceful, but she just looked relieved not to be here. And Ma Beakin looking at me across the coffin in that way of hers, her eyes all narrow and screwed up like a pellet, giving me the herb potion I'd asked for to bring on my monthly. She said how nice my Ma looked, and how lucky she went quiet before she found out – she nodded at my belly. But I never took her potion. I got afraid of hell and what God would do if I killed His little seed, and then it was too late to change my mind. 'Well, I'll be at the birthing, then,' she said, when I gave the herbs back – I was afraid to keep them in case they brought bad luck. 'I was with your Ma when she had you and I'll see in her grandchild, God rest her soul.'

I wish she was here now, Ma Beakin. I wished I wasn't up in this big house all on my own with a stupid ring on my finger which everyone knows is a lie. I wish she would be in at the birth of my little William and I wouldn't have to go among strangers who won't care if I live or die.

October

It's raining. And getting cold. I'm warmest in this little porch room. Lisa knows I sit up here, but she doesn't mind. As long as I keep out of her way. There's a room full of books downstairs and on Sundays, when she's not here, I go in there and take a few to read up here. There's nothing else to do. The books are very old. Some of them are boring but one or two are interesting. There's one full of rules about 'etiquette'. Bloody silly, most of them – how to eat, how to walk, how to hold 'polite conversation'. I tried out the soup-eating yesterday, sipping it from the side of my spoon, just to see what Lisa would say. And she noticed, though she didn't smile or anything, just nodded. But then scolded me for wiping my bread round the bowl.

Little William is moving a lot now. All the time. Just like Flo said it was when she was with hers last spring – before she stopped talking to me, stupid cow. Even after she had it, she still looked fat as a pig, like she'd another stuck up her. But I'll show her. I'll show them all. She'll still be living at her Albert's Ma and Da's, even when he comes back, if he comes back, and he'll just go back to being the postman and they won't have got any better. But I'm going to be here with my little William, who's going to be a proper gentleman like his Da, and no one will be able to say any different. And the Master's going to have to let us stay here and when he dies all of this will be mine, because little William will be his only grandson and he won't get another. So, I'll show them all that laughed at me and hounded me out. I'll have the last laugh.

October

I don't listen to the wireless any more. Lisa listens in the kitchen but I don't want to hear all that horrible news – it's bad for little William. Lisa says the City's burning. Good. I hope one of them lands on the Master to pay him back for taking my William away from me. Because no one will get me to believe that he didn't stop William from coming back and marrying me like he said he would. He knew enough nobs like himself, he could have arranged that William kept that pass he'd got to come and see me. No, he killed William, killed the father of his only grandson, sent him out to fly over the sea when they were rescuing the Army. William should have been here. He should have been with me. Married. But the Master had him sent out and killed and made his grandson a bastard. But I'll get my own back. When little William's grown, then I'll tell him what his grandaddy did to him, I'll make sure he knows, and if the Master's still alive, we'll make him pay for what he did.

Oh, God. I'm getting hard, like Da. I don't want to be like him.

October

I wonder what the cottage looks like now Ma's not there to keep it. His things all over it, I should think. She was always picking up after him, though I told her not to. 'Let him do it,' I said to her. 'You're not his servant.' But she didn't take any notice of me. And though I told her to leave, though I told her I'd leave with her, though I told her I'd look after her, she kept on working in the dairy, even though her shoulder was black and blue from where he'd hit her.

Ma Beakin said she'd had the swelling long before anything Da did to her. 'He just speeded things up,' she said, when she stood by me in the graveyard, a month after the funeral. 'You should be grateful for her release, Maddy. Your Ma was in a lot

of pain.' 'Yes,' I said, 'and most of it from what he gave her.'
But she shrugged – 'God works in mysterious ways,' she said.
Then she poked at my belly. 'You take those herbs quick, my
girl, before it's too late. Or you'll be a bigger fool then either of
your folks.'

But I didn't care what she said or what she thought. I'd had
a letter from my William saying he'd come and we'd be wed.
He'd got a forty-eight-hour pass and I was to be ready. And I
carried that letter in my pocket and, even though my Ma was
just dead and I should have been crying, I was singing inside.
The baby would be all right. William was coming to marry me
and the baby would be all right. William coming to marry me
and get me away from Da. William, coming to marry me. Me.
Me. He was coming to marry *me*.

October
I'm getting suddenly fat. And I'm hungry all the time. I keep
thinking of all that butter we'd make in the dairy. I can almost
taste it. All I get here is a dab of marg from the rations. Lisa
hardly gives me any but I need it. Little William needs it. He's
kicking and pushing against me all the time and only quietens
down when I eat. If I had some money I could go out and buy
something for myself. I would go now, even to the village, I'm
that hungry. But I haven't a penny. Lisa keeps all the money
and the ration books locked away somewhere – I don't know
where. And she watches me all the time like a hawk, unless I'm
up here where she knows there's nothing I can steal. As if I
would take one of those stupid old swords and sell it. Silly cow.

The funny table in here is full of sewing things – needles and
cottons and buttons and things. And there's some cloth with a
pattern marked out for an embroidery that's been just started –
some flowers. There's a bundle of threads – yellow and pink
and red – so I'm going to go on with it, make them all roses,
bright and cheerful, as a cushion for little William. Make a
change from writing in this silly book and reading about
manners and how to talk properly.

We've got nothing for William. I don't know what they think I'm to do with him when he comes. I'm not putting him in a drawer, like Ma Beakin did with hers when they came. No. That's not good enough for my William. He's going to be a proper gentleman right from the start and he's not sleeping in a bottom drawer, like a village brat.

Lisa's still going on at me about the way I eat and drink. 'You're not to gobble your food like a pig,' she said yesterday when we were having tea – but I'm not to call it tea, it's supper. And – 'Ladies leave a little of their food on their plates to show they're not so hungry. It's good manners. The Master will expect you to know that . . .' Bloody bitch, so she can scoff it herself when I'm gone, I should think. But I left just a scrap even though I was so hungry I could have eaten it all, hers and mine. Bloody Master, what right has he to make all these rules? But Lisa actually smiled and even offered me a second cup of tea – which I was meant to refuse but I didn't. Looked bloody strange, she did, like a goose with that swallowed-up grin on her face. She looks better with her usual scowl.

November

The leaves are falling fast now, all the trees are bare, though the beeches are still holding on to some leaves, like they do for a while before winter. They rattle and rub together like chapped hands. I don't like it.

On the farm now we'd be sorting out the barns, going through the potatoes, picking out the seed. Ma'd be turning the cheeses in the dairy, the cows would have dropped off the high summer yields, place would be almost quiet – kitchen all warm with the stove stoked up and my room all cosy with the heat coming through the floor.

Stupid. And Da would be down the Arms with the dairy money – Ma's money – drinking it away. And he'd be back in the night, shouting and swaggering and finding something to be angry about. Stupid, stupid, stupid Maddy. You forget what it was like, don't you? You forget the strap on you and locking your door and wanting not to listen to him doing it to her and her little squeakings, like a new puppy that's too scared to shout.

November
It's cold. I'm wearing all my clothes but none of them fits. I'm getting too big. I don't like it. Ugly and lumbering like a great cow.

And Lisa's put curtains up for the blackout and she says we're not to use too much coal because of the war, so it's doubly cold. Anyway, I found a coat in one of the cupboards. A nice coat. Thick and warm, all fur with a soft collar that felt just like Charlie when he used to come purring on to my bed and sleep on the pillow beside me. So I started to wear it. But Lisa got furious. 'You take that off,' she shouted. 'That's the Mistress's.' 'But she's not going to wear it in the grave, is she?' I said back, because I was cold and angry and it seemed stupid to keep it in the cupboard when I knew she'd been dead years. It even smelled of mothballs. But for once I wasn't going to give in. 'I need to be warm,' I shouted back. 'It's bad for me and bad for the baby if I'm cold. So I'm wearing this coat and anything else I find until I've been given something new. And,' I went on, 'I'll take whatever I can for the baby. He'll be here soon and there's not a stitch of clothes ready for him. You can tell your precious Master that even in my village they at least have the baby's clothes ready by now. Doesn't he care about his grandson?' And I stormed out and left her standing there, with her mouth open like a chicken whose head has been cut off but whose face hasn't noticed yet.

November
I'm scared. Little William's growing so big, much too big. It was all right before, when he was just a little bump, but now I can't even see my feet. I can't bend over or tie my shoes, and it's hard to get in and out of chairs or pick things up from the floor.

And what's going to happen? He's going to get bigger and

bigger still before January and then how's he going to come out? I'm much too small for him to come out of me now. I'm scared. If I was in the village I could talk to Ma Beakin, maybe get her to give me something to make him smaller or me bigger, so that he'll come out easy. I could ask Flo even, just to tell me if it really is so bad when babies are born. But I can't go down there now, not while I'm so big. And there's no one here I can ask. For all this wearing of the bloody ring, I haven't seen any doctor.

Oh, I've seen plenty of sheep and calves being born, but it looks different for them, they don't seem to feel the pain so much. I'm so scared. How can a baby this big come out of me? I wish I'd taken Ma Beakin's herbs. I wish I'd never had this baby. I wish I'd never met William.

December

Christmas soon. Now we'd have salted the pig and we'd be making the cake to store for tea on Christmas Day. We'd beat up the best butter and new-laid eggs and I'd be stoning raisins and cleaning currants until I could see those little black specks even when I closed my eyes. And the kitchen would smell all warm and full of spice, and the bowls of dripping from the pig and the sausages and hams hanging from the rafters. That was a good day, Cake Day. 'I think we'll be making the cake today, Maddy,' Ma says, and she takes down the big brown bowl and sends me over to the dairy to fetch the butter and find the eggs. And then there'd be the big pudding and she'd get me to stir it and make a wish as I dropped in the sixpence. And then the mince, with always a bit left over which wouldn't fit in the jar and we'd just cook up a bit of pastry for us two and eat it hot in little pies, just to try it out . . .

No. It's no good remembering. I'm not there. I'm alone in this cold house which smells of wax and polish and the windows are dark with the blackout and the planes scream overhead, reminding me of William.

Sometimes, just sometimes, I wonder if maybe he isn't really dead. Maybe he got out of that plane and he's been captured and when the war's over he'll come walking back down the drive and I'll see him from up here and run out to greet him . . .

Stupid. I don't know what's got into me today. Ma's dead. William's dead. I'm on my own here with no money and no name and nothing of my own – a bastard child in my belly that nobody wants. And I'm trying to make out I'm like a princess in a fairy-story when I'm a nobody and a stupid fool.

December

A parcel arrived today with things in for me and little William. So, my outburst had some effect after all. These are the first things I've got for little William. Nice warm things. Coats and jumpers and dresses – though what he'll want them for, I don't know. And bonnets and mittens and terry towels for napkins. There's even some wool and needles for knitting, not that I'm much good at it. For me there's some warm dresses – big ones – and a cardigan, and a coat and a nice lilac skirt. Nice things, proper heavy, thick material. Of course I can't wear the skirt now, but later, when I'm normal, I'll look like a proper lady in it.

William's things look so pretty. All little. He'll be here so soon. And Lisa says we're to look in the attic for the old cot. Maybe we'll set it up in the little brown room and I could move in there with him, and leave that horrible big room. It'll be so nice when little William comes. I won't be on my own all the time. I'll have company, someone of my own. Someone of my very own whom no one will ever be able to take away.

December

Horrible bombs everywhere but not here. Lisa says if we get bombed we're to go under the table in the dining-room, as we haven't got a shelter. It's thick as a tree trunk, so it won't break in a hurry.

We practised getting underneath it to see if there's enough room. It was funny, I couldn't help giggling. I haven't been under a table since I was trying to dodge Da when I was little, and there we were, two grown women, crouching like we were kids – and me as big and clumsy as an elephant. Even Lisa laughed a bit and she said she reckoned we'd be all right as long as I didn't end up having the baby down there. But I stopped laughing then, and I don't know why – maybe because we were down there looking equally silly – but I suddenly blurted out that I didn't want to have the baby there or anywhere, that I was afraid of all the pain and the hurt and that I might die of it. She hauled me out of the table and sat me down on the antique chairs that normally I'm not even allowed to touch and I thought, Oh, God, now I'm for it. But though she was angry it wasn't at me. She said it was time I saw a doctor, that it was no good my being so scared as it'd make things worse. And I asked if she'd seen a baby born. 'My sister's had three,' she said. 'The last were twins and she never had an easy time of it. I'm sure I wouldn't want to have any.' Not that she'd have had the chance, I thought, a man'd think twice before looking at her. 'But what'll I do?' I said. Then she laughed a cold sort of laugh, like Ma used to when she was picking herself up off the floor after Da'd been at her. 'You'll manage,' she said. 'They all do.' Then she went back to the kitchen and we didn't say anything more.

December

It's really cold now. Lisa's made up a fire in the parlour and we sit in there, but it's still not warm enough. When she goes off on Sunday, I'm going to get a load of wood from her store in the shed and burn the bloody lot.

My bosom is so swollen now it makes me feel sick to see it. I don't think William would like it. He said he liked them all small. They're like udders in spring now and there's lines and marks all over my belly and my belly-button sticks out like a door handle. I look ugly.

I'm trying to do this knitting, but I was never any good at it.

Not like Ma, who'd whip through a pair of socks in an evening.
The embroidery is coming on, though. I do it up here in the
porch room, even though it's so cold. I've nearly done all the
roses and I've left a space to stitch 'William' on in blue thread.
It'll look so nice.

December

The doctor's just left. Nasty, sneering little man. He called
me 'Miss Madeleine', even though I've got this bloody ring
on my finger. His hands were cold and he pushed at my belly
and made William kick and punch till it hurt. He said William
was lying the wrong way and that if he didn't 'turn', I'd have
to go into the Mother and Baby Hospital. Bugger that. I'm
not going in that place with all those snotty madams. I can't
understand it. My belly's big enough, so I don't see what's
wrong. He said I had to go out for walks to make the baby
turn. Then he went into the kitchen and had tea with Lisa
and I could hear them whispering – the Master this, the
Master that – and I stood outside and tried to listen, but they
must have heard me, because all of a sudden they talked
about the war instead.

December

Thick snow everywhere. Lisa made a path but she wouldn't let
me help. It's so cold. I'm sure it's the cold that's bad for little
William; it's what's made him be the wrong way round. But
he's been kicking and moving a lot, so maybe he's round the
right way. He'll be a standing-up baby just like his Da.

Lisa and I stay in the kitchen most of the day, and she
helps with my knitting. She's as quick as Ma. She's made a
bonnet for little William – pink though, but I never said
anything. And she's being more canny with the rations, or
there's more of them. She says she'll get extra for me – milk
and eggs when little William is here. We don't talk about the
war. One of her sister's boys is out there, but she doesn't
say anything about him. Quite a little routine we've got now,

and I'm almost forgetting what it was like before I came here, as if this is all there's ever been.

December

I've been thinking about when William's bigger. He'll have to go to school. But I don't want him to go round here, where people will talk. So, I've thought what I'll do is teach him his letters and numbers myself, just like Miss Sykes taught me. It'll be good to have him learning from me. Then, when he's bigger, he'll have to go away to one of those fancy schools like his Da went to. The Master will have to see to that, he can't let his only grandson not be brought up as a gentleman. He'll have to see that I mean to bring my little William up properly, just as if I was William's properly married wife.

December

Terrible pains today, like my guts being pulled out and twisted. Like the monthly only much, much worse. Lisa fetched the doctor but by the time they came back it was over. He checked me all over with his cold hands and said that straight after Christmas I'm to go into the Mother and Baby Hospital until I'm ready to give birth.

But I won't. If the pains come again I won't tell anyone. I'm not going into that hospital, where they'll all look at me like I'm some sort of insect.

The only good thing is that I'm to have a fire made up in my bedroom. It's not such a bad room when it's warm. If it was in brighter colours and a pretty counterpane on the bed, it would be all right really. Lisa was sitting with me earlier. She's gone down now to make the tea – supper and listen in. She's knitting something else for little William, only this time it's in yellow wool, which is better. She says it's from an old jumper she doesn't want any more.

Christmas Day

Lisa wanted me to go with her to her Ma's but I said I didn't want to. So I'm sitting here in the parlour with a really big fire and I'm warm for the first time in months. And I've found a bottle of brandy and I'm drinking that and feeling tipsy and funny.

I can't help thinking of Da, what he's doing, if he's been invited anywhere for the day. He won't have cooked anything for himself – he hardly knew how to make a cup of tea, let alone a Christmas dinner. Serves him right.

I've two pairs of thick socks on – William's socks. They're the only things of his that I've found and I'm not telling Lisa. It's awful. I've almost forgotten what he looked like. I've forgotten how his voice sounded and how his body felt. I've forgotten how he smiled at me when he called me his Rose. And I mustn't forget. I have to remember so that I can tell little William what a good, strong, brave Da he had, and how he loved his little son, even though he never saw him, not once.

January
It must be the crash that's brought this on. It's too early. Maybe it's another false alarm and it'll go away. I won't give in. I won't –

Jesus, this pain, and my back aches. But it can't be ready yet, it's too soon. I'm going to stay up here till it stops. I'll write about the plane from yesterday, that crash in the garden.

I can still see bits of the wreck all over the front. I can see all the foreign marks on it. God, it made a terrible sound when it exploded. I thought we were being bombed. And when Lisa and I ran out, there was blood all over the snow and I saw bits of the pilots all on the lawn – an arm, with its glove on, just lying there on the ground . . .

It's just the shock, that's all. The pain will stop in a minute. I'll get Lisa to make me some sweet tea – that's what Ma used to give, I remember, when my hand got caught in the mangle. Lots of sweet tea and the pain will go away and it'll be all right.

Lisa said they might have to bury the pilots in the woods. There's so many bits of them they can't gather everything up. But I went white and she stopped and I thought I would faint –

maybe I'll faint now. Oh, God, the pain, the pain, I don't want this –

January

She's in the room at the other end. I don't want to hear her if she cries. She hasn't stopped crying since we've come back. I've shut all the doors, because I don't want to hear her. I'm not staying awake all night just to watch her crying.

January

The nurse is angry with me because of her not feeding. But she won't feed from me. I've even put sugar on my nipples and she still won't feed from me. Every time I go near her she just cries. If I pick her up, she cries. If I change her napkin, she screams. If I give her the bottle, she won't take it. Only Lisa can give her the bottle and then she takes it all and falls asleep.

January

She hates me. And I hate her. All that pain for this ugly, puny, yellow chicken of a baby who screams when I go near her. She cried as soon as she saw me when she was born. On and on and on, her face all red and her head all bald and her ugly yellow body curling up in temper like a bit of burning paper.

January

I think they've made a mistake. She's not my baby. They've given me the wrong one. This isn't my little William who danced and kicked and punched inside me. My little William is bonny and fair and smiles at me. They've given me the wrong baby. I'll tell them and they'll give me back my little William. Poor little William – he's probably missing me like I'm missing him. I must get him back. They must give him back to me.

January

The nurse says I should be out of bed and she's cross that I'm not looking after my baby properly. But I tried to explain to her

– she isn't my baby, there's been a mistake – but she looked at me like I was mad, so I didn't dare say anything more. And there's Lisa going on about how she's just like the young Master when he was born. I know they're wrong. They're doing this on purpose because they know I can't do anything. It's a plan to get me out of here because I've got a girl baby instead of a boy baby, which I should have had.

February

I'm still sore down there from where they did things to me. It hurts to walk. Lisa's moved into William's room to be near the baby. I've stopped even pretending to get up for her in the night – she only screams when I go near her.

Lisa says she's written to the Master, but she's waiting for me to choose a name before she sends the letter. She says I've got to come up with one quick or he'll be angry that he hasn't been told. So what? He's going to be angry anyway. Now he's going to get me out of here, I know it. Because she's not a boy. It would have been all right if I'd had my little William, but without him I'll be turned out – what does he want with a girl baby?

February

Lisa says she's to be called Lydia. It's a name she likes and she's chosen. I don't care. It doesn't make any difference. She still screams when I'm near her. And what am I going to do when the Master turns me out? What will I do with Lydia? I don't want her. On my own I'd have a bit of a chance – I'm strong and I could get work – but not with her. I keep hoping that maybe a bomb will fall on his fancy War Office and he'll be killed and then I won't have to leave and it'll all be all right because all this will be mine. I know it's bad but I can't help hoping.

March

My hands are all red from the washing. That's all I do now –

washing and cleaning and cooking, just like Ma. I don't do anything with Lydia, Lisa does her, fussing and cooing, and the stupid baby smiles back at her like she's her bloody mother. If I come into the room, than she's off screaming like a devil. It makes me look stupid, me, her own mother who nearly died giving birth to her.

And I'm still as fat as a pig. Can't get into any of my old clothes or the lilac skirt the Master sent me. No word from him about Lydia. He's just biding his time. Any day now there'll be a letter with instructions to Lisa to have me turned out. It's not fair. It's his fault I'm not properly married and now he's going to throw me out of here with no money or anything.

Oh, I wish Ma was here. It would be all right if she was here. Lydia would be all right, she wouldn't cry so much. And Ma'd know why I was still hurting when I walked. I miss her. Miss the way she did things, her glasses all steamed up over the jam and her calling in the cows for milking so that they never played up with her. I miss her so much.

April

Lisa says she's leaving. She says it's time she did something for the war effort and she's going to work in one of the munitions factories. But she can't leave. What'll I do with Lydia if she's not here? So I said to her – 'Aren't Lydia and I more important then the war effort?' But she plumped herself up like a stupid cockerel and said I was old enough to look after the baby myself.

But I can't. If I'm alone with Lydia, she just screams all the time. And maybe it's all part of the Master's plan. Maybe he wants Lisa to go away, so that when he comes down to turn me out, there won't be anyone to stop him. Or maybe he just won't send any money and we'll starve? Lisa *can't* go. I'll beg her and beg her and she just can't go.

April

It's warm today. I sat outside with Lydia on a rug and for once she was quiet and sucked her thumb and dozed a little. So she should be after the night she gave me. It was just like when she was first born – nothing I did made any difference, so I just shut the door on her and left her to scream.

I could move into William's room now that Lisa isn't here to stop me, but I don't dare. The Master could come back at any time and if he saw me in there he might get angry and turn me out.

No, I'm just keeping very quiet and doing all the cleaning that Lisa told me to. He's still sending money, but at any time, Lisa said, he could come down here and then . . . Well, I've decided, if he comes down here he's not going to find a tenant-farmer's girl and her brat. He's going to find a lady and her daughter. I'm going to be so proper and genteel that he'll want me to stay. And I'm going to make sure Lydia is well-behaved and good-mannered and knows all the right things to do. He'll see the wife his son chose. He'll see how he should have let me marry his William. So, I'll show him and I'll make sure Lydia shows him, and then we'll stay here and be safe and when he dies it'll all be ours.

May
Not much point writing in this diary any more. It's nice and warm. Trees all out, birds chattering. There's all new plants coming up in the garden, but they're having a struggle with all the weeds over them. God, what I could do with this place. I could make a proper flower garden, something William would be proud of.

I'm going through that old book of manners and learning all the things from it. I've been practising going up and down the stairs with a book on my head and eating with a penny under each arm to keep my elbows in. I'd like to change the way I speak too, but that's a bit harder. I read aloud from the books in the study and try to remember what William's voice sounded like.

If he was here he'd be so proud of me. We'd sit on the fancy chairs in the parlour and he'd say how clever I was and how much he loved me. If he was here, I could even learn to like Lydia a little. But now, when she looks at me all scowling and cross, I can't help but get angry back. She has never smiled at me. Selfish baby. And I'm doing all this for her. All this to stop her from being just another village brat, to give her an inheritance, something that belongs to her. When she's old enough, then she'll understand what I've done. But I'll have to be strict with her. She's going to be a proper lady and that takes learning.

July

Just to say it's more than a year since I met William. A year since he's dead. Poor William. And I can't hardly remember what he looked like.

August

So, Da's dead then. Well, I can't help thinking it serves him right. I hope he had as much pain as he gave her, because I can still see the bruises he made – how I'd help her up to bed and sponge her with witch hazel. The colour of those bruises, purple like peonies and yellow like chrysanthemums, and her eyes all red from crying, but she wouldn't have shouted so as not to let anyone hear, in case they punished him. Well, I hope he's being punished now. And I don't want them laying him next to her. She had him all her life and I want her to be free of him at the end.

August

I was in the kitchen, making lunch for me and Lydia, when there was a rattling at the back door and in walked Ma Beakin. I was so struck I nearly dropped the china. 'I've come to sit with you, Maddy,' she said, settling down into a chair. 'It's not right for you to be all alone with your Da being buried this afternoon.' She looked different, not so plump, older, and – I don't know, but suddenly seeing her and hearing her voice – it brought back the village and Ma and I just started crying, blubbering like a baby. But she didn't even blink, just pulled me towards her and patted and petted me so that I could smell the bread smell of her clothes and I cried and cried until there were no tears left. I felt stupid then, but she stood up and made me sit in the chair, and while I cleaned myself up she bustled about the kitchen like she'd been there all her life, finding the pot and making tea. Then Lydia woke and she picked her up and of course Lydia was immediately quiet and smiled and giggled like she never does for me.

We had tea, Lydia sitting on Ma Beakin's big lap and reaching out for her cup and Ma Beakin laughing as she took it out of her reach. It made me angry. I've been trying to teach her that it's bad manners just to grab for things and I don't want it turned into a game.

She started talking about the village. Her young Jack's been killed and her Dot's Alan. 'Her kids don't have a father now,' she said sadly. And I thought, Well, Lydia hasn't ever had a father, but no one's cried over that. I didn't say anything, just drank my tea, though she'd put too much sugar in it for what I like now. She poured hers into the saucer and drank it like a cat making noises, while all her gums showed. I'd forgotten that.

Then she started. 'You should have made the peace with your Da, Maddy. You should have come back to look after him. He needed you.' 'He'd have killed me,' I said, pointing to Lydia. But she shook her head. 'He'd have got used to it in the end. You know him.' But that's just it, I knew him and she didn't. And she started again. 'What are you doing in this place, Maddy? You don't belong here. And you can't fool me with your fancy airs and graces. Come back to the village. Now your Da's dead and the farm's gone back, you can stay with me. I'd look after you and the little one, for your Ma's sake, you know that.' 'Oh, yes,' I snapped, 'and the whole village pointing at me and laughing to my face.' But she shook her head. 'It's all changed now, Maddy. No one would mind. It's all different now.'

To ignore her I got the feed ready for Lydia, but she took it out of my hands and fed Lydia herself. And of course the little madam ate it all properly – not like she's been doing with me lately, spitting it out and throwing it around. 'She could do with a bit of fattening,' Ma Beakin said, poking her like she was a piglet at the mart. 'She's that way naturally,' I said, and tried to take her back, but she started crying and it made me angry to have her show me up like that.

We stayed in the kitchen – she said she didn't feel comfortable in a parlour. She told me more gossip. Mr Greeson's not running the shop any more, his daughter-in-law's got it now. Madge Greeson, I remember her, sour little cat. And Flo's got another baby due soon – 'Maybe two by the look of her,' she laughed. 'All of us on rations and she's the only one that thrives on it.'

Then she put Lydia on the floor with a bit of crust and began again. 'Come back with me, Maddy. You're lonely here, you're not happy. Come back. Don't be proud, like your Da. Come back before it's too late.' 'Before what's too late?' I asked. She frowned, getting short-tempered. 'Well, look at you,' she said. 'You sound like you've got a plum in your mouth. You look like you haven't done a stroke of work in months – all fat, not like you, Maddy. And I don't know what you think you're doing dressing up in those fancy clothes.' I was wearing one of the Mistress's lace shirts – they're pretty and what ladies wear. 'You're not yourself, Maddy,' she went on. 'You've a face as long as a steeple and your baby is all thin and yellow and it's not right. Don't be a fool. You don't belong here . . .' On and on and on, until suddenly I got angry and I stood up and said, 'Well, you should have thought of that when I first knew about the baby. No one wanted to help me then, no one wanted anything to do with me. Well, I'm not going to forget that. I've gone my own way and I'm going to do very well and you're just envious.'

She stood up then and picked up her string bag and just sighed. 'I came to sit with you while your Da was being buried, Maddy. It didn't seem right to me that you shouldn't know anything about it, that's why I sent my Susan up to tell you.

And I'll say this, he was a miserable sight in the end, your Da, but no more miserable to me than the sight of you cutting yourself off from your own people. You're a fool, Maddy. You're stubborn, like your Da, and you'll end up lonely and unhappy, just like him.' Then she left.

But I won't end up like him. I won't end up like any of them. I won't have Lydia playing in the dirt of the farmyards. She's going to have shoes and speak properly and learn lessons and know things and not be a farmer's brat, like the rest of them. And I'm going to have bettered myself and they'll all be sorry when they see me in this big fine house which will be mine. They'll see I was right. I'm going to make my own life. I won't stay in their mucky rut. I'm going against the grain.

Sophie

Dear Soph,

Just a very quick note before I leave. THIS IS THE LAST LETTER I'LL *EVER* WRITE FROM HERE. God, I'm so excited. Leaving the Home is like getting out of prison – not that this place has really been prison, of course, and as you always say, we were lucky to be able to stay here and be together and not get split up and fostered or adopted by revolting people – but you know what I mean, to be free of all the rules and the bells at meal-times and bed-time and all the time. God, I'm just so excited. Were you this excited when you left? I can't say you looked it, but then you never do, do you? Anyway, it was different for you, because you were coming back here at weekends, so you weren't really properly leaving. Not like me. I'm going to be completely on my own in a totally new place without you or anyone I know, and though I'm TERRIBLY excited, I'm also a bit nervous as well. But you will write, won't you? PROMISE YOU WILL. PLEASE.

Anyway –

Sorry, had to break off there as Matron came in to inspect my packing. Well, you can imagine what that was like – I'd just thrown everything into the case and sort of sat on it till it shut, but was that good enough? Oh, no. Shock, tutting, shaking of head. She unpacked the whole thing and now it's all folded so carefully I'll be terrified to disturb her arrangement. And then, would you believe it, she announced that now I was leaving I could in future call her – 'Ann'. *Quelle privilège.* But really, after all these years of calling her 'Matron', of her *being* Matron, I really don't think I could even think of her as anything else. And 'Ann'? Isn't she a bit stout to be an Ann? Don't worry, I was very polite and promised I'd keep in touch. 'Your sister always writes so regularly' – i.e. I expect you to do the same. Must I always be struggling to match your stainless reputation, Oh peerless elder? And she left in the end with a lot of fussing.

Oh dear, this was meant to be a quick letter. I'll stop now. Please write to me as soon as you can – like right now. I'll be dying to hear from you. But I'll write when I get there anyway. I wish you were here to tell me I'm being silly. Please write SOON.

Lots of love, Stella

PS Thank you so much for the little card you made. I showed it to Sharon and she didn't know which way up it went either, but it's lovely all the same. I've got it in my bag and I'll put it on the wall as soon as I get one. Sorry this letter is so terribly about me. How are you? Still in the PINK phase? I do like the card even if I don't understand it.

Your ignorant little sister, S.

Dear Soph,

I know you won't have had any time to reply to my first epistle, but I wanted to tell you about this place immediately, while it's fresh.

I'm sitting in MY room, which for the first time EVER I don't have to share with anyone – not even you of the punctilious nature. So I can throw my clothes all over the floor and leave my books open on the bed and sleep in my boots for all anyone cares.

The last couple of days have been incredible. Loads of people, mazes of buildings, vast library – I just get lost all the time, but discover the most extraordinary pockets of places – a lab full of ferns with electrodes stuck in them – measuring thoughtwaves? And a gym with two great grunting giants slapping each other about on mats like washing, then they stand up and bow – that's Judo. Don't worry, I'm not quite ready for that yet . . .

I'll tell you about the journey. My luggage managed to get on to the wrong train all by itself and only at the last minute did

I stop it going on a holiday of its own up north – maybe it's got relatives in the mountains . . . Then I met some people on the train also on their way up here. Annette, immensely tall, long sheaves of chestnut locks, all lanky and sophisticated and terribly superior, and would you believe it, she's reading chemistry. I wouldn't have thought she'd have done anything more than file her nails and glance at the odd magazine. Then Emily, exactly as you'd imagine – short, plump and ringlety, very friendly and comfortable, doing history. Then a few others as we got nearer, until finally PAUL – tall, dark and handsome? Not exactly. Rather, short, slight and spotty – a bit like Glyn at the Home, but he's also doing English and is very excited about a drama group which he wants to set up and which he's already invited me to join.

Anyway, we all got sorted into our various halls of residence – just a fancy name for blocks of bed-sits. Actually, mine's all right. I've got a view over a courtyard with a huge tree in it. I don't know what species but I'm sure you'd love to paint it, it's got lots of perspectives . . . I've got Arabella on one side of the wall – blonde, the Ophelia type, all seaweed hair and looks like she's going to fall asleep at any moment. She's reading biophysics – what is it about the sciences that gets all the future models? And – Margaret on the other side – short, brush hair, rather abrupt, spectacles, reading classics. My room has its own little desk, a basin, a kettle and one comfortable chair. I share the cooker with three others in a communal kitchen. It still looks spotless, but after I do my exploding apple slab . . .

So, then a few of us went out to the PUB and chatted and had fun and I thought – if Matron (Ann???) could see me now – as I flicked the ash off my cigarette and sipped my cherry brandy . . .

I must stop now. Actually, I'm rather tired. Tomorrow I'm having my first tutorial and as it's absolutely *de rigueur* to fall in love with one's tutor, I want to look my absolute best, so that he can reciprocate . . .

Do write soon. This is a terribly long letter. I'll be checking the post every morning. Sorry this is so much about me. I do hope you're all right. I thought of you this evening when I was in the pub. Don't you get fed up with that wine-bar job? Couldn't you find something else to do with more money? Teaching?

You see, I do think of you.

Lots and lots of love, Stella.

Dear Soph,

Thank you so much for your letter (even if it was a bit short). It was SO good to see your handwriting waiting for me. Yes, of course my letters have been 'overexcited', but what else do you expect, it's all so new and different, nothing like the Home at all, so don't come down on me too hard, Soph, please . . .

Actually, I do mean it about your washing-up job. It seems pretty silly considering how clever you are and talented and everything that you have to do something so silly just to earn money. I think you could earn a fortune just teaching people how to LOOK at things before they even start painting. You know, like the way you used to talk to me about it. But I suppose I can see what you mean about wanting to do something mindless so that your imagination is left free to roam. I mean, I could probably do with a spate of washing-up right now. I'm so up to my ears in work. I haven't done anything other than write, read, eat and sleep for the last week and I feel very worn out – mentally.

I've got PILES of books to be read. Will have to spend YEARS in the library just sorting out the bloody reference numbers. And the essays – honestly, Soph, I'm beginning to have my doubts. I mean, I got in here by the skin of my teeth and now I'm going to have to work really hard just to keep my head above water (great mixture of metaphors there – or is it similes . . . ?).

Anyway, I've got this lovely tutor, Mr James – he's nearly ninety, so don't worry – seems vague and dotty but really rather sharp under all that. It's not at all how I thought. I mean, I have to do most of the work on my own, while he just checks up on me from time to time. A bit hard. Self-discipline was never my strong suit, as Matron was always reminding me. I don't know how you manage yourself with your painting. I couldn't. I can only do this because I imagine that Mr James will breathe down my neck if I don't. You must have a will of steel – but then, I know you do anyway.

You remember Paul, whom I met on the train? – (this is a test to see if you actually READ my letters) Well, he's finally got organized and has set up a reading for this play he wants to put on and I'm invited to audition. I don't know what play – probably something obscure.

I must go now. I've got a lecture in exactly three minutes and there's nothing worse than creeping into a hall with a hundred eyes all staring at you while you try to be invisible.

Write soon.

Lots of love, Stella.

Dear Soph,

Yes, I'm writing out of turn. Actually, I'm afraid this is a rather difficult letter. I've got to ask you a favour and I feel pretty awful about it.

The thing is, I'm broke. I seem to have spent all this month's money in a fortnight and now I've literally got nothing. I'M TERRIBLY SORRY. I know I've been stupid. It's just that I wanted to go out to the pub with the others and I can't just sit there and let them buy me drinks, so I end up buying a round as well and it's really a bit expensive. I don't know how they all manage. I suppose their parents help them out. I mean, they all act as if they've got plenty of money, even though they all complain they haven't a penny. I suppose they feel safe because they know their parents will bail them out if they get stuck. And they just assume the same for me. Of course, I don't say anything about parents and no one asks – everyone's so afraid of being thought nosy that you could live here for years without them even knowing your name. I just say I lived in a big house in the country and leave it at that. Of course, I tell them all about you, my famed-to-be sister. I've quite dazzled them with you.

Anyway, I'm just waffling on. I'm sorry. The thing is, would it be possible for you to lend me just a little to keep me going till next month? I WILL PAY IT BACK. I feel awful for asking when I know you're saving everything you can to spend on rose madder and raw sienna. I'm sorry. I know I'm disappointing you. But I've learned my lesson. Already I'm staying in and drinking tea in the Common Room. And I've stopped smoking – I didn't like it anyway, it just looked good, you know.

I hope you're all right. What are you working on now? You never say. I wish you'd tell me, describe it a little, so that I can imagine it and be there with you. I went past an artist's supply shop today and thought of you. I like the blues best – cobalt, ultramarine, coeruleum – such heavenly names.

I'll stop now. I've an essay to write and loads of reading – you see what a model student I am.

I'm truly sorry to ask about the money. Really I am.

Love, a very contrite, Stella.

Sophie, you're an angel. Thank you a million times. I promise I'll pay it back. I just saw this card and thought you'd like it. I think the colours are rather like yours. I'll write properly soon. Thank you. Thank you. Thank you.

ALL MY LOVE, Stella.

Dear Soph,

Actually, I've been thinking rather a lot about what you said in your last letter. Yes, I suppose I am 'affected' by our lack of parents. I mean, I hadn't really thought about it before. At the Home everyone was the same – all of us in the same parentless boat, as it were – so it was normal and none of us thought anything of it. But here, with everyone slagging off their parents – it's *de rigueur* – all I can think is that they're lucky to have them at all. But I don't say anything and I don't tell any of them about my life in the Home because it sounds so odd now and I don't want them to find out about it and realize I'm 'different'. It makes me feel embarrassed. Did you feel like this when you were at art school? What did you say about it when people asked? What do you say now?

It's getting very autumnal – leaves falling, nights drawing in. I should be able to quote some ancient poem about it, but honestly if I see another line of verse I'll throw up. Remember how we'd collect conkers and then put them in the boiler so they'd explode? And the times we'd sit around the fire at study-time and scare ourselves silly with ghost stories while Matron went out to make tea . . . I had a letter from her the other day. And do you know, seeing that neat little handwriting actually brought a lump to my throat. AWFUL.

Anyway, did I tell you about the auditions? Well, I'm sorry to say it seems your little sister isn't going to make her name treading the boards. I was in a rather off mood – I seem to be getting a few of them at the moment. Well, I really fluffed the reading, so I've ended up with a minute part – just as well, really, I'm so busy anyway. But I'm understudying the lead, so maybe I'll put poison in her coffee . . .

I do miss you. I suppose it's just that I'm all on my own here. At the Home we had each other – we were so lucky in that, when all the others were on their own. I suppose now, being on my own, I mean with you not being here, is why the whole parents thing is getting to me. It never did before.

I've got all your pictures and cards up on my wall. I wish you'd do a self-portrait – but a photograph would do (this is a hint). Is that how artists do self-portraits – from photographs? I think it's very enterprising of you to be sending slides off to all the galleries – and very brave too. What do they say? Are they nice about them?

Sorry this is a very flat letter. I'll stop and do some dull medieval poetry. I do hope you're well. I'm thinking of you. Please write soon – and at length?

Love, S.

Dear, dear, dear Soph,
You've no idea what a wonderful surprise it was to see you. I

was so thrilled – even if I did spend the first hour in tears – I was just *so* pleased to have you really here. I think I've missed you more than I'd realized.

And I feel much happier now that you've seen it all. (I told you you'd be inspired by the tree in the courtyard, but I'm claiming that picture . . .) And you've no idea how much my stock has risen here since your visit. Arabella was hugely impressed by your knowledge of colours – well, you're an artist, what does she expect? But she says she's now thinking of changing the whole direction of her thesis to look into the chemical origin of pigmentation or something like that. Whatever it is, you certainly inspired her. I've never seen her look so less drowned.

Anyway, I want to say two things.

First, I think you look FAR too tired. I'm sure you don't want me to lecture you, but I'm going to (Matron would be proud of me). I think you should find another job which isn't so wearing. You can't paint all day and wash up all night for months on end without a break. PLEASE LISTEN TO ME. I'm worried about it. PLEASE THINK SERIOUSLY ABOUT THIS.

Secondly, about the parents issue. I suppose you're right in some of the things you said and I'm glad we talked, but I can't help feeling angry at myself for remembering absolutely nothing about them when you seem to remember so much. I mean, if I could just remember one or two things even – a look or a sound or a smell, anything – but I can't. And it seems to me to be so unfair, not so much that they died in that stupid boating accident but that I can't remember anything about them beforehand. All I can remember is that ghastly nightmare woman I was put with and her hideous green kitchen and being cold and knowing something was horribly, horribly, wrong because you weren't there. And then when you were with me again and you promised you'd never go away – God, the relief, you can't imagine. And then the Home and Matron, and it was all more or less safe after that. But nothing about our real parents, nothing at all. And I think I'd feel – well, more real, if I at least remembered something. It's stupid, I'm sure, and I've never minded before, but it's just here, now, it makes me feel like a hollow Easter egg. Oh, I don't know, I'm sorry, I'm just maundering on.

Anyway, I've a lecture in half an hour and I have to order my notes. It's already dark and not even tea-time yet. I don't like this weather. I wish it was summer and you could come up and we could go boating – *de rigueur* here . . .

So, anyway, thank you so much for coming. I know how much a painting day means to you and I was terribly thrilled that you gave it up and came to see me. I'm sure you don't miss me half as much as I miss you – you'd be fine without me but I couldn't live without you. Please listen to what I say about your health.

I love you.
Stella.

Sophie, that's incredible, wonderful, amazing, stupendous, terrific, outrageous, splendid, fantastic, cacophonous, revolutionary, princely, right-out-there-with-the stars . . .
S.

Dear Soph,
Here is a list of questions. Please answer in the space provided and return immediately.
1) When will the show be?
2) Is it all your own work or are you sharing it (Sorry if this is an ignorant question, I don't know how this sort of thing works.)
3) How many paintings will you show?
4) Will they be for sale?
5) How did you get asked? Chance? Friends? Art school connection?
6) How long will the show be on for?
7) Will it get lots of publicity?
8) Are there any prizes or grants or awards you could apply

for as a result of doing a show? Sponsorship?

9) Are any of the old paintings going in, the ones I know?

10) Can I do anything to help? Bring a bus full of friends? Lobby rich collectors? Publicity? Rent-a-crowd?

11) Do you know how proud I am of you and how I KNOW you're going to be famous one day . . .

PLEASE SUPPLY ANSWERS TO ALL THESE QUESTIONS *NOW*.

By the way, does this mean you'll do less work at the wine bar? I hope so.

I must dash. I'm going to a dance this evening in a jazz place. I've been so good with money – AS YOU KNOW – that I can afford to splash out for a night. Do write when you can between canvases.

Much love, your very proud little sister, Stella.

Dear Soph,

Your letter's been sitting here for ages – isn't that a change, usually I've got the reply written before I've even finished reading it. Sorry, I've been busy with – but I'll tell you later . . .

Thank you for answering all my questions, even if a bit briefly. It does seem a long time to wait till spring and I appreciate now that it's not a big academy exhibition and just a very small space in a studio complex – but for all that, I'm still proud of you. And I do think you should try to get some proper people in there – you know, helpful people, critics or agents or gallery owners or big shots, you know, and the papers and . . . All right, I won't go on, but I want it to be a success, however 'small' it is. Really, Soph, you make a lousy saleswoman.

Anyway, what do you think I've been doing? Dancing. Yes. It wasn't a jazz place I went to, it was a salsa/rumba place and the music was heavenly. Really, I don't think even you could have sat still to it. I SO enjoyed myself. I was dancing the whole time. It felt so good, the music just fed me with energy. I've been again twice and I'm going again tonight. God, it's heaven after all this cooped-up stuffy learning and freezing in this bloody room. You must go with me when you come up next.

I'm so glad you've cut down on the wine-bar days. I hope you're feeling better. You've got lots of time to get paintings ready for the show. By the way, have you chased up about the bursaries thing? There must be loads of funds with pots of gold ready to give to deserving artists?

I'm SO looking forward to seeing you at Christmas. It'll be the first we've ever had to ourselves, so let's have it just the way we want it – lots of cakes and chocolates and roast potatoes . . . And I'll lock the door so you can't go into the studio on Christmas Day.

Must dash – I've work to get through before I can go out tonight.

Much love, Stella.

Dear Soph,

Yes, it has been rather a rush here. Essays to complete, books to return, notes to borrow. And DANCING. Yes, I'm still struck. I met some new people there, really good dancers. The ground practically smokes under their feet. They go to a class in the evenings and I think I'll join them next term. I'll make some time. It's such a relief after racking my brains about medieval literature, which I'm really not so keen on. I know, I know, I'm skating on thin ice, so I'll change the subject.

In answer to your questions:

Yes, I have bought Christmas cards – bloody dented my finances.

Yes, I have sent one to Matron.

Yes, I will let you know when I'm arriving.

No, you don't have to meet me.

Yes, I am managing all right for money, thank you.

But I'm afraid your present will be terribly small. But at least I don't have to borrow from you to pay for it. I do have some scruples.

Please don't overdo it at the wine bar. I know it's good for tips at this time of year, but I don't want you to be so exhausted

when I come that all you do is sleep. I'll lock up your pencils –
that'll keep you awake . . .

Love, S.

Sophie, well, I'm sorry if you were 'offended' by my letter. I
don't see why. Of course I don't mean to 'order you around' or
'limit your independence', as you say. I think that's very unfair
of you. Just because I don't want you to exhaust yourself. And
I'm not being 'possessive'. I just care about you, that's all. But
you're so wrapped up in your painting you probably don't even
notice me and the way I feel.

S.

Dear Sophie,
I'm sorry too. I suppose it's just Christmas. It brings out the
worst in me – everyone talking about their families. I'm sorry.

Of course I don't mind if you want to paint on Christmas
Day. You can do whatever you want.

Anyway, I'll get the late afternoon train and should be in
around eight. Don't worry if you're not at the flat, I'll sit in the
pub on the corner and chat up a stranger – I'm getting very
good at it now.

It's very quiet here – everyone gone, just me and the caretaker,
Bert. He's actually got quite friendly now – this after a whole
term of smiling and saying hallo to him, a protracted courtship.
'Keeping an eye on you, Miss . . .' You know the sort, like Frank
at the Home, surly on the outside but with a fondant centre.
Why is it these caretakers are always called Bert, or Frank, or
Jack, or Fred? Maybe it's a requirement of the job . . .

No need to mention the row again. I'll see you on Saturday.

Much love, Stella.

To my dearest sister, who's so brilliant and wonderful. Happy
Christmas. This is to keep your hair back but still look glamorous
while you work on your masterpieces . . .

All my love, Stella.

Dear Soph,
Just a note to say how much I enjoyed our Christmas. It was simply perfect.

Your new picture is up on my wall and looks marvellous. I'm so glad you're getting back into drawing and 'real' pictures again. I know you'll hate me for saying this, but I will venture to hint that I never really thought all those abstracts were quite your style at all. Landscapes and portraits – especially portraits, yes. But weird splodges of colour? I mean, just look at that wonderful tree picture. Really, Soph, I was so astonished. It all looks so exact, so beautiful, all the faces and everything. Can I have a copy of it in the new slides you're having done? Are you still sending them off, by the way, even though you've got a show organized? I suppose it would be a good idea, because maybe one of the big galleries will come and offer you another show.

Anyway, now you can settle in for another term's worth of letters. Much as I adore you and adore seeing you, the best thing about the written page is that I can't feel you disapproving of me so much in it. (God, what a bloody awful sentence. Mr James would have a fit . . .)

Must go now,
All my love, S.

Dear Soph,
Sorry it's been so long. Thanks for your LONG letter – a whole page and a half, you're getting garrulous . . .

Now, first, what's this about this Mr Stein person? I didn't quite understand from your letter. I understand he liked your slides (I told you the tree picture would be lucky), but I don't quite understand what you said he wants you to do? Is it another show? (Oh, my dear, *another* show, the public are just clamouring . . .) I mean, of course I'm very pleased – God, nobody deserves good luck and success more than you – but I would like to be certain that this man with his mysterious 'project' is – well, you know – all right. But millions and millions of congratulations though, anyway, just to get a reply from one of those stuck-up gallery idiots is really something. (Is he foreign?)

Anyway, I've been up to my ears in it here. SO much work to do. Ghastly. Essays just pile up and I don't know when I'm supposed to do them. I'm looking forward to the holidays already.

And some heat. God, it's bloody freezing here. Their idea of a warm radiator is my idea of a gravestone. I'm off to the dance club tonight for the evening class – that'll warm me up.

I hope you're well – oh, and sorry, I can't remember what I said about your being disapproving. I'm sure it doesn't matter. Half of what I say is a joke anyway. So please don't let it upset you.

Do write soon.

Love, Stella.

Dearest Soph,

You mustn't let stupid idiots like that put you off. He's probably a failed artist himself, that's why he's a critic. You shouldn't allow one of those worms anywhere near your studio. They're all bastards, they just want to haul themselves over your dead body. Their opinions would fill a library, but their talent wouldn't cover a postage stamp. I *know* you're good, the tutors at art school *knew* you were good, the studio giving you the show *knows* you're good. And think of that Mr Stein – he wouldn't be interested in you if he didn't think you were good. *So listen to all of us.*

But of course you're upset about it. After all, he's probably had lots of practice in gunning artists down, so he knows exactly how to do it. So, take a day or two off – sleep, EAT (I don't think you do enough of that . . .) And let yourself recoup your energies before you start again.

Please write and let me know what's happening. Don't worry about spilling it out to me, I do it to you often enough and I'm only too pleased to help you for a change.

REMEMBER: I LOVE YOU AND I THINK YOU'RE WONDERFUL.

Stella.

Dear Soph,

It's so lovely to come down and find a letter from you, especially when I don't expect one.

This 'commission' possibility from Mr Stein sounds very exciting. What does he want? When does he want it? Will you get paid a lot of money? (Not that that's ever a consideration of yours.) Have you met Mr Stein yet? Or maybe that's not the done thing? Is it all arranged through letters? (But please be careful. I know this sounds really, really silly, but make sure he's trustworthy.)

Anyway, I'm so glad to hear you're feeling more confident and with this 'commission' on the horizon, I'm not surprised. But don't worry about not painting for a while. Have a rest. I think you probably need to have time off to refill the cistern.

As for me, I now have the perfect balance between work and play. Twice a week I go to the dance class and on Saturdays I go to the club. The rest of the time I'm up to my ears in old works of – to my mind – rather dubiously great literature. Really, I have to admit, I'm not madly interested in this course any more. I know I shouldn't say this, but I'm happier dancing. You know I was never much of an academic. Dancing makes me feel alive in a way I don't think I've ever felt before. And the people in the class are much more adult and interesting than the pretentious students around here. Last night I got chatting with a guy, Martin, whom I've been doing some paired work with, and quite naturally, without even thinking about it, I found myself telling him about the Home. He didn't bat an eyelid. His parents were refugees from some coup or other and he was separated from them in a camp for four years till they met up again here. So, telling him about my lack of parents was quite straightforward really. I felt I could really be myself with him.

It's still terribly cold here. I'm wearing all my jumpers and look rather like an overstuffed rainbow. How do you cope in the freezing studio? Or does the fire of your inspiration keep you warm?

Write soon.

Much love, Stella.

Dear Soph,

YES. YES. YES.

That's all I need to say, really, so I'll just sign off now . . .

No, I really do think it's a good idea. You need a break. God knows you've been working your guts out for the last three years during art school and now with wine-barring and everything. It's about time you took a holiday. Your show isn't till spring, so you can come back with plenty of new inspiration for that. And this Mr Stein project – *if* it comes off (I'm a bit dubious about that man) – isn't till summer by the sounds of it, so now is an absolutely perfect time.

Of course I'll miss you, but I'll be all right. We'll both write and a couple of months will just fly past. You'll have to send me loads of postcards, so that I know what you're seeing. But will it be warm? It's no good hopping from one freezing country to another.

And don't worry about your 'dead feeling'. After all, you're not a machine, you can't be expected to turn out painting after painting, picture after picture, without a break. Even a car needs petrol. And of course you'll find some new inspiration out there – isn't it the traditional artist's retreat? And there are loads of Old Masters you can check on – I know, I looked it up in the library, the place is absolutely bursting with ancient genius.

But I am a bit worried about the money. Are you sure you'll be able to manage? I know you're very good with money (unlike some people . . .), but I don't like to think of you suddenly stranded over there in the middle of a load of gesticulating natives . . . God, if I had any spare money I'd give it to you like a shot. I'm just sorry I can't help. It isn't the grape picking season down there by any chance?

Things are just carrying on here – essays, dancing. We're planning a sort of display for the end of term – maybe you'll be back for it? And there's talk of a tour . . .

I do have to be careful with all this candle-burning at both ends, but so far I'm managing to stay afloat (real Eng. Lit. sentence, that one . . .).

Do write soon – you won't go without leaving me an address, will you?

Love, Stella.

PS I've just thought – isn't it from around there that our parents came? Maybe we've got a few relatives tucked away. You could look them up. Wouldn't that be exciting? Maybe Matron would be able to give you some clues . . .

Dear Soph,

AN ADDRESS PLEASE. ALL I'M ASKING FOR IS AN ADDRESS. POSTE RESTANTE – PO BOX – ANYTHING. I WANT SOMETHING I CAN WRITE TO. PLEASE.

All right, of course I don't expect you to go looking up old relatives if you don't want to. It was just a thought – a silly one, it's really not important. But you are lucky to be able to remember some of the language – of course, I can't remember a word.

Yes, the dancing's still hot. I'm doing special exercises now to limber up and get more supple. Every morning I creak my way through them – I ache even behind my fingernails – but apparently the difference does show, though I'm not nearly as catlike as some of the dancers. Really I should have been doing this from childhood – tell that to Matron, not quite country dancing . . .

I've bought a special new dancing skirt as a treat, blue with spangles, very short and I look very slinky in it. And Martin says my 'line' is much improved – whatever that means . . .

Write before you leave with all the addresses.

Love, Stella.

At the Hall

Dear Soph,

Thank you for the address. I hope you have a WONDERFUL TIME. I shall be thinking of you A LOT. This is the first time we've ever been away from each other for so long.

Please write when you can – and when you can't. And get someone to take photographs of you in front of ancient buildings like a proper tourist. And come back looking relaxed and happy.

ALL MY LOVE, Stella.

Dear Soph,

Thank you, I loved the postcard. It looks heavenly out there, all that blue. You're so lucky.

You probably won't get this for weeks, being between addresses, but I wanted to tell you the latest between Martin and I. Well, you remember the talk Matron would give when we reached a 'certain age'? About 'seeing men'? At the end of it I was so confused I thought if I so much as LOOKED at a man I'd have a baby (I think she was better at domestic science). Anyway, I now know it's got nothing to do with looking. He's very wonderful and considerate and I'm not going to drivel on about him any more or this will sound straight out of a ghastly teen magazine. But before you ask, yes, we are taking precautions – well, he is and –

No, I can't go on about it. I wish you were with me and then I could tell you. But I feel very happy about it – and happy in general, really. I just wanted you to know.

So, write soon – when you get this, but I'll write before, anyway. I'm thinking of you and hoping you're having a wonderful time.

I miss you.

All my love, Stella.

Sophie,

They won't let me write. Someone else is writing this. Where are you? I've been in an accident. Matron's here. Please come back. I'm very scared.

S.

Sophie,
Someone else is writing this. Haven't you got the telegrams? They tell me they've sent at least three. I've been in an accident. I can't move. They won't tell me what's wrong. Please come back.

    S.

Sophie,
It was such a relief to hear your voice. I wish you were here now instead of tomorrow morning. I'm so scared. Nobody tells me anything, but I can't move my legs or feel them or anything. It's like they're just not there. Please come soon. Please tell me it will be all right. Matron's here, but she won't say anything either. It's all a nightmare and I want to wake up. The only way I can keep the panic down is by writing to you, even though you'll be here before this is even delivered. It's just for me, really. Oh, please be here soon . . .

Sophie,
Matron will deliver this to you at the hotel on her way out tonight. I just want to say that I'm so grateful that you're here and I'm so sorry I spoiled your holiday. Soph, I'm so scared. I can't tell you when you're here because you look so scared too. But you won't go away again, will you? And it'll be all right, won't it? Please say it will.

    S.

Sophie,
I'm sending this directly to the flat. No, like I said this evening, I know you have to go back there for clothes and things. Matron will stay till you come back and then she says she has to go.

    I keep going over and over the accident in my mind, thinking if only I'd stayed in the class a moment longer – or left sooner – or anything. I know it's my fault, but I'd taken that short cut over the main road so often I didn't think – I never thought – oh, Sophie, what have I done, what have I done?

At the Hall

Please tell me it's going to be all right and come back quickly. I'm upset all the time and then I get angry and then I start crying and then I can't stop and that makes me even angrier. Nobody is telling me anything and I'm so scared. I need you.

S.

Sophie,
I've even tried phoning the wine bar but they don't know where you are. Why can't you have a bloody phone put in your flat? Why aren't you back here? Matron left yesterday and you said you'd be back here by lunch-time. What are you doing? You should be here.

S.

Dear Sophie,
Well, all right, I'm sorry, like I said this evening before you left, I can't help getting angry. You just don't know what it's like.

They've put weights and pulleys on my legs, but they still won't tell me anything. How long am I going to be like this? When will I be able to get out of bed?

When you come this weekend, I want you to find out *exactly* what's going on. I want to know how long it'll be before I'm back to normal. However long it takes. Please. Do this for me. I'll do everything they want as long as I know what I can aim for.

And please hurry back. I know you have to work and everything, but it's terrible just lying here through the week and waiting and waiting for you at the weekend.

S.

Sophie,
No. Don't come this weekend. I don't want to see anyone.

S.

Sophie,
Well, what do you expect? How do you think it fucking feels

for me? Imagine if you were suddenly struck blind? Never walk again, Sophie. Never, ever again. I'm a fucking cripple. For life.

S.

Sophie,

Martin came to see me yesterday, but I told him I don't want to see him again. I don't want to see anyone and I don't want anyone to see me. Except you. But you don't want to see me, do you? You expect me to be 'brave' about it. Well, I'm not bloody brave. I'm so angry I could scream. And I did today. I threw the flowers across the room and told them I didn't want them to bring me any more. I don't want to see them all dying around me.

Everyone just looks at me with disgusting pity in their eyes. I can't stand it. I don't want to be in this place. How long am I going to stay here? Till they find a miracle cure? Where am I going to go?

S.

Sophie,

You'd be a lot more use to me if you were here and not running around chasing money. Fuck the charities. I don't want to live on fucking charity.

It's all right for you, isn't it? You can just walk away from here and go back to your nice little flat and get on with your fucking painting, which is all you really care about anyway, isn't it? You don't give a damn about me as long as you get your show ready and keep that mystery Mr Stein sweet for his big 'commission', which sounds like a real fairy-story he's stringing you along with if ever I heard one.

Well, screw you, Sophie Dario, you cold-hearted bitch, never mind me, never mind I'm your sister, your only flesh and blood. You're an artist and that's all that really matters to you, isn't it?

S.

At the Hall

Dear Soph,
Please come back – please, please.

They took me out in a chair today. I didn't want to go. I wanted them to leave my bloody legs alone, but they wouldn't listen to me. They strapped me in and wheeled me through the corridors so everyone could get a good look at me. We went outside. It was cold. They wheeled me up and down the path, saying how pleased I must be to get some fresh air and weren't the snowdrops pretty. But I just wanted to go back – I just wanted to come back here to my bed and hide. But they wouldn't listen – they wouldn't listen and I couldn't do anything.

I've threatened that if they do that again I'll go on a hunger strike.

Oh, please, Soph, please come back. Forget all the horrible things I've said. Please, please come back and protect me from this. I'll be all right if you're here. Please.
    S.

Dear Sophie,
I've just got your letter now (you can phone here, actually, if you want). Well, what a piece of luck with that bursary – it was one of my ideas, wasn't it? I mean, before all of this. You see, I do have some good ideas for you sometimes, don't I?

But will it be all right to use the money for me? I mean, I know you can say that you want to move somewhere quiet with a proper studio and everything for yourself, but won't they think it's all a bit fishy?

Never mind, I'm sure you know what's right. I trust you. And it doesn't have to be a very big house – as long as it's away from people. Surely we – you – could find somewhere cheap to rent if it's out of the way enough? And you won't have to keep the flat on as well, because you'll be with me, so I'm sure we'll be able to manage financially.

Anyway, I'll leave it all to you and just try and be patient. Please come and see me soon, even though I'm sure you'll be busy looking at places. It makes such a difference when you're here.

Stella.

Sophie,
You've got to get me out of here. They're trying to prove I'm nuts so they can lock me away.

They sent a shrink along today. I told him I didn't want to talk to him and that he could shove his psychiatry. 'So, you're experiencing some feelings of anger?' he said. 'Do you want to share it with me?' Jesus, did he think I was a complete imbecile? I was so furious I picked up my jug of water and emptied it over the patronizing bastard. Ha. You should have seen his face. Looked like he was experiencing some anger all of his own.

I've got to get out of here, Soph. I *will* go nuts if I stay here. Haven't you found anything yet? Please find something quickly.

S.

SOPHIE,
ONCE AND FOR ALL: I DO NOT WANT TO SEE ANY OF MY FRIENDS. I THOUGHT YOU UNDERSTOOD THAT. JUST BECAUSE I'M A FUCKING CRIPPLE DOESN'T MEAN I'VE GOT NO FUCKING CHOICE AT ALL.

S.

Oh, Soph,
It looks wonderful. I can hardly believe it. Can you bring some more photographs with you when you come? And that Glass Room on the side there – that's just perfect for you, isn't it? As a studio, I mean. And all that sea everywhere – just think of the wonderful paintings you'll make of it all. And no other houses anywhere near – oh, it's perfect. How did you find it?

Oh, Soph, this is the first breath of life for me since the accident. You can't imagine how much it means to me to get away from here, to have some peace, to just be with you. When can we go there? Soon? *Please*. It can't need anything doing to it, it looks fine. I don't want any of those cripple aids put in. Let's just hurry and get in there.

I can't wait for the weekend. Clever you.

Stella.

Dear Sophie,

God, I'm so excited. I keep telling myself – next weekend we'll be there, you'll come here to the hospital as usual but this time you'll be taking me away. It will be all right, won't it? I mean, nothing will come up at the last minute and stop this?

The chaplain came round today. I told him that unless he could make me pick up my bed and walk, he wasn't much good to me. I think everyone here will be pleased to see the back of me. The feeling's mutual.

I'm a bit surprised you're keeping on the flat. Are we going to be able to afford it? The bursary, welcome though it is, surely won't stretch that far? And why do you need the flat? There's that lovely Glass Room for you to work in – much nicer than that poky, cold box-room studio. I thought you'd be relieved to see the back of that place.

But I don't want to pester you about it. I'm just so grateful to be getting out of here. I'm really very, very grateful to you, Sophie. And I want to say that I'm sorry about some of the things I've said to you – about your painting and everything. You've been very patient and I've been revolting. I know. I'm sorry. But I'm so scared all the time – and everyone else seems so scared too. That's why I don't want to see anyone. They don't know what to say and just look embarrassed. But you won't get like that, will you, Soph? I promise I will try to be less angry – and I'm sure this sea house will make all the difference to me. But, please, don't you put a face on to me as well. I can't bear it when you do that. I don't want to lose touch with you. You're really all I've got now.

I also want to say that the nurses will come night and morning – the hospital's arranged it – to wash me and move me and all that. I don't want you to do any of it. I mean it. It's revolting and it's their job, not yours.

I wish I could send you my love but I don't seem to have any. I'm dried up and full of prickles like an old thistle.

I'm sorry.

Stella.

The Glass Room

Oh, Soph, I could watch the waves for ever. I watch them and watch them and feel all that awful time in hospital being washed out of me.

I like sitting in here best – in your room, when you're out. I like looking at all your paints and brushes and pencils and things all around me. So many brushes, I never really knew you had so many. And I imagine you walking around and getting blue in your hair and dabbing at the canvases . . .

How can I explain to you how much better I feel having you with me all the time? I wish I could give you something. But I won't, I won't even say anything, because I don't want to make you feel uncomfortable. But if I could tell you – if I could let you know – if I thought you wouldn't mind – I'd thank you and thank you and thank you for just being my sister . . .

Dear Sophie,

Of course I didn't mean what I said and I'm writing now so that you'll get this tomorrow while you're still there. It was just a shock, that's all. I didn't expect you to be going back to town so soon. But of course I understand you've got things to do there and I'm very sorry I was so angry. Please don't let's be in a bad temper with each other.

S.

The Glass Room

Soph, I'm sitting here in your room, watching the sea, and I realize that it's got a secret and if I watch it for long enough I'll find out what it is.

I've been thinking a lot about our parents. They must have loved the sea too, doing all that sailing. Maybe it's something I've actually inherited from them. And it struck me too that it would all be very different if they were alive, wouldn't it? I mean, you wouldn't have to look after me, because they'd be there to do it. I wonder if you've thought of that.

Right now, the sea is stretching out all around me and there's no one on it and I feel clean and free and peaceful.

Your paintings look a bit forlorn. They miss you. You haven't worked on them for a while. Of course I won't actually say anything to you, because I know you don't like it. But, oh, Soph, I wish you'd paint the sea. If I was an artist that's what I'd do – I'd paint the sea over and over again, the sea telling me its secrets . . .

Dear Sophie,

Do you think we could have some PRIVATE signs made? Some people came all the way up the cliff path today and I saw them looking in at me through the window. I DON'T LIKE THAT. I'm sure a few signs wouldn't cost a lot – maybe you could just paint them on some bits of board?

Otherwise, I'm all right. I play patience a lot. It's a really good game. I had three hands come out completely today without cheating, isn't that clever? Actually – I wasn't going to tell you this but I really feel I must – I think I've discovered a secret. It's about the sea and the card games – I mean, I think they're linked. I'm not sure how, but there is a connection between them, I know it. I feel pretty certain that fairly soon now I'll understand exactly what it is.

I hope you're well and working hard for the show. Of course I understand that it's easier for you to work there, where things are familiar, rather than here, but maybe when the show is over and you've finished the work for it you'll be able to start here on a new project.

I look forward to seeing you at the weekend.
Stella.

Sophie,
I mean this. If you mention a bloody shrink to me again, I'll
smash up your painting things here in the Glass Room. I don't
need a bloody shrink. I'm a cripple and no shrink is going to
change that. If you're so keen, you see one.
S.

The Glass Room

Soph, I wish you wouldn't draw me. I wish you'd talk to me
instead of drawing me. I wish you wouldn't be so distant. Why
can't you be like you were before? I never hid anything from
you before – like these Glass Room letters, like my little trick
with the nurses when I tell the night one that the day one has
taken me out and vice versa.

I wish you'd paint the sea. The sea wants you to paint it. It
keeps asking me why you're not down here painting it and it's
gone all flat and mournful . . .

Dear Sophie,
Please come back. I fell out of the chair this morning and
couldn't get up till the evening nurse came. They think I've
cracked some ribs. Please come back and get me out of this
hospital. Please.
S.

Dear Sophie,
No, I don't mind if you stay away for the weekend. I'm sorry I
disturbed your week by making you come down, even though
it was nice to see you.

I still can't sleep very well, but they've given me some new
pills. Come back when you're ready.
Stella.

At the Hall

The Glass Room

Soph, the sea is in a strange mood today. It looks very calm and then suddenly it draws back its teeth and spews out the water as if it's disgusted. It's like a very dense game of patience where most of the cards are hidden and I can't tease them out – sort of stillborn . . .

Sophie,
Why do you have to go on? It ruined the weekend. Why do you have to go interfering with me? I don't interfere with you, do I? I don't want to go on with that degree course. What for? I wasn't really interested in it anyway if you must know. And cripples don't get good jobs, so just leave me alone.
    Stella.

The Glass Room

Oh, Soph, you *want* me to lie to you. You *want* me to tell you I've done things. You *want* me to pretend, to make you feel better. I'm just about to write you a long letter – to post. But most of it will be a pack of lies, which is what you want to believe. I wish I didn't have to do this for you . . .

Dear Sophie,
What a surprise to get your letter. In answer to your questions:
    Yes, I have done my exercises.
    Yes, I get taken out every morning.
    Yes, I'm eating.
    Yes, I'm reading the books you left.
    Yes, I've written to Matron.
    No, I haven't written to Martin.
    Yes, I have looked over my old notes.
    Yes, I will get in touch with Mr James about postal tuition.
    So, you should be very pleased with me. I wish it wasn't so warm though. I don't like this weather – almost spring. I don't

want spring and summer and all that green.

I hope your painting is going well. Have you sent out the invitations for the private view yet? Don't forget to send one to that Mr Stein. Are you getting excited about it? I am.

Love, Stella.

The Glass Room

Oh, Soph, I've just realized what the sea is saying. It says your name over and over – Sophie, Sophie, Sophie. Sometimes long and rolled out, sometimes soft and quick. But always you. You're around me all the time, my Sophie . . .

Dear Sophie,
Just to warn you before you come down – I'VE CUT OFF ALL MY HAIR.

Don't be shocked. It's wonderful. I did it on my own with some scissors, but when the day nurse came she was so appalled that she did some neatening up of her own – seems she started life as a hairdresser. But it's really short. And it feels marvellous. The sea approves. It staged a magnificent display of crashing waves like applause all afternoon.

So, don't be surprised. I look like a nun. See you at the weekend.

S.
PS Yes, I've done the exercises, etc.

The Glass Room

Oh, Soph, it *is* spring. I hate it. Hate all that braying green and the puffed-up clouds and the sea lying flat on its back, all calm, like a cat purring. And the flowers interfering, poking up over everything where it had all been so bare and empty and clean. It all nags and nags and nags at me to go out – but I don't want to go out. I DON'T WANT TO.

You haven't even pretended to work in here for ages. It's

all dusty. You're never going to work here, are you? You don't even like visiting at the weekend.

My period came today. Do you know that technically I could still have children. They could have spared me that . . .

Dear Sophie,
Thanks for your note. That's all right. I don't mind. I'll see you next weekend instead. I'm fine.
   S.

The Glass Room

Soph, it's midnight. There's a full moon. I'm here in your room and the light is coming in through the windows and washing me. I can feel it very softly, like feathers all over. I imagine I'm in the sea and I'm weightless and being stroked and the sea is shushing all around me.

I like the night. No one sees me. I'd like to stay up all night and sleep all day.

Oh, Soph, I so miss you. Of course I don't say anything, but I so miss you – miss you as you were, as we had been. Because it just isn't the same any more, even when you are here. You just look bored and trapped and like you're having to restrain yourself and force out some patience and being nice. I'm just a burden on you. I pretend I've done the exercises and the study and you pretend to be pleased about it and that's how we could go on for years and years.

It's getting cold now. It's strange there's no warmth in the moon. It looks as if it should be warm – all white and shining and clean. But it's cold. Like the sea is cold. And you're cold . . .

Dear Sophie,
You looked so happy walking away this morning, so excited about the private view, and I was really pleased to see you looking so good. Of course, I'm thinking about you like mad and will do so all weekend. I really, really hope something good

comes out of this show – there's no one else on earth who deserves success more than you. It's a shame that Mr Stein won't be there. I suppose he'll come another day and you'll meet him then. Sorry, Soph, but please be careful with him. He does strike me as being rather fishy – this commission and everything, and now not meeting. I mean, you don't *know* him at all, do you? All right, I'll drop the subject now.

Last week there was the most wonderful full moon. Did you see it? It looked so clean.

I do hope you can forgive me for not coming in the end, but I just couldn't, not with all those people and everything. I do hope you can understand that.

Have a wonderful time – be a star, be the great artist I know you to be. I'm so very proud of you. And please don't worry about me – don't even think about me. And I won't expect to see you until it's over.

I love you.

Stella.

The Glass Room

Soph, I've thought of you all day, I've imagined you in that sea-green dress walking round the show, looking lovely and really impressing everyone.

And I hope you haven't thought of me. I hope you've been able to forget this house and your ugly sister sitting in her chair like a scrawny bird. Because I know that if you think of me, then your day will be spoiled, and I don't want that.

It's not going to get any better, Soph. If anything, I'm going to get worse. And I can't bear that. I'm so sorry for what's happened. I'm so sorry for becoming this hag.

Oh, Soph, you've no idea how much I've missed you. Every second, every minute, every hour and day and week that you aren't here. I've missed you so much that it hurt, literally hurt, and nothing can help that.

I'm such a coward. I'm not brave, like you. All I ever wanted in life was a good time. And you. But even you I would have let go of eventually. For all my dancing around, I'd have got married and had children and settled down. But not now.

You have your painting. You will always have your painting. It's the most important thing in your life and it always has been. I'm glad you've got that. It makes me feel better for all this. But you will paint the sea, won't you? One day? Paint it how it looks to me – like a bed that's warm and comfortable and safe. A welcoming place.

The sea is very quiet today – untroubled. I feel close to it, I want to be part of it – belong, like Mama and Papa, to those waves.

I'm getting sleepy now. The pills are working. I've got your pictures here in your room all around me and your photograph is smiling on the table.

Know that I will always love you, my Soph. Whatever, wherever, I am. And I know that you have always loved me, my sister.

Dear Sophie,
Please forgive me for this. I really think it's the best for both of us. I'm sorry.

Please put me in the sea. Forgive me.
Stella.

III

MOSAIC

He came to my room every night at the Hall. Every night when it was dark and the moonlight twisted patterns among the rosebuds on the walls, slowly, carefully, the handle of my door would turn and, soft as a cat stalking, he would approach my bed, my shadow lover, my silent shade. Stealthily – one, two, his feet lifted up and set down on the bare boards. Tensile feet. Feet that gripped my body like a second pair of hands, prising me open, pushing me apart, so that he could enter me even more smoothly. Feet that were crisscrossed with a network of scars – the beatings, he said, but that was later, much later, when he was talking. Till that time he lay beside me in silence, his feet alongside my own, nudging my legs in unconscious pleasure, like a baby flexing its fingers as it sucks from the breast. His feet that are soft and tender, even with the ridges and scores that are the pattern of his history.

Not a word from him. When I whispered his name, when I opened my mouth to cry out with a cry drawn from me by the power still locked in his bullman body, when I started to call, he would cover my mouth with his, eating the words from me, gobbling them with his tongue, grinding them with his tough teeth. Speak to me, I pleaded silently. Speak to me. But his fingers drummed a tattoo of silence against my cheek and his tongue darted into my mouth to prevent me betraying him.

He'd be gone when I awoke.

In the morning I'd look for marks on him. Marks where I'd bitten his soft skin or torn his back, the deep-red blooms I'd branded on his neck. But always he appeared at the old woman's table fresh and clean, like a new canvas, without any sign of blemish, as if when he washed he dissolved all our intimacy

169

away, leaving nothing for me to lassoo him with. He smiled courteously as if we were guests at a hotel. He smelt of cologne, this polished, secret man who dabbed the napkin carefully to his wide lips, lifting off every stray crumb. Even his clean, manicured fingers were scented. Fingers that had dabbled inside me and licked away the taste as if it was the sweetest honey.

All that summer by the sea I'd had nightmares of finding Stella's wrapped and weighted body washed up on the shore. I would see her lying there, waste matter the sea had rejected. Lying there, waiting for me . . .

But they had taken her body far out to sea and I had not glimpsed more than a smear of dirty grey canvas as my sister slid heavily into the cold waters.

I didn't leave a wreath or a posy. There was no marker to show where she lay. But that night, when it was dark and I was drunk enough, I took all my drawing things – the pencils, brushes, bottles of oil and turps, rags and tubes of paint, charcoals, pastels, chalks – and I broke them and tore them and flung them into the waves. The sea smacked its lips and my little tokens were swallowed whole, like the insignificant minnows they were.

But by the time he had arrived to take me to the Hall, the new boxes of pencils and pastels and charcoals were tantalizing me, even though I hadn't opened them. There they were, laid out on the table in the Glass Room, and despite the scorn of the silent, empty house I knew I wanted to work again. I hated myself for that knowledge.

The gorse was still in flower, its heavy coconut scent gripping the end of summer. His car waited at the foot of the cliff, like a sleek grey cat, purring.

'Sophie? Sophie Dario?' His voice was marked with a softly gruff accent and he was smaller than I'd imagined. Older. His hair quite white and his face sculpted by age. But a strange, mesmerizing face. I felt that somehow I already knew him, that there was something in him that I recognized.

I looked away from his face and his too keen eyes, down at his hands, noticed the veins standing out as if reaching for air. He wore a cheap-looking ring on his little finger that contrasted oddly with the stamp of gold at his cuffs. He stood very upright, proud, confident, his suit expensively discreet, impeccably pressed, looking very out of place on the cliff-tops. I noticed his shoes were scuffed by the walk up from the shore, the polish dimmed slightly.

'I'm so very pleased to meet you at last,' he said, holding out his hand. It gripped mine very firmly and I found the sudden contact almost shocking. 'I am very sorry about – '

'It's all right,' I said, and dropped his hand quickly. 'It's – it's all right – thank you, Mr Stein.'

'Simon – please.' He smiled. 'Mr Stein – it is so hard.' His accent tinged his words with a beguiling persuasiveness. I was reminded of the courteous, charming, slightly stilted language of the letters he'd written me, his handwriting surprisingly neat, almost feminine, scrolling over the page.

'You've been very – kind to me,' I said.

'*Ach* – ' He waved a hand dismissively. 'I have done nothing. But you are a very talented artist, Sophie.'

'I – I don't know about that.'

'But I do.'

There was a pause. The sea turned slowly below us; the wind ruffled my hair. It felt very peaceful standing there with him, restful.

I turned away. 'I – I'd better get my things – '

'You received the materials I sent?'

'Yes – it was very generous.'

'They are – the correct sizes – thickness?' he asked.

'Yes – yes – I – '

'I could not completely remember – ' he broke in eagerly. 'It is such a long time since I have bought artist's materials and I had to try – to think – '

'You paint – draw?' Maybe this was what spoke to me in him.

'No.' He turned away abruptly. 'I will see to the car.'

Inside the house I picked up my bag and looked around. The place was shuttered, dark, dusty. I was conscious of a feeling of escape, but touched the bulky padding of the letters in my pockets to remind me of my penance. Never again would I abandon her. I locked the front door and the burden of the house shifted on to my shoulders. This time, though, I would not put her down.

He drove lightly, easily, as if it was a simple matter to manoeuvre his large heavy car though the narrow country lanes. He held the wheel with careless confidence between the fingers of one hand whilst smoking fat untipped cigarettes with the other. He chatted blithely about artists he knew and the gallery world with which he was familiar, but I was feeling uncomfortable and didn't say much.

'Nervous?' he asked after a silence.

'Yes – a little.'

'Maybe – ' He hesitated. 'Maybe you feel afraid? Maybe you think you will not know how to work again?'

'Yes – ' I looked at him in surprise. 'That's right. You know, I haven't so much as touched a pencil since – since – '

'And you fear your talent will have left you?' He smiled kindly. 'I don't think so, Sophie.'

'You know, I would have given it all up,' I said suddenly. 'All of it – I don't know why you've taken this trouble with me?'

'I don't like to see good talent sacrificed,' he said, and then went on quickly, 'And, Sophie, believe me, you would not have given it up – '

'Oh – but – '

He shook his head. 'You're too much of an artist – it is in your blood – it *is* your blood, you could say. You would have begun to work again eventually – I think you know that. All I have done is to make things – a little quicker, that's all.'

I looked at him curiously. 'You seem to know a lot about this sort of situation. Have you yourself ever – '

But immediately as I watched, a smile rose like a diver ascending very hurriedly and his face that had worn a depth of gentle gravity was now closed, though a genial good humour danced over the surface, bright and careless as sunlight on the sea.

'No – no – not at all.' He laughed loudly. 'But you see, Sophie, in my line of business I meet many good artists like yourself and I hear all the problems . . .'

He went on, but I wasn't listening. There was something about his determined affability that I found off-putting. I suddenly felt very alone.

I touched the letters in my pocket for reassurance, but they were cold and stiff and crackled reproachfully. Despondent, I leaned my head against the window while the car shot into the early evening silent as a bullet.

She was sitting with her fingers sunk in the soil of the vine beside her, as if it were a pet she was stroking. She was surrounded by plants. Limp ivy trailed over the arms of her chair, tall ferns peered over her shoulders. She looked old, weary, supported more by the straight back of the chair she sat in than by the force of her own body.

The room was cluttered and dark, the furniture cheap, ugly. There were two huge vases of dead flowers – roses? – on the mantelpiece, their fallen petals crinkled like confetti.

It was not at all what I had been expecting.

She nodded to me briefly as we came in, dismissed Simon to make tea and gestured to the shabby sofa with a grubby hand.

'So,' she began in a mannered voice, 'Simon tells me you're very talented.'

'Well – I really wouldn't like to – '

'I've seen your work,' she broke in, 'the slides Simon sent me. I thought they were very good – not that I know anything about this sort of thing, of course.' Her hands were locked together, the fingers wrestling with each other. Large, rough hands.

'I – I understand you want me to make some drawings of your grandchildren,' I said, when the silence became too uncomfortable. 'Are they here now?'

'No.' She shook her head. 'No, it's all changed now – that's all over with now.'

I waited, but she didn't continue. 'Does this mean – ' I began haltingly – 'that you don't want – I mean, Simon hasn't mentioned any change of – '

'Simon doesn't know anything about this – yet,' she cut me off roughly. 'I'll explain things to him later – he'll understand. No,' she went on, looking at me keenly, 'I still want you to make drawings for me, Sophie, but not *of* my grandchildren – it's too late for that now. I want these drawings to be *for* my grandchildren.'

'I'm – I'm sorry, I don't understand.'

She leaned forward. 'I want you to make drawings of this house – the Hall – that's what I want you to do now.'

'Draw your house? But – but I was expecting – '

'You don't mean to say it's beyond your capabilities?'

'No – I mean – Well, it's just rather a surprise.'

She gave a grim smile. 'I like surprises. Of course,' she went on briskly, 'I'm not asking you to draw it as it is now.'

'No?'

She shook her head. There was an eager tinge to her eyes as she leaned even closer to me. 'I want you to draw it as it was.'

'As it was?' Now I was even more confused.

'You see, it didn't always look like this – ' She straightened up, gesturing to the chaotic clutter around her. 'It was all very different once.'

'But – look, I'm sorry, I really don't understand.'

'Of course, I'll be able to help you,' she swept on. 'And Simon will help – he won't mind staying on for a bit. We can both tell you what it was like – we'll describe it for you.'

'But – '

'I want these pictures to be my legacy – ' She was suddenly fierce. 'My legacy for my grandchildren. When I am dead, they will get the pictures and then they'll understand – they'll see what their grandmother did for them, what I was able to achieve. How, despite everything, I managed to keep this house – the Hall. Because I did it all for them – and their mother. And it was worth it, Sophie – ' Her eyes gripped mine – 'it was worth it. Nobody can say it was in vain, however much I've suffered and whatever's happened now. It was all of it – *all* for them.'

I didn't dare move, speak. I saw the jagged hurt in her eyes and suddenly there was my sister, my arching, springing sister with her blue-black hair and her shining eyes, skewered to her chair, her face sharp and pointed as a ferret, eyes narrow as a weasel, hair cropped as a convict. My lovely sister, my dancing sister, pinned to her chair like an animal with bared teeth dangling from barbed wire.

I shivered.

'I'm sorry.' Her voice was unexpectedly gentle. 'It isn't very easy for you, is it?'

We exchanged a look, but I didn't want to see the sympathy in her eyes any more than she would have wanted to see the sympathy in mine.

'Do you mean,' I gathered myself together slowly, 'that you want me to draw things – which aren't here?'

She nodded. 'They were here once – not now.'

'It sounds very – '

'What?'

'Well, I've never been asked to do this before,' I said lamely.

'You're an artist, aren't you?' she replied tartly. 'You can imagine things, can't you?' She paused a moment, looked at me carefully. 'I had thought – that you might appreciate a challenge.'

Of course I could have refused, could have walked out of that room and – and? Returned to my mausoleum? Imprisoned myself again with that reproachful ghost and the sea taunting me inside and out, waking and sleeping, never resting, never still. No. I wanted to rebel, wanted to let this freak wave carry me till I was out of my depth. She was right, this old woman, I was challenged by her odd commission to draw the past, that maybe by setting her past on paper I might lay my own.

'All right.' I held her gaze. 'All right, I accept.'

'Good.' She smiled for the first time and her face that had been so dour was suddenly alight. 'Then let us begin.'

Is it strange that I was so pliant, so malleable? Is it strange that I didn't hesitate, didn't question? I suppose, looked at from the outside, it does appear unreasonable. And yet at the time it seemed natural – right. In a drawing sometimes, I will make a line, a hard crude line, that looks ugly and out of place but later, when the drawing is finished, that line is seen to be the keystone of the whole picture.

So it was for me at the Hall. So it was when the handle of my door turned in the night and he came to my bed. So it was when I gathered up the disparate chippings of that house and made a mosaic of them.

It was not easy to capture the old woman and yet I felt compelled to try. Sometimes her face was plain, hard as rocks in winter, grey and brown, thick and muddy and dull. Then, looking out to her garden, it would change and, like light flashing over a landscape, she would be suddenly beautiful. And yet she was not a beautiful woman. Large, heavy-footed, her big hands swallowing up the fragile teacup from which she sipped with an awkward delicacy. She wore no rings or jewellery, she dressed carelessly in old skirts and frayed cardigans. Her grey hair was loosely pinned at her neck, so that it fell thinly on her shoulders. But her face – cut hard and then suddenly molten; set as stone, then warm and dimpled as a baby.

And as I watched her, listened to her, lived alongside her, I felt myself developing a strange allegiance to this stubbornly imperious old woman who had invited an artist into her home like the aristocracy from which she could have descended.

She got used to my sketching as she spoke, painting the house for me in words – 'The grandfather clock – it was there, in the corner by the door. Very large, the face had a sun and moon on it. And swords, weren't there, Simon? You remember those? All up the walls with the shields and the flag. And in here there was all that fancy furniture – took ages to keep clean. But you liked them, didn't you, Simon? They were the first things we – you – we did business with. And that cabinet with all the little knick-knacks inside – I used to get Lydia to clean them, her hands were much smaller. Remember the embroidered covers on the sofa, Simon? Remember how very taken with them you were? Come on, Simon, you think, remember – help me remember. It was all so long ago . . .'

He sat beside her, loosened his tightly genial face and with a gentle patience prompted her to describe another house for me to draw. Another house that did not have this ramshackle, dusty façade, a house that was clean and polished and filled with rare and lovely furniture.

Three is a strange number, one is always left out. Though we sat together, ate together, I was not really included in their conversations. They shared jokes and reminiscences in a way that rubbed grit over an open wound – just so had I talked with Stella. And slowly, as if he were caressing a late plum, the old woman began to shine under his attention.

But at night my spirit lover came to my room. I took him in my hands and kneaded his flesh until it hardened. I squeezed and pummelled and pressed the thin, soft skin until he gasped, pushing my fingers away, then hungrily replacing them. And I thought – ha, now you don't think of her, now you think only of me.

But as we lay pushed up together in that narrow single bed, as the moonlight watered the rosebuds, making them climb ever faster in their vain flight up the walls, he seemed to smile at me from beneath his heavy lashes as if he heard my defiance and it pleased him.

One morning I came down to find the hall strewn with boxes like lily leaves over a pond.

'There's a lot to do,' the old woman said as she dragged a crate into the front room. 'You'll just have to ignore it.'

Soon there were rows of chests like railways pointing to the door. We stepped over them, through them, winding our way as if in a maze.

All day the old woman bent over them, packing them full with gardening books, catalogues, small hand-tools, old bulbs and seed packets, crockery, pictures, ornaments – almost anything that seemed to come to hand. Then in the evening she suddenly pulled open the lids and began to lift it all out, like Sisyphus, unwrapping all her careful windings of newspaper and old cloth until the floor was spread with objects and she had found – maybe an old magnifying glass. 'Ah, no, not this – Lydia will want this,' and, muttering, she carried her prize back to a cupboard.

Simon followed behind her, never minding that his suit was getting dusty or his shirt – rolled up at the sleeves – was stained, his waistcoat buttons done up wrong, ash falling down the front.

'But what are you doing, Madeleine?' he asked anxiously. 'I don't understand. What is this?'

'Don't ask me any questions, Simon,' she replied roughly. 'This is none of your business. I don't want you to interfere.'

'But what is all this?' he persisted. 'Changing the commission, all right; so Lydia and the children had to go back to town suddenly, I understand – a bit of a mystery, but I understand. But this, Madeleine – this packing – all this?'

'I said don't ask me, Simon – I'm not explaining anything.' She bent to lift another box. 'If you want to help, just get out of my way.'

'Well, if you don't want to tell me anything – '

'I don't – not now – not yet – '

'All right,' he conceded unhappily. 'But let me carry that box for you . . .'

The landscape of the house was changing all around us. One day a clock would be on the wall and I would read the time. The next day it was gone, swallowed up in a wave of cloth and paper. Then, in a day, two days, it would reappear, like a drowning hand reaching for a rock, but on a different wall, showing a different time. The house like a snake sloughing off an old skin.

He had already left my bed, slipping away before dawn while I feigned sleep to give him cover for his silent exit. But I couldn't sleep. I was sore, he had been rough, squeezing my breasts and snapping my nipples, pushing hard into me and covering my mouth with his to gulp up my cries.

It was that pale half-light before the dawn, the time when the light returns grudgingly, filling the sky with colour like liquid poured into an empty bottle. An ivy branch was tapping furiously against the window and when I got up to look I saw the trees flailing in the fierce wind and rain of a sudden storm. I picked up my sketchbook to make a quick drawing – I couldn't sleep anyhow. Maybe I could catch something of the line of trees lashed by the wind, the rows of roses bent over backwards.

But then I saw the old woman.

She was pushing her way forwards against the wind. Stamping across the garden as if forcing the earth down with her booted feet. She was cradling a great bunch of stakes in her arms and, as I watched, she made her way to the rosebed, flung down the stakes and, holding each plant firmly, began trussing them to their new supports.

She worked methodically, one plant after another, taking no notice of the storm that whipped the hair over her head and tore her coat open so that I could see her night-dress beneath. She looked like a sea captain, in her element, leaning on the wind as she worked, her boots weighted to the ground.

This is the real woman, I thought, as I snatched drawings of her. Not that prink-fingered lady who sipped her tea, not that irritable, indecisive, fussy woman who packed and unpacked her possessions. No, here, in her garden, her legs solid as trees in the soil, her hands deft and sure as she gripped her plants. This is the woman, I thought, to whom I feel my loyalty. And I decided to make a portrait of her to go with the commission, a strong, clear, determined portrait that would be an inspiration.

By the time she had finished, the morning light was clear and I could see the rows of roses standing to attention, tight in their swaddling clothes. I looked to see some expression of pride, some satisfaction on her face, but as she tightened the last of the supports and turned back to the house she seemed to sag. Her head drooped, her shoulders wilted, her coat fell open, exposing the slur of her breasts. She shuffled away from the roses furtively, guiltily, as if from the scene of a crime, her bare head battered by the heavy spears of rain.

It rained. The house was surrounded by water, like a moat. We were cut off. And diving beneath the waves, my burden released from gravity, I could almost find a sort of peace.

It was an aquarium, an underwater world where we three drifted past each other and bubbles emerged from our mouths instead of words. We nodded slow, aqueous nods that bobbed up and down like seaweed on the tide. Then we'd drift in the wake of another current, the old woman picking up objects, moving them, putting them down so that the sea was changing all around us.

In my drawings I began to net the house, fitting a shell over the tender mussel of the Hall. In the nights he and I swirled over each other like sea mist. There was the steady drip of water from the eaves. Moss crept over the windows, the rooms greened with damp. I slipped under the surface. I breathed water. I slept . . .

At the end of the corridor upstairs was a small closed door. Curious, I went inside. It was a tiny room, hardly bigger than a cupboard. A small window looked down the long avenue of trees that lined the drive. There was a low armchair and a mushroom-shaped sewing table that leaned drunkenly on its central leg. Unusually in this house of makeshift furniture, the table was old, antique, though the delicate inlay of leaves and flowers was cracked, the surface scarred with rings. The room was shut up, still, quiet. Quiet as if it hadn't been opened for a long time. A different quiet from the muffled silence of the house.

I sat in the deep-buttoned little chair and looked down the drive, observing the narrowing lines of the trees as if I would draw them. I felt the letters heavy in my pockets.

I was waiting. Waiting? For what? For whom? To see – And what would I say when I saw her? What would I say as she ran down that avenue, waving her hand up to me at the window? Are you well? Are you happy? Where have you been? Could I tell her that I missed her? That every day I thought of things I wanted to tell her? Or would I beg her to forgive me? And what would she say? Stare at me with her dark eyes and her mouth thin and bloody where she'd bitten her lips. Ugly. Cropped-headed. Her hands clawing at me. 'Don't leave me, Soph. Oh, Soph, don't go . . .'

Because though I had escaped the sea house, hadn't she followed me, whining and keening, sniffing my scent like a bloodhound? Hadn't she swum across the water to find me, nimble as a fish, agile as a seal, her feet finned, her legs swishing like a mermaid's tail? Didn't her face haunt me from behind the mirror, her mouth twisted upwards in an ugly grimace, as if the fish had started nibbling her lips and then moved away to even more succulent parts . . .

I took out her letters, looked at her eager, chaotic, familiar handwriting – handwriting that was twisted of my heart – and I found myself weeping as I had not wept before. As I had not wept when I watched her body slip into the sea, not wept as I sorted her things in that rattling sea house where there, outside, was her hair tangled in the seaweed, her body petrified in the rocks, her voice shrill in the cries of the gulls. My sister, my stupid, stubborn little sister, for whom I thought I would have died but whom instead I had betrayed, run from. Now, in this house which she had never known, in a time which had moved on without her, now I was crying for her, for my cravenness that had caused her death, my fear, my cowardice in the face of her need.

The old woman must have been standing there for some time. I didn't hear her come in, just a stir behind me, and I stood up suddenly, the letters falling from my lap.

'I'm – I'm sorry.' I made as if to leave, but she was in the way of the door, looking round the little room with an expression of surprise.

'The porch room,' she said. 'I'd quite forgotten it.'

She lifted the lid of the sewing-table, and took out a piece of cloth. 'Still there – my God.' She laughed, but the sound was harsh, mocking. 'See that?' She held it out. 'I made that. You wouldn't believe it, would you?'

It was an unfinished square of embroidery. A pattern of roses – red and pink and yellow – around a central word – WIL – picked out in blue with another L only half stitched.

'It's – very pretty,' I said uncertainly.

'Pretty? Pretty awful, you mean. And there's a diary around here somewhere. I used to sit in here writing it when I was carrying Lydia. God, I was a fool then – a stupid fool. I'll burn that too if I come across it.'

Roughly she shoved the cloth back into the table, then suddenly pointed to the letters at my feet. 'Are they yours?'

'Oh – well – yes – '

She eyed me shrewdly for a moment. 'They're from your sister, aren't they? The one who – '

'Yes – ' I was anxious to pick them up; they looked so vulnerable and exposed scattered there.

'You ought to get rid of them,' she said tightly. 'Learn from me – make a fresh start. There's no point holding on to things.'

And then she was gone and I was alone in that no man's land over the porch, looking down the long avenue of trees where in the flurry of leaves lifting and turning I thought I could see waves rolling in.

The drawing I made of her was not triumphant. Not even strong and decisive. No, the drawing that finally fixed itself to my paper was of a defeat.

She was sitting in her big chair, staring wanly at the fire. Her face was flat, her hair uncombed, her body wilting. She looked beyond pity, beaten. Truly the old woman.

Simon came in as I was finishing. He looked over my shoulder and when I glanced up I saw alarm cracking his good-humoured façade. He winced. 'Very realistic,' he said drily. But the look he gave me was scalding and I put the drawing away in my portfolio guiltily, as if I had committed a crime.

And what had Simon been doing? All those days we were locked in the house by the bars of rain. Sometimes he drove out alone and, busy with the drawings which were developing, deepening, I hardly noticed his absence. Certainly I no longer needed him or the old woman to pick out the meat of the house from the bones which surrounded us. I had it in my mind's eye exactly and there were days when I was so absorbed I didn't even feel the pleasure of working again, only the gift of lines flowing from my pencil. I felt righted – like a bottle that had been tipped on its side and now stood straight. I had fallen back into my work as if my summer's renunciation had never happened. It was my heart, my breath, my blood – I couldn't live without it. I didn't even think to be grateful to Simon for returning me to it.

He hated the boxes and frowned when they got in his way, kicking them angrily with shoes that were no longer sleek and shiny but scuffed, dull. In fact, his whole appearance had gradually metamorphosed into a careless, shabby replica of the old woman and her house. He no longer looked so out of place with his neatly pressed suits and his starched shirts. His trousers were crumpled, his shirts unironed, when a button fell off his waistcoat he carelessly tossed it away. One evening sitting in the front room, he suddenly pulled at his tie – the bow uncoiling like a snake. '*Ach*, this thing strangles me,' he said, undoing his collar. 'For what should I wear it?'

And he had remained open-necked ever since.

Despite the old woman's obdurate secrecy, every day he made fresh attempts to make her explain her strange behaviour. But it was useless. His cajoling lapped around the rock of her silence impotently.

Until finally, one evening, he said with a sigh, 'All right, Madeleine, you will not explain this – situation to me. You do not have to. As you say, it is not my business.'

'That's right,' she said stiffly, avoiding his gaze and staring proudly into the fire.

'You can be stubborn – I can be stubborn too,' he went on. 'You can tell me nothing – but you cannot stop me helping you.'

'There's absolutely no need, thank you.'

'You are leaving the Hall?' he said, suddenly sharp. 'You are going – where, Madeleine?'

She didn't reply.

'You have another place to live?'

She shrugged.

'You do not have to explain this to me, old friend,' he said more gently. 'You have my word – I will ask no questions. I only want to help, that is all.'

'Why?' She looked at him.

He smiled. 'When I started in business here you were my first good customer – you trusted me, you treated me properly. To you it did not matter that I was a foreigner. You behaved kindly – like a lady. Do you think I was not grateful for that?' He paused. 'Then let me help you now, Madeleine. I have a villa in the South. It is empty. I bought it some years ago as an investment, but I never use it. Of course – ' He hesitated uncertainty – 'it is not what you are used to. It is hot there although it is by a lake. There are lemon trees,' he added with a shrug, lighting a cigarette and looking away as if embarrassed.

There was a long pause as she studied him. 'You're a good friend to me, Simon. I don't know why.'

'A good friend you would talk to.'

At the Hall

But she continued to regard him steadily. 'You have been better to me than my own family.'

He shook his head sadly. 'Nothing is better than family, Madeleine,' he said.

One afternoon he returned to the house with his arms full of shopping bags. 'Today is a special day for me,' he said. 'It is my family day. Tonight we celebrate.'

He cooked an elaborate meal and served it to us in the dining-room, which he'd dotted with candles so that the sombre place looked less forbidding, the harsh stares of the old portraits softened by the gentle light.

He pressed us to eat and drink. 'Try a little more, Madeleine, this is a speciality of my family . . . Sophie, let me fill your glass, it is looking lonely without wine . . .' He was charming, entertaining, telling us stories and anecdotes and jokes. But I felt irritated. I wanted to cut through his veneer – his polish that kept me sliding away from him. I wanted to break the division he'd made that kept me smiling politely at him during the day and lying silent beneath him at night.

'Where do they come from, Simon?' I asked in a moment's silence. 'Your family – are they here?'

I heard the hiss of the old woman's breath but he replied evenly enough. 'No, Sophie, my family are no longer alive.'

'Oh – I'm sorry.' I felt as if I'd stubbed my toe. 'I didn't mean to – '

'It was a long time ago – it is over now.'

'But – but – all of them?' The wine had made me bold. 'Surely you have other family?'

By now his eyes had narrowed, until in the flickering light he looked like a sharp, pointed bird. The old woman was shifting uncomfortably, but some stubbornness kept me pushing recklessly at the wall of his defences.

'Are they buried here, at least?' I asked. 'Can you visit their graves?'

'No.'

'They're abroad then?' I must have been drunk. 'It must be a comfort to you to be able to visit them when you travel – you know, to lay flowers and everything.'

He sat very still and the candles, burning steadily now, illumined his face with sharp flares of light that glinted his cheekbones and glittered his eyes.

'They were – cremated,' he said slowly, his voice very low. 'Their ashes – scattered. I cannot visit to pay my respects.' He looked away. His hands were still curved round his wineglass but limp, as if he didn't feel it between his fingers.

I closed my eyes feeling very ashamed. 'I'm sorry,' I whispered.

He nodded. 'You see, Sophie, I am like you – there is no sign on the grave of my people.'

'And – you're alone?' I said after a moment. 'You really have no other family?'

'That's right, Sophie. Alone. Like yourself.' He looked at me and I saw I had breached the wall.

I saw him lying across the bed suddenly as a shape – a comma, a question mark. And automatically, without thinking, I reached for my sketchbook and began to draw.

He lay very still and when I switched on the lamp he only turned his face away, shielding it with his arm. The broad sweep of his back quivered as I ran the pencil over the page. Yes, this was alive, each line singing and true, the rhythm of him sounding a determined march on my paper.

All bodies hold a rhythm. Some are staccato like a bird, others ripple like a slow lake. He held a clenched fist inside his skin – a heart that would not stop beating, resilient, fibrous. I wanted to catch that heart now, while he was naked and vulnerable, and pin it to my page.

He made as if to move.

'Don't,' I said curtly. 'Wait.'

He lay stiff as wood while I carved.

Then he moved again, this time swinging his legs over the side of the bed, so that he sat with his back to me and his head bowed over. Immediately, I tore off the old sheet of paper and began again. A good pose, better than before. The curve of his back like a wave curling over and his shoulderblades, with their thin covering of skin, like rock beneath a fine film of sand.

'If you could just raise your head – just a little – '

'Don't.'

It was the first word he'd ever spoken in my room and I discarded it as lightly as a spent seed husk.

'I won't be long – I promise. If you could just lift your arm.'

I wasn't even looking at his face, just the sinews of his neck, the lines with which I scalpelled his nerves to my paper.

'Yes, that's good – that's very good. No – don't move.'

'Sophie – please – don't – '

But I was slicing through lines and planes and surfaces.

'You know, you're very good,' I said. 'Have you done this before?'

I only stopped because I saw his shoulders shaking.

'You're cold.' I put down the pad and picked up a blanket. 'I'm sorry. I should have thought of that. Here – ' I draped it over his shoulders. 'Maybe I'll just do a bit of you – an arm, or a leg, or something.'

But it wasn't the cold.

He was crying. Simon, that self-contained man, was crying, weeping, sobbing here in my room in front of me.

'Simon?' I hardly dared approach him. 'Simon – I'm sorry if I – '

I tried to take his hand, but it was clenched shut, his fingers clawed over his thumb. Even his toes were gripping the floor, as if it were a perch he was afraid of falling from.

'Simon?' I tried again, putting my arms around him.

His skin was clammy with cold, as if he were underground. He looked grey, ashen. His body suddenly withered: the muscles that before had pressed so hard against me were wasted, the skin falling away from his bones. His genitals, shrivelled and weak, reproached me for spying on his nakedness.

'Simon?' I coaxed. 'Won't you –'

'He used to draw me.' His voice was flat, expressionless. 'He used to – draw me.'

'Who?'

There was a long silence.

'Simon? Who?'

I could hear the first of the birds cracking the dark with song and I was thinking, It will be dawn soon, he will have been with me all night . . .

When suddenly he replied. 'He picked me because – because I had been an artist. I hadn't told them that, of course. Artist – intellectual, a lethal combination. I'd told them I was a shoe-maker and they'd sent me to a shed to sort shoes: a mountain of shoes, ordinary people's shoes – worn shoes, shoes some with the heel a little loose, shoes some carefully polished – all in a heap, empty shoes. Every day I was afraid I would find their shoes – my mother, my sister – but they were already gone, everyone was gone – finished, ashes for fertilizer. Sometimes, when they were very busy with the transports, they made us take the shoes away even before – before—' He faltered. 'But I was lucky – it was a good job, indoors. I would not have lasted long as one of the labourers.' His voice was harsh. 'And then one day that officer came walking through the shed, laughing, joking, slapping his leg with his horse-stick – his horse-stick with the silver head. He came up to me, stood right in front of me. There was a crumb on his tunic – a crumb of real bread, very white on the grey of his uniform. And I was praying with all my will that before he took me away, somehow that crumb would fall off and I would eat it. But he was asking me questions – Where did I come from? What was my profession? And I didn't care any more – I was going to die anyway – so I said, "I am an artist, Mr Captain, Sir." "An artist? Follow me."

'I had no choice. He walked very quickly. I thought he was selecting me for a special death – knives, dogs, clubs. But I didn't want to be beaten to death like an animal, even then. So I asked him – I addressed him – you cannot have any idea what that means, can you? I asked him, "Please, Mr Captain, Sir, where are we going?" But he didn't get so angry. Of course he hit me, but the blow was not so hard. He only laughed. And that was what was so dangerous. When they were laughing it would not be funny – not for us.'

He stopped, wiped his mouth. Now I could smell the death on him. Now, without his cologne, his pomade, there was a dirty, greasy, metallic smell.

'He took me to a room. It was very clean. I was thinking how my blood would make a mess – and all the time I was looking for the dog, the knife, what he would do to me. He made me take off my pyjamas – they would be kept for another prisoner, he would not want to take them off my corpse himself. I stood there naked. He looked at me – all around. With his horse-stick – his horse-stick he – he touched me. With his horse-stick he – '

There were flecks of spittle on his chin. He cupped his genitals. 'Only with the horse-stick he – he – lifted, he – pushed – '

When he started again his voice was bleak, stripped. 'I had to stand on a stool. And then he would draw me. If I moved he beat my feet – not my body, just my feet – with the horse-stick. I don't know why he chose me. There were others he could have used – fresher, healthier bodies, new from the transports with the flesh still on them. But he chose me. Sometimes he even gave me bread. You could say he saved my life, that officer.'

The room was greying with morning. In the thin, cold light he looked haggard. An old man. White stubble pricking his face.

'I wanted to live – and I lived,' he cried suddenly. 'Others died. Not me. I said to that God up there, Take them, not me. And He listened. Sometimes I wish He'd never heard.'

The words chilled me. As if he had put his fingers unerringly straight on my heart and twisted it. 'Take her, not me . . .' Yes, some ugly part of me had also been relieved by Stella's death, which had released me, set me free from what could have been a lifetime of bondage. And suddenly I was afraid, with an old stirring fear that clenched inside me, gripping my pity and squeezing it mercilessly. I thought I had wanted to know this man, to see behind the mask he wore. Now I felt I knew him so well I could see his intestines. But did I really want the weight of that knowledge? The burden of a new dependence?

He was twisting the small ring around his finger. 'Part of the fence,' he said tonelessly. 'I cannot escape. For what did I survive?'

His eyes closed wearily and there was silence.

Then gently, very gently, as if he were a fragile child, I pushed him back on the bed, swinging his legs over so that he lay full-length. He was very cold. I chafed his hands and rubbed his feet and piled all the blankets over him. Then I pulled up a chair and for the first time I watched him – Simon Stein, my lover – sleeping.

He slept long, a heavy stone sleep that selfishly I was grateful for. After a while I dressed and left the room, taking my portfolio with me. The drawings were finished, but I thought that maybe by altering a line here or there I could use them to lever me out of his nightmare and into some sort of order, some routine. But the smoke from his crematorium chimneys clouded my sight. I could smell death and decay even in the gentlest parlour pictures.

I took the portfolio back up to my room, opening the door carefully to rest the case just inside. I didn't want to see him. What would I say? Offer condolences? Those pitiful drops people had squeezed out for me – 'Oh, I'm *so* sorry. Such a *terrible* tragedy . . .' Little tin words that rattled discordantly and failed to cover the wretched squawks of their embarrassment.

But he was awake.

'Sophie?' he called just as I was closing the door. 'Sophie – is that you?'

I came inside, just a step, still keeping the door open.

'Yes, that's right, it's me.' A pause. 'How are you feeling?' I cringed, but was unable to stop the banalities tumbling out of my mouth like jesters. 'Did you sleep well? Is there anything you want? Anything I can get you?'

Yes, there it was, the terrible need to efface the guilt of impotence by taking some action – 'Are you sure we can't do anything for you? Shopping? A nice holiday maybe . . .' Who can bear to stand idle and watch another grieving?

'You've slept a good long time,' I rattled on, avoiding his eyes. 'It's nearly afternoon now. Are you feeling any better?' I winced.

'Yes – thank you.' His voice was even. 'I slept very well.'

'Oh – good.'

Silence again. I stood by the door, clenching my fingers.

'Sophie – ' he began at last, his voice soft and low. 'I must – you have – Why won't you look at me?' he said suddenly.

I looked up immediately, tried to focus on his face, but my eyes kept sliding off his features. Dimly I recognized that he looked tired and sad, but then the officer with his sketchbook came between us and I looked away.

He sighed. 'Your drawings?' He gestured to the portfolio. 'Finished?'

'That's right.'

'Let me see.'

He sat up and I took the portfolio to him. It was easier, with the sheets of paper spread over the bed, to avoid his eyes. He looked through them all slowly, one at a time, then he stopped suddenly. He had found the portrait of the old woman.

'Oh – that's the one I did – '

'Yes, I know.' He pushed my hand away.

'You – you didn't like it.'

But he was studying it carefully.

'I wasn't thinking of including it,' I said, adding with a brittle laugh, 'It's not really very flattering, is it?'

'But truthful,' he said thoughtfully.

I was suddenly aware of his proximity and shuffled the sheets together roughly.

'Not so quick – not so quick,' he protested. 'There's no hurry, is there?'

'No – of course not.'

With a deliberate movement, he covered my hand with his. It felt tender, as he had never touched me before, not seeking to excite, not twisting cries from me, but gentle, familiar, known. It terrified me. I stood stock-still.

'You have been very kind to me, Sophie,' he said. 'It has – not been easy for you, with me. Forgive me.'

This was almost intolerable. I suddenly realized that his previous polite distance had suited me exactly. I didn't think I could bear this warmth – this gratitude.

'It's all right,' I said with a ghastly cheeriness. 'It's fine – really.' I tried to move out of his grasp, but he was holding me tightly.

'I want to thank you.'

'Oh – there's no need for all that.' I finally pulled myself free and started backing away.' I felt the door frame behind me. 'Really – there's absolutely nothing for you to be thankful for. Well, I'll just let you be then,' I said with relief. 'You can stay here – I won't disturb you.' Oh, no, God forbid I'd disturb him – God forbid I'd allow him to disturb me.

'Thank you'

'No, no – really.'

And then the door had closed and I was tearing down the stairs and shooting out of the house like an arrow.

Hard, hard, I lashed myself as I ran down the lane. 'You're like iron, Soph – you've got no heart . . .'

I stumbled across the frosty fields, welcoming the cold that might scour me clean – of what? The stain of my history? Or the ink of my fear that had seeped through the pristine white cloth of my concern for her – 'You don't care, Soph, you don't care – you just want to be free of me. Well, go back to town then. Go away, I'm fine . . .' And had I pushed aside her paper protests? Had I reached out to gentle her cropped head? No. I'd slipped on a bright gingham apron of smiles to cover my guilt – then ran back to town, cradling my independence.

Independence – God, I would spit on it now if I could. Don't touch me – I'm independent. Don't need me – I'm independent. I made a tower and walled myself in and called it independence, while down on the plain my sister howled and beat at the doors.

And now Simon – looking at me, being grateful to me, threatening me again with those fine chains that I could see running through his fingers, the links bright and strong, ready to lock around me.

But no – not again, not again. This time I would not be frightened away. This time I would not sacrifice myself for that independence. This time I would stand my ground, I would resist the wind that wanted me to pull away from him. This time would be different. This time it would be all right.

It was dark when I got back to the house. I stood in the porch, knocking the mud from my shoes, and it was some minutes before I realized that his car wasn't there.

I ran inside, up the stairs – stupid, stupid, as if I didn't already know what I'd find. My bed was empty, the blankets folded and tucked militarily tight over the barren mattress. I stood in the centre of the room sniffing the air, as if I might just catch the scent of him. Nothing.

I went into his room – that little wood-panelled room that was warm and musty like the inside of a cupboard. His things were gone. And I thought – yes, here is the price of my independence.

Desire hung between my legs heavy as a ripe plum. I wanted him. I wanted the weight of him crushing me so that my body might receive his imprint like a fossil. I wanted to lie with him in that narrow bed, close as ships in harbour. I wanted the cream and toffee of his voice as he rolled my name around his tongue and spoke to me, whispered to me, tendered me. I wanted the salt of his breath as he licked the sweat from my temples and combed my lashes through his teeth. I wanted the stubbornness of his chest with the muscles slacking like the strings of an instrument discordant with age. I wanted his full mouth with the smile that betrayed him so that never again would I be taken in by the arch of his eyebrows as he looked at me askance.

The tall, thin woman stepped out of the cold and my aqueous world shivered into slivers of malachite. She stood in the hall, perched on her high-heeled shoes as if on a ladder, her hair topaz blond, her face a frozen snap of ice.

She stared at me for a moment, glanced at the open sketchbook on my knees.

'You must be the artist,' she said. 'Sophie – somebody-or-other, isn't it?'

'Yes – I –'

She looked away from me. 'Where's Madeleine?'

But just then the door of the front room opened and the old woman emerged. She was wearing her thick gardening coat; it was streaked with mud and her boots were clogged with earth, her hands filthy.

'Madeleine –'

'Lydia –' She turned quickly. 'What are you doing here?'

'I thought I'd come and see you.' She took a step forwards.

The old woman closed the door behind her sharply. 'I wasn't expecting you,' she said coldly.

They stood opposite each other, stiff as a drawing in hard pencil. They made no move to embrace.

'I – I wanted to talk to you,' Lydia began hesitantly.

'Really?' the old woman raised an eyebrow. 'What about?'

'You know.'

'Lydia, I cannot imagine to what I must owe this sudden desire for my company. Please tell me.'

Lydia's hands flexed by her sides but, taking a breath, she steadied herself and pointed to the boxes. 'What is all this?'

Her mother sighed. 'Really, Lydia, I paid quite enough for your education. Don't play the fool now, please.'

Lydia flinched but stood her ground. 'I want an explanation, Madeleine,' she said. 'For God's sake, what do you think you're doing?'

But her mother was unmoved. 'I do not intend going over all

this again,' she said stonily. 'I did not expect you to come down here. You chose to do so, that's up to you – I can't stop you. But just leave me to get on with my – '

'Oh, stop being ridiculous,' Lydia snapped. 'You know full well that I'm just not going to allow you to let this go on any longer.'

'You have no power to stop me, it's as simple as that.'

'Look, Madeleine,' Lydia began again, more gently, 'I don't want this to go on – really I don't. I honestly never thought that you'd seriously – that you'd mean to go through with it. But then when I saw Simon last night and he told me that – '

'Ah, so that's what made you come down,' the old woman broke in. 'I wondered. That must have been a nice surprise for you – seeing Simon,' she added caustically.

'I – well – he – he showed me the pictures,' Lydia stammered. They both looked at me.

'Oh – ' I said uncomfortably. 'I – I hope you liked them.'

There was a metallic glint in Lydia's hard blue eyes. 'I'm sure you'd have made very short work of the twins,' she said curtly.

Before I could respond she had shifted back to her mother, who was picking pellets of mud from her fingers and scattering them carelessly on the floor. 'Look,' she tried again, 'I haven't come down here to talk about those pictures – or Simon – or anything else. Just tell me what it is you're expecting me to do – or say – or whatever – so that we can forget this whole – misunderstanding and get back to normal.'

'It's too *late* for that now,' the old woman said tonelessly.

'It isn't too late, Madeleine, it's never too late.' She took a few steps forward, pushing the boxes out of her way. 'Come on, Madeleine, what do you say?'

But the old woman just shook her head. 'I tell you, Lydia, it's too late now.'

'Why?' She was standing over her mother now, looming menacingly tall. 'Why do you say it's too late?'

'Oh, for God's sake, Lydia,' the old woman cried out suddenly. 'Why did you have to come down now? You weren't going to see it – it was all – '

'Weren't going to see what – what, Madeleine?' She reached for the door handle.

'No – don't – ' The old woman had her back to the door and feebly tried to push her daughter away. 'It was all going to be cleared away – it was all – '

'Get out of my way – Madeleine, get out of my way – '

'Lydia – please – don't – '

But Lydia, like one defying a god, roughly shoved her mother aside and opened the door.

There was silence. Then a sudden cry.

We went in after her.

She was standing by the glass doors. She didn't even turn as we came in, just stood there staring out. 'My God, what have you done?' she whispered fearfully. 'Madeleine – what have you done?'

I looked outside. There in the dim afternoon light was the scene of a massacre. For a moment, before I could make any sense of it, I thought it was almost comical it was so bizarre, so utterly unbelievable. Where the rosebed had been, so neat and ordered, with the plants all in rows like sentries, there was now a churned mass of earth and grass. Bushes were splayed ungainly over the ground, their leaves torn, their late flowers battered, soil still clinging to their twisted roots, which looked obscene, wrenched so harshly out of the earth. The horizon of the garden now stretched unbroken all the way down to the woods. Not a plant was left standing.

Lydia turned on me. 'It's all your fault,' she spat furiously. 'Look at it – look what you made her do. Those bloody pictures – raking up the past like that – it's all your doing – you made her – '

'Oh no, you're not going to blame anyone else,' the old woman broke in fiercely. 'This was my decision – mine – and

I'm proud of it. You never liked my roses. I wasn't going to leave them to you.'

Then she dashed outside and, as we watched, began pulling the plants into one large heap with a frenzied energy.

'We've got to stop her,' Lydia cried. 'We've got to – '

She made as if to follow her mother but then, realizing her shoes, kicked them off with a curse and ran into the hall, where I heard her fumbling amongst the boxes.

When she came back, she was wearing a pair of Wellington boots that looked misplaced beneath her neat navy-blue skirt. She was pulling on an old tweed coat and tossed another coat and a pair of boots to me. 'Come on – put these on. Quick, quick.'

'We'll just have to plant them all back again,' she said decisively, as we stepped outside. 'You talk to her – distract her – get her away. I'll start the planting.'

She walked briskly towards her mother, who was busy with a fork, flinging more plants on to the pile.

'Coming to join me?' The old woman greeted us with a manic cheeriness. 'Jolly good. I thought you might.'

'Now, Madeleine,' Lydia began with a great show of calmness and reason. 'Why don't you just sit down and have a nice rest? You've obviously been working very hard. Sophie will stay with you. Then we'll all go back to the house and have a nice cup of tea together . . .'

But the old woman just laughed and carried on throwing the bushes one on top of the other. She disappeared round the far side of the pile.

The heap was much larger close too and the plants looked pathetic all pushed up together. I was reminded of the piles of corpses Simon must have seen.

And then suddenly the old woman called out. 'Stand back – stand out of the way – ' There was a gagging smell of petrol and the heap soared into flames.

'Jesus – Jesus – what are you doing?' Lydia screamed. Like an animal desperate to escape a forest fire, she ran impotently to and fro round the heap. 'What do you think you're doing?'

But the old woman was standing resolute, ruthlessly pushing the plants into the hottest heart of the blaze. The fire illuminated her face with a harsh glare; her mouth was set, her feet planted, her back straight, as she watched her beauties burn.

'Well, Lydia,' she shouted, 'I'm burning my boats now, aren't I? Something you and your precious grandfather could never do. I'm finally getting free of you – and your whole damn clan. I'm burning it, burning it all. Want me to burn the house down for you as well while I'm at it?'

'No – Madeleine – no – '

'But you don't care for that old place, do you? You couldn't give a damn – '

'I do – I do – Oh, Madeleine, why are you doing this?'

The roses twisted and writhed, the sap singing, spitting. Every so often the branches would convulse and lift, as if by some eerie force they were being resurrected. Thick swathes of smoke billowed in the wind.

'Oh, Madeleine, I never wanted this,' Lydia cried, her face very stark in the bright light.

'Well, maybe it isn't about what you want any more, my fine Lady Lydia,' the old woman spat. 'Always what *you* want, isn't it? Like the way you are with the twins – taking them away from here when it suited *you*, never mind that they wanted to stay with their grandmother. What *you* wanted, Lydia, not what they wanted.'

She was picking up the half-burned fingers of plants in her bare hands and flinging them on to the fire. Lydia flinched as the bright, hot missiles darted past her.

'And what about their new school?' the old woman went on. 'That nice new school *you* wanted them to go to. Happy there are they? Really? Enjoying themselves? That's not what I've been hearing.'

'What do you mean?' Lydia was suddenly alert.

'In their letters.' The old woman spoke slowly, deliberately. 'In the letters Christopher and Catherine have written to me.'

'Letters?' Lydia stood aghast. 'They've been writing – to you?'

Her mother nodded. 'And I can tell you, Lydia, never mind the stories they've been spinning to keep you happy, they're not the jolly little boarders you think they are.'

'I don't believe it – it's not true –'

'Oh, but it is.' There was a cruel smile on the old woman's face. 'Want to see the little tear stains?'

'But – but they said – they said –'

'Well, let's face it, Lydia, they can't talk to you, can they? You wouldn't listen to them – you never do. And I'll tell you one more thing—' The old woman paused, kicked at the fire. 'You look at your children, Lydia. Who do they remind you of? Not you – no, you look like your precious grandfather. No, it's *me* they take after – their grandmother. So you see—' She laughed harshly – 'you're just a chip off the old block after all. Like grandparent, like grandchild – you've been following in old footsteps. Round and round like animals in a ring, that's what we are.'

The blaze had quietened now, most of the plants already crumbled to ash. In the pyre, flowers of flame bloomed and died. Smuts and cinders were tossed about in the wind.

Lydia was edging away. 'I'll go inside,' she said, her voice small, broken. 'I'll leave in the morning.'

'Really?' her mother called out after her. 'You'll leave? I don't think so.'

Lydia glanced back over her shoulder, but her face was hidden in the darkness. She made some motion with her hand and, stumbling across the broken ground, went into the house.

The old woman leaned heavily on her fork and gazed at the charred remains of her roses wearily, as if she was just waiting for the job to be finished.

Lydia knelt between her mother's knees and bandaged her hands. They were torn from the roses and blistered from the fire. The old woman sat in her chair with her head leaned back, her eyes closed, her hands held out limply. When Lydia lifted them, she allowed them to be raised; when laid down, she allowed them to rest. She showed no interest in her daughter's ministrations.

It was a grey, heavy day. The sky was thick with snow and the ugly circle of charred twigs was almost completely hidden by soft white drifts. I think we were all grateful for that.

'Is this too tight?' Lydia broke the silence, but her mother simply shrugged. Lydia laid the finished hand gently on her mother's knee and began the process again. Carefully she bathed the fingers, picking at the edges of the wounds with tweezers to draw out the tiny thorns, then she patted each one dry and dabbed them with cream, smoothing it tenderly around the cuticles and down into the joints.

She was wearing an old brown cardigan over her white blouse and a pair of thick socks over her stockings. As with Simon, the house seemed to have succeeded in imposing its own dress code upon her. She was smaller too without her shoes, and her face unmade-up – was softer, less angular. It was her mother who now looked hard, her face closed in, distant, as if with the fire she'd burned the life out of herself.

Picking up a fresh bandage, Lydia began weaving it around her mother's fingers. 'I'll stay on for another day or two,' she said casually. 'If that's all right?' No response. 'You know – make it a bit more – ' She paused to lay the bandaged hand on her mother's lap. 'A bit more – homelike. What do you say?' Her mother blinked. 'It won't take me all that long,' Lydia went on in a rush, 'to unpack the boxes and – '

'Lydia – don't.' The old woman's voice was hoarse but firm. 'Don't – please.'

'But really,' Lydia persisted. 'It won't take long at all – just so that you can feel at home again and – '

'Lydia – please.'

'No, really, Madeleine, I mean it. It'll be all right. You see – '

'*I* mean it, Lydia. Don't go on.'

'But I want to explain.'

'There's nothing to explain.'

'No – please, Madeleine, you don't understand.' Lydia knelt up and touched her mother's knee, like a suppliant. 'There's something I want to explain to you – look at me, please? There's something I want you to understand. Oh, please, look at me?'

The old woman's head turned, slow as the door of a vault opening. 'What?'

'You see – ' she began haltingly. 'I'm – I'm – I don't want us to go back to how it was – '

'Good, then we can just – '

'No – ' Lydia broke in. 'No – you don't understand what I've got in mind. You see – ' She leaned forward eagerly, so that her chin, dog-like, pressed against her mother's knee. The sight was disturbing. The old woman sat stock-still, her distaste emanating in bilious waves, but Lydia seemed quite impervious.

'You see,' she continued, 'what I've got in mind is so much better – better than anything you could think of. I've been thinking about – well, about last night – and everything you said. No, don't – ' She held up a hand as her mother drew breath. 'Please – let me explain. I've – I've been thinking that I don't want us to follow in those old footsteps. I don't want us to go on making all the same mistakes and ending up the same way. I want us to make a new start – a fresh start, for you, me, the children, all of us. I've been going over and over it in my mind all night and – '

'Oh, Lydia, don't go on,' the old woman protested wearily. Her face was tired and pale in the stark light of the reflected snow. 'Please – leave it now.'

But Lydia wasn't to be put off. 'No,' she said strongly. 'Madeleine, you will listen to me for once. Just hear me, please – just hear me out.'

The old woman shrugged resignedly and made no further attempt to interrupt.

'Well – last night – ' Lydia began hesitantly. 'You see, last night it – it suddenly came to me how this whole thing could be resolved – transformed, really. You see – you see, what I thought was that I could *sell* the house in town – sell it and use the money to restore the Hall – to make it how it used to be – like in those pictures – ' She flashed a glance at me, her eyes burning. 'I could make this house my career,' she went on, 'restoring this house – *our* house – to all its glory. You do understand what I'm saying, don't you, Madeleine? I mean, we would all move in here with you – all of us, living here together – a proper family. Oh, think of it, Madeleine, it would be so wonderful. The children would love it and you'd love to be with them – watching them growing up – and Dan could have the peace and quiet he's always wanting . . .'

She was looking up at her mother but didn't seem to see the appalled expression, how the old woman's mouth had tightened, even her bones sinking away. Lydia pressed on oblivious, blinded by the light of her own face, leaning forward even as her mother was leaning away, her voice bright as a hammer tapping on and on.

'I want to tell you – I want you to understand – that I'm so sorry for what I've done – for what I've made you do, the roses and everything. I don't know how I'm ever going to be able to forgive myself. But we can plant new roses in the spring, can't we? They can symbolize our fresh start. We'll all plant them – you, me, the children, everyone – we can all do it together. And I'll *give* you the Hall – I'll make it over to you properly, so that it will be your home – our home. And later – ' She was slowing, hesitating – 'later when – if – if – ' Her voice dropped – 'if you get ill – we'll be able to look after you. You really shouldn't be on your own any more, you know, it's not safe. You – you do understand what I mean, don't you?'

She must have taken her mother's awful stillness as an assent, because she kept on, relentless as an avalanche, a dam-burst.

'We could all be so happy together – it could all be different. I could see it so clearly last night while I lay awake in the Ship Room. I felt – oh, I don't know, almost as if it was – well, being suggested to me.' She looked down shyly. 'As if I was being told how to make it all right . . .'

The old woman was shaking her head as Lydia came to an

end. 'My God,' she said softly, almost in wonder. 'You're just like your grandfather. No, not that one – ' she put in quickly as Lydia looked up. 'You had another for all that you never knew him. My Da. My drunken, illiterate, tenant-farmer Da. On and on he'd go for what he wanted, but then when he'd get it handed to him on a plate – like I've handed the Hall back to you – well, what do you know? He wouldn't want it any more. Just like him, you are.'

'Oh, but I do, I do,' Lydia burst out. 'I do want the Hall – but I want it with you. I want you to stay here with me and – '

But the old woman wasn't listening. 'I never really spoke to you about the other side of your ancestry, did I?' she said reflectively. 'Never told you much about my Ma and Da – the farm, how we lived then. Never even said much about William, did I?'

Lydia looked away. 'Nobody spoke much about him,' she said, her voice very low. 'Except at school – when they found out – '

'But he was a good man, your father,' the old woman went on quietly. 'Just unlucky – very unlucky. And he'd have made a good father too – and a good husband, given half a chance. But – ' She sighed. 'I can hardly remember him now – all those years ago – it was over so quickly. I hardly even knew him. Just a few days, that's all we had together, just a few days – and then there was you.' She paused, looking down at her daughter – a look that wasn't anger or bitterness or even reproach, but bleached of feeling, like cardboard. 'You and *him*,' she added heavily. 'Your precious grandfather.'

Lydia drew a breath. 'Let's not talk about this,' she said hastily. 'Just tell me what you think of my idea. It's a good one, don't you think? Let's talk about that.'

'But that is exactly what I *am* talking about. How you want to put my head in that noose again – '

'But it wouldn't be like that. It would be different. I'm different – '

'It's his blood running through your veins, Lydia,' the old woman said tightly. 'And it's your house, after all. You'd end up as subtle as he was. My God – ' She laughed coldly – 'how he hated me. And no matter what I did – how I dressed or what I said – he always saw me as a dirty tenant-farmer's brat who'd got his only son into trouble. He hated me – and I hated him. I thought it would be the happiest day of my life when he died. I thought, at last, at last, I'd be free. But I was wrong. You see – ' She tipped her head on one side as she looked down – 'he'd left you behind, hadn't he? His little replica.'

'Madeleine – don't, please.' Lydia had twisted away, but her mother's voice was as insistent as her own had been. Like a tap dripping – steady, monotonous, inevitable.

'I thought I'd never have to see him again – never have to feel his disapproval, his loathing. But every time I looked at you, there *he* was, staring at me out of your eyes.' She shuddered. 'Because you were his little girl, weren't you, Lydia? From the top of your head to the tips of your shoes, you were all his. Any wonder I kept you in that school, as far as possible away from me? But that was wrong too, wasn't it? Everything I did was wrong – always wrong. And it's too late now. Oh, it might have all been different if he'd let William marry me. Because he stopped that, you know. I was always certain about that. Your precious grandfather made sure his son didn't get the leave he might have had to marry me. Oh, yes, you can blame him for that fair and square. At least his son didn't marry beneath him, never mind the bastard he fathered – '

'No – ' Lydia had got to her feet. 'No – No – I won't listen to any more of this. You've spat on my feelings, you've told disgusting lies about Grandfather, you've insulted me – him – everything. Well, leave then. Do what you like. Go to hell for all I care.'

The old woman looked after her as she stormed out. 'She's never been happy,' she said, her voice very flat. 'She's my own flesh and blood and I've never made her happy.'

I heard his car and, without hesitating even for a moment, as if the engine hooked me by the neck and pulled me out of bed, I snatched up my dressing-gown, ran out of the room, down the stairs and out of the front door to meet him.

It was early. The sun melting the snow that dripped silent and self-effacing as it shrank back into the earth.

The car pulled to a halt and I stood there – 'You're independent, Soph, you don't need me . . .' I stood there – 'I'm not important to you, Soph. No one's important to you . . .' I stood there, my bare feet bolted to the cold ground as though hands gripped them. Stood there, though a chorus of ancient reflexes tried to pull me away.

But when he stepped out of his car, smiling as he caught sight of me, I fired the final arrow of my independence. 'Where the hell did you run off to?' I shouted at him. 'How dare you just leave me here, expecting me to wait for you?'

But the arrow glanced off him harmlessly and he stretched out his hand as he came towards me. 'Don't chide me, Sophie,' he said gently. 'I've missed you too.'

Fight, screamed the chorus in my head. Fight. Fight. But the touch of his hand, dry and slightly cold, but curved so exactly around my own, seemed to dissolve those ancient bindings and the chorus began to disperse, melting away like the snow.

'I – I was afraid – ' I stammered. 'I thought when you'd left that I'd driven you away.'

He was holding me close to him openly, there, in front of the house, in front of anyone who might want to see. I could feel the deep heaving of his breath as he wound his fingers tight in my hair and pulled me hard against him. 'Ah, Sophie, but you have been like manna in the wilderness.'

'But – but – I've been – so – so – ' I clenched my eyes in shame. 'I don't deserve this – I don't deserve – '

'Ah, Sophie,' he soothed. 'Sophie, my love – we are going to be so happy you and me. We will be together. At last, now I am giving up the gallery and we will – '

'No – no – ' I pushed him away. 'No – you can't do that.'

'Sophie, but what is this?' His soft accent caressed my name. 'What troubles you?'

'I don't know – I don't know–' I stood there confused, bewildered, fighting away the chorus. 'You can't just give up your work like that. It's your life – your–'

'*Ach,*' he waved a hand. 'It's just a shop for sausage-makers.'

'But what will you do?'

He paused, his head on one side, then said slowly, 'When I was an artist, even though already I was building up a good reputation, my father he was always complaining: "You are wasting your life, Simon. You are throwing it away. Why don't you do something useful instead of all this art rubbish." So, when I was freed and came over here, I got myself a business. I worked hard, made plenty of money – all so that my father should have been pleased with me. But—' He shrugged – 'it's enough now. I'm too old for such games. Now I want to be happy – now I want to live my life.'

'But – but you were happy before, weren't you? You were living well, weren't you?'

He shook his head. 'That wasn't living, Sophie, that was surviving.' He reached out to finger my hair. 'That is not the duty we owe the dead.'

Instinctively my hands went to my pockets, but the letters weren't there. I was without them – for the first time I was without them. 'Her letters,' I cried. 'Upstairs – I must–'

'Leave them.' He caught me as I turned.

'But – but – I can't just—'

'No more punishments.' Gently he drew me back towards him. 'Your sister would not want that. She would want you to live...'

His voice rumbled as he pressed my head against him and suddenly then I could hear the sea as it pounded the beach the last time I saw her. She'd been watching me through the windows of the Glass Room, waving and smiling as I walked away to my show. She must have known then what she was going to do, because it was all so carefully planned, but she was leaning forward eagerly in her chair, her silly cropped head glinting blue-black in the spring sunshine. And for a moment, just a second, we exchanged a look – a real look, a knowing, familiar, loving look. And I thought, Yes, it will be all right – when this show is over, I'll come back and stay with her and it will be all right. And all the poison of her fury, all the gall of her need, all my own failure and guilt and inadequacy were washed clean in that look of hers that was so full of love and understanding and forgiveness.

Simon's voice had finished burring, but I held on to him tightly. After a moment he kissed my head and said, 'And do you know what I will do with my life now?'

'No?'

'Now I will learn to be an artist again . . .'

I looked up at him. There was a brave, vulnerable look in his eyes which resonated within me like a plucked string. And then I knew that I wanted him with me, stitched to my side. That I was bound to him as one drop of water running down a pane collides with another and joins together indivisibly.

We sat on the sofa amongst the old newspapers and burst springs and we held hands, stupid and tender and raw as all the lovers who have ever been.

Little bubbles of protest kept rising in my head like the effervescence in champagne – Oh, this is silly . . . It's too . . . But how could we possibly . . . And then they'd pop and the thoughts would disperse as though they had never been.

After a while I looked at him and said, 'When are we going home?'

She was wearing a heavy fur coat and the amber hairs glistened and flickered as she walked down the stairs. She moved very upright, her head lifted, her hair neatly pinned at her neck. She was pulling on a pair of black gloves.

She was no longer the old woman.

'Madeleine,' Simon smiled as she came to a halt beside him. 'You look beautiful.'

'Thank you.' She looked at him. 'You've been very good to

me, Simon,' she said suddenly, 'despite what I've done in the past. If I can ever do something for you – '

'Mend this quarrel, Madeleine,' he urged. 'The past – that is not important, we all do what we think best at the time and later we see the mistakes. But now, this time, you still have a chance to make it right.'

She shook her head sadly. 'It's too late for that, Simon,' she said. 'I'm sorry, it's really too late.'

There was a pause and she glanced up the stairs to the row of closed doors on the gallery. Then, taking a breath, she said decisively. 'I don't think there's any more need to wait. If you could just take me to the station now – ' She broke off as a key turned, a door creaked open and high-heels clicked pertly along the wooden floor to the balustrade above us.

'Lydia,' Madeleine called up, her voice bright as a cocktail hostess. 'I'm so glad you came out. Won't you come down? My train's leaving shortly. I haven't much time.'

Lydia looked down at her. 'I wouldn't want to keep you,' she said coldly. 'You're obviously in such a hurry.'

Madeleine's hands clenched by her sides, tight and shiny as two black beetles. 'Lydia, do come down,' she coaxed, the glitter flaking from her voice. 'I'd like to talk to you.'

'There's nothing to talk about.'

'Well – just to say goodbye then.'

'What for?'

'As a favour to me – a gesture – '

'I don't owe you any favours, Madeleine.'

Simon clicked his tongue impatiently. '*Ach*, for God's sake, Lydia, stop behaving like a spoilt – '

But Madeleine interrupted swiftly. 'Do you think you could take my case into the car now, Simon? And while you're there, I'd be very grateful if you would check the packing of Sophie's pictures. I don't want them to get damaged on the journey. If you could, please?' she added firmly as he hesitated. 'I'll join you outside in a moment.'

He frowned but obediently lifted her suitcase and she

followed him with her eyes until he was safely out of the house. I made to leave too, but she caught my arm. 'No, wait, Sophie. I want to talk to you before I go.' She glanced anxiously at her daughter, standing above her, proud as a figurehead on the prow of a ship. 'Just wait here with me for a moment, Sophie,' she appealed. 'Please.' So I took a place in the shadows, to make myself as unobtrusive as possible.

They stood for a time, tense and silent as two fighters in a ring, then Madeleine began gently. 'Please come down, Lydia. It's so difficult to talk like this.'

'Who said I wanted to talk?'

Madeleine's hands flexed, but she kept her voice steady. 'Very well, then. You don't have to say anything to me, but there is something I would like to say to you.'

'Oh, yes. Another insult? Another rejection? More bad-mouthing Grandfather? No, thank you, Madeleine, I really don't think there's anything you can say that I'd want to hear.'

'I want to offer an apology.' Madeleine's voice was firm. 'I want to apologize to you, Lydia. I think – I think I can see now that I really haven't been much of a mother to you over the years and – and I'm sorry.'

There was a brief pause, like the sea drawing back, and then, 'Sorry? Is that it – sorry?' Lydia's voice was harsh as sandpaper. 'All those years when you were bloody foul to me and now you just expect to say "sorry" and make everything all right?'

'I – I don't know what else I *can* say.' Madeleine faltered. 'I don't think there's anything I can do, is there?'

'Oh, no – no, there's nothing you can do. I'd say you'd already done more than enough – rejecting my offer, ruining the garden. No, Madeleine, you just sail out of here and don't you worry about – '

'But you've got the Hall now,' Madeleine broke in. 'What more do you want?'

'The Hall *is* mine,' Lydia shouted. 'You haven't given it to me as a present, it was mine to start with.' She brushed the hair out of her eyes; her hand was trembling. 'Well, I'm not going to salve your conscience for you, Madeleine,' she hissed. 'I'm not going to smooth away the wrinkles so you can sleep nice and easy at night. I want you to suffer – like I've suffered, like *he* suffered when you finally got your hands on him and he was too weak to protect himself. Why the hell should I forgive you? I don't feel any forgiveness for you – not one tiny jot.'

'But Lydia – please,' Madeleine cried. 'I don't want to leave it like this. I've done the best I could –'

'No—' Lydia slapped the balustrade with the flat of her hand. 'No, Madeleine. You're the one who wants to leave. Just walk away – go on. I'm not going to stop you. But if you want me to forgive you – I won't. Not now – not ever. Grandfather was right to hate you. You climbed over dead bodies to stay at the Hall and I'll never forgive you for that.'

Madeleine's face was white with livid red patches, as if her daughter's words had physically hit her. But she stayed on her feet, she kept fighting.

'Lydia – listen to me. What I did, I did for you – I did it *all* for you. Your grandfather might never have left you the Hall if I hadn't stayed here with you and made sure –'

'No, no stop it—' Lydia broke in. 'I won't listen to any more of your lies. I don't want you to talk about him. I don't want you even to mention his name. I loved him –'

'I know you loved him. I know he meant the world to you. But that's over now. He's dead – buried out there in the woods.' Her voice was twisted with anguish. 'Please don't carry on that feud now, please. You don't know what it did to him. He was so riddled with anger and hatred and bitterness at the end. Don't end up like him Lydia. Please, I'm begging you—' She broke off, leaning against one of the boxes, her face in her hands.

But Lydia had stopped suddenly as if she had come up against a wall. She was staring, shocked. 'In the woods—' she whispered. 'What do you mean? He's in the woods?' She looked at her mother crouching below. 'But – but you said – you *always* said the pilots were in the woods. Madeleine – ' She shook the balustrade urgently. 'Madeleine, you said that he was – that his ashes were – Madeleine, tell me – '

'What?' Madeleine moaned. 'What is it? What have I done now?'

'The pilots – ' Lydia urged. 'Madeleine, you said the pilots were in the woods – '

'Of course the bloody pilots weren't in the woods,' Madeleine snapped, straightening up and wiping her eyes. 'Do you honestly think the Ministry would have allowed – '

'But you said – '

'I said a lot of things.'

'But – but you said he was cremated – his ashes scattered. You said – '

'Dear God, Lydia, must you go on?' She looked at her daughter bitterly. '*Him* – *him*, it's always been *him* with you, hasn't it? Couldn't you ever have thought of me?'

'But where – ' Lydia persisted. 'Madeleine, for God's sake – tell me where he is.'

But Madeleine stared at her daughter for a long time before she replied. Then she said stonily, 'He's buried down there in the woods – where I told you the pilots were. He didn't want to leave the place either.'

'But – but – why didn't you tell me before?'

'I didn't think it was the sort of thing a young child should know,' she said heavily. 'And obviously I had to stop you playing down there, because I was afraid you might – '

'But when I was older – then – now – it would have made such a difference.'

'Would it? Really?' Madeleine looked at her. 'So you'd have come down here to visit the dead instead of the living? No, Lydia. He was dead and I wanted him kept dead.' She gave a bitter laugh. 'A fine success I made of keeping him below ground.'

There was a sudden sharp tooting outside. Simon had started the engine.

211

Madeleine drew herself upright with a deep breath and looked around her. 'Well, Lydia, you've got him now. I've lived with him for all these years and now, thanks to you, I'm finally leaving him behind.'

But Lydia didn't respond. She stood dumb, staring out at the dusk through the stained-glass window on the landing below her.

Madeleine turned to me. 'I want to thank you for your pictures, Sophie,' she said quietly. 'You've made this house beautiful for me. I hadn't expected that.'

I shook my head. 'But – but I'm sorry for all this,' I said lamely. 'It seems so – so – I'm sorry for both of you.'

She gave me a look that was both proudly indifferent and scorchingly sad. Then she moved to the door.

'But *where* are you going?' Lydia called out suddenly. 'You haven't told me. Where can I find you if I need – '

Madeleine stopped but didn't turn round. 'Simon knows where I'll be,' she said. 'Ask him. There isn't time now.'

'But – but – ' Lydia was leaning over the balustrade, her hair falling into her face. 'But – you can't just go – you can't – '

'It's too late for all that now, Lydia.' Madeleine spoke with fierce restraint. 'It's too late – it's always been too late for us.'

'And what about all this – ' Lydia's face hardened as she gestured to the chaos of boxes and packing cases. 'What do you want me to do with all this, eh? Sort it out and send it off to you? What was all this mess about, Madeleine? Tell me.'

Madeleine looked from side to side at the boxes – but not above, not at her daughter. 'I suppose,' she said slowly, 'I suppose I was just trying to see what it felt like – leaving. I suppose – I just wanted to make it real.'

'Well, you're making it real enough now, aren't you?' Lydia scorned.

Madeleine paused. 'All right – I've changed my mind.'

'Oh – ' Lydia's cry was a mixture of shock and joy. 'Really? You mean – '

'I mean you can keep it all,' Madeleine cut in. 'Have it – do what you like with it. You might even find one or two things that will surprise you.'

'And what about the children?' Lydia flung out her final weapon. 'What do you expect me to tell them when they ask about their grandmother?'

Madeleine was suddenly still, as if that last wild spear – totally unanticipated, totally untrained – had indeed found its mark in the very heart of her. But then her back straightened and her fingers unclenched. 'Tell them – tell them I'm dead – tell them I've gone away – tell them whatever you like,' she said. 'Let's face it, Lydia, you don't want them to have anything to do with their grandmother, do you?' And, without waiting for a reply, she opened the front door and walked out.

There was an exchange of voices outside, the heavy slamming of doors and then the slow crunching of gravel as the car was driven away.

Lydia stood motionless, the breeze from the open door slapping her face, careless and rough as the waves that had lapped over my feet after they'd swallowed my sister.

But then, when the last sound had been fully absorbed into the dark and there was only the rustle of the wind in the trees, then – calmly, slowly, as if there was no longer any impediment – she walked down the stairs to the front door.

She shut it hard and leaned back against it. Her face was hidden in shadow but I could see her shoulders settling down like sand in water.

Suddenly I felt very tired. I just wanted to escape this house and go home.

'I'll be leaving when Simon comes back,' I said, moving towards the stairs.

She nodded absently as, idly flicking open the lid of one of the boxes, she peered inside.

'I'll – I'll just go and pack.'

But she took no notice and I was half-way up the stairs when her sudden shout arrested me.

'Oh – look,' she cried. 'Look – ' She was holding up a small glass object: a dome? a paperweight? I couldn't see very clearly. 'He gave it to me – Grandfather gave it to me for Christmas. It wasn't in my room when I came back from school that time after she'd had it repapered. It wasn't there and I thought it was gone, like everything else, but it was here all the time – I can't believe it – she must have taken it – ' She rummaged again in the box. 'What else is there? What else did she steal?'

But I was feeling sick and sad and I turned away, leaving her kneeling there on the floor like a votary, her arms deep in the boxes as she pulled out their contents, spilling them in a sea all around her.

'You'll sell the Hall?' Simon asked.

'No,' she yelped. 'Of course not. Well – I can't. Under the terms of Grandfather's will I'm not allowed – '

'*Ach*, wills.' He waved a hand. 'These things can be managed, you know.'

'Yes – well, I'll see. More tea?' She leaned forward to refill our cups.

She'd lit a huge fire in the hearth and there was a mound of crumpled catalogues beside her. From time to time she threw another ball into the blaze, nodding with satisfaction as it burned.

I felt uncomfortable watching her, this parody sitting in her mother's chair. It felt wrong to me – like a cat with its fur stroked backwards. And yet she fitted it all so well, so exactly, queening it here in the room that had been her mother's domain. She looked happy.

'It's your life,' Simon said, taking out a cigarette. 'I'm not going to interfere.'

'That's right, Simon.' She smiled. 'Best not to interfere, you know.'

There was nothing more to say.

In the silence I studied her as if for a drawing. Her face glowed from the fire, her hair burnished gold, her eyes blinking heavily, contented as a cat. In a few years, I thought, her hair will grey and she could be sitting in this room, looking out at the first of the new season's roses . . .

'Drink your tea, Sophie,' she urged. 'You don't want it to get cold.'

I gulped at the strong unstrained brew too hastily and, though I picked the leaves from my tongue, I couldn't free my mouth from the aftertaste.

It has been a clean, sharp winter. Frost on the glass. Cold. My breath condenses even inside the house. In the evening I light the fire and it crackles and sings, the twigs snapping like fingers. He brings me driftwood from the sea. The branches are stripped and twisted into Baroque shapes and he laughs when I say I cannot burn them. The house clutters up with these sea-sculpted relics. They are bleached white – white as bones picked clean.

When the sun shines over the sea in the afternoon, it pours through the window of the Glass Room, where he lies asleep while I paint. Stella was right about the sea, but I struggle to capture it. The grey and the mauve and the sudden blue of the water. The white and sulphur yellow of the sky and the little splash of crimson when the sun goes down.

He takes up a pencil sometimes, then puts it down. But his fingers itch and soon I think he'll be able to draw without fear of the faces he might reproduce. He is growing a beard. He grumbles and says he looks like a prophet. And sometimes we quarrel and sometimes he is angry. Sometimes, like the sea, he is sullen, curling up on himself and turning away – he is old, he says, old and dirty with death. And sometimes he chases me along the shore and, when he catches me, tips my head back and pulls kisses from my lips, like a child sucking grapes from a bunch.

In the night, when it is cold, we curl up close together and I hold his old scarred feet between my own as he laps and rocks at my body. His ring bites into my breast. But soon, very soon, he will take it from his finger and fling it far out into the sea.

Then it will all be quiet. The stars will come out over the

water and the soft stroking of the waves will smooth out the features of our beloveds until their faces are as sheer as pebbles on the shore and they are forgotten.

Caulifl
brocrie
avocoto
spinach
Bussel sprouts
flax seed
spirulina
Hempseed
fish + shimp

Pro Plant Complete Shake

DR. Gundry